EXHALE BLACK SHEEP

Strength to Live Again

LuGina C. Horton

LuGina C. Horton

EXHALE BLACK SHEEP

Strength To Live Again

EXHALE BLACK SHEEP
Strength To Live Again

Copyrighted Material
Created, published and distributed by LuGina C. Horton
First Printing, 2020 Exhale Black Sheep Strength to Live Again, A Eve G. Novae Series

First published in the United States of America in 2020 by LuGina C. Horton
In accordance with the Library of Congress U. S. Copyright Act of 1976, the scanning, uploading, and electronic sharing of any part of this book without the permission of the publisher LuGina C. Horton is unlawful piracy and theft of the author intellectual property. If you would like to use material from the book (except for the use of brief quotations in a book reviewing purpose).
For More Information, prior written permission must be obtained by contacting the publisher LuGina C. Horton. Thank you for your support of the authors's respectful rights.

Cover design by LuGina C. Horton
Interior Design by LuGina C. Horton

LuGina C. Horton

6260 E Riverside Blvd
Suite #134
Loves Park, IL 61111
Luginac.horton@gmail.com
Visit www.luginachorton.com

ISBN: 978-1-7353414-0-8 (hardcover) - ISBN: (large print hardcover) - ISBN: (ebook) - ISBN: (audiobook)

Disclaimer: The book is meant solely for entertainment purposes. In no event will LuGina C. Horton be liable to any reader for any harm, injury, or damages, including direct, indirect, incidental, special, consequential, or punitive arising out of or at any time in connection with the use of the information contained in this book. This publication is intended to provide helpful and informative material. It is sold with the understanding that the author and publisher LuGina C. Horton are not engaged in rendering legal, medical or other professional services. The author and publisher LuGina C. Horton specifically disclaim all responsibility for any liability, loss, or risk, personal or otherwise, which is incurred as a consequence, directly, or indirectly, form the use or application of any contents of the book. No action should be taken solely on the contents of this book.

Dedication

To my best friend, and my greatest inspiration. The leader and example of love for all of my life. The one who chose to become the giver of my life. Mother, my mother, the late Merline J. Horton. Jack...I appreciate your teachings of life principals and for allowing me to glean and gather the benefits of your God and the very fields of your true womanhood. You are the best part of my rise from day-to-day; knowing that you are forever with me. I live because you lived.

    To my beloved daughters, and one and only granddaughter, Sheduia V. Sockwell, Rae' Aja B. Horton, Amari S. Richardson, and Ms. Mi' Heir N. Mack, the Ladies who have allowed me on purpose to arise before their very lives the embodiment of principals and qualities of this work. Their love, support, time, respect, and confidence in me over the many years of mothering them have helped me to not only understand my purpose of life, however, but also to know the very essence of my gifts; to build lives as it relates to love, trust, and truth of God's Kingdom. And it's been a gift given for me to walk therein. I have dedicated my life to being a mother and leader with the hope that they, too, will become on purpose, women of noble worth and like qualities to reposition the lives of others.

    To my Grandparents, the Battens, Flores, and the unique men and women of my family and dear friends, to your own strength of individuality, thanks for the times of shared love, joy, and laughter. Too Sheila, Khaneidra and Melinda our love is forever and can never be overlooked or forgotten. Thank you for helping me experience the best side of me.

To the women of third-world nations, especially my friends of Nairobi Kenya, Africa; perhaps targeted by cultural, economic, and circumstances of natural and spiritual hardships. For the various challenges you face daily in an environment that has yet to convert to new changes. May you arise from hindrances and have great experiences of laughter from joy within, balance, and the fulfillment of becoming the very best you inside of you.

Lastly, to the people who have gone a great distance with me to keep my writing career possible and in full force- **my remarkable and supportive readers**; for years, I've always wanted to wrap my heart written out on paper enforced by a title and spine. My dream to become an author could not have happened without your continued support and all of you. I love you and will forever give thanks and love to you **ALL** beyond.

Always In Grace,

Lugina C. Horton
KINGDOM MASTER BUILDER

Globally God's Kingdom Leader

E-mail: luginac.horton@gmail.com

Facebook: www.facebook.com/luginahorton

Facebook: https://www.facebook.com/ILiveToBuildLives/

Instagram: instagram.com/exploreluginachorton

Website: www.luginachorton.com

Acknowledgments

Every accomplishment in my life would be counted as an airless space without the relationship of my spiritual leader, best friend, and father of wisdom. My dad Ambassador Luegene Batten, because of you and you're fearless leadership, I have expanded. My position in the earth has become that of great substance. I'm glad to say you are my father and have always fathered me even beyond times of life failures. You have been right there. You fathering me has allowed me to know that I'm as rare as a red rose in the middle of any winter. I will forever need your guidance, Father Abraham. I love you, and I will always love you.

I appreciate the encouragement and truth from my late Pastor Mary Allen, the late Joy Lambert, aka Joy-Joy, Ms. Dorsey Thompson, aka Mama D, Nadine Hicks, my childhood inspiration for success Auntie Princess Diana Denny, Vernett Guerin, LaTisha Jones, Erin J. Sanders, LaKeyshia Miller, Susan Levingston, Vicki Joyce Richard, Heirreonna Streeter, Dorothy Hawthorne, Vanity Thomas, and Andrell Bragg-Shaw aka Dena. All of the many individuals who gave of themselves directly or indirectly in my life, like all my Aunties and Uncles whom I love with all of me. Indeed your place in my life has been and will always be necessary. Thank you for circling yourselves around me in wisdom, gifts, talents, and, above all, love.

Most of all, every day in my rising, I'm wrapped in grace to the Creator of all things, my God and heavenly Father, and His Son Jesus Christ. He has given us all the greatest gift ever—the inner workings of the Sweet Holy Spirit. Our teacher to lead us in all truth for opportunities of a lifetime on purpose.

I, LuGina C. Horton, Am a Pastoral leader with a Philanthropic heart,

Challenges in life have caused me to seek words enriched with faith, words that will convert the abandoned hearts of those whom I am privileged to teach, counsel, and encourage by way of my global kingdom influence. Which I believe will cause a change course of life; A life filled with faith and hope.

As a leader, I am committed to the continual growth that caused me to shift one journey to another. My journey has been filled with life-changing decisions that have been difficult, leading me to lean on the source that birthed the journey I find myself on at this very time.

Through this journey, I have been led to a place of pure love, trust, and truth and there is a mandate for me to shift those whom I have the pleasure to lead, and empower to enter this place of pure love, trust, and truth so they too may experience the abundant life.

The message of the Kingdom Ambassadorship

Therefore I, LuGina C. Horton, will observe the following to take place as a committed conclusion to the growth in my vision for all mankind.

This vision is a desire to create a pure place for those who I am given the pleasure to lead, a place of agape love. A place of trust and truth that all may lead in their area of gifting. Business leadership to Philanthropic leadership to Pastoral leadership; my journey has been evolving, causing me to make difficult decisions, but through it all, I landed in a place that has clear guidance, that is, the Kingdom of heaven, motivated by the Kingdom of God, imparting and departing the constitution of the country of my citizenship.

Globally God's Kingdom Leader
Lives in Rockford, Illinois.
You can visit LuGina C. Horton at her Website,
www.Luginachorton.com,
find her on Facebook www.Facebook.com/luginachorton,
https://www.facebook.com/ILiveToBuildLives/
and follow her on Twitter @BloomBuildlives,
Instagram instagram.com/exploreluginachorton
E-mail luginac.horton@gmail.com
For all love notes!
LuGina C. Horton
6260 E Riverside Blvd #134
Loves Park, IL 61111

Introduction

As people, we have created all over the world in our minds and put into action the rise and fall of the known and don't want to be known as the black sheep. Within every family, nationality, community, church, boardroom, neighborhood, business, and further. An ancient old norm has been inhaled in the thoughts of every believer. There is no accepted space to live in the moment that's not prepared for you. From the families where the overlooked and undervalued roots are about to be exposed, one woman's struggle to strengthen what remains. Eve is every woman. For years we have known her to be the mother of all living. Who battles with what she walks away from and the truth she abandons to follow. It is the suppressed need to be like the core she was birthed out of. After failing to realize it is more than her with her. She speaks life into what came out of her; all women. Some will laugh, and because of pain, some will cry. But will they all rise?

Even though all five childhood friends Eve, Lauren, Olivia, Kayla, and Andrea grow up in the same neighborhood. They were not raised in the same house. Now that they have left the hive and have experienced love from multi-facet relationships. From more than the Sisterhood, everyone's trust has been tested, and the truth is calling for an upfront answer. Will you or will you not believe the truth, the whole truth, and nothing so help you God, the unadulterated naked truth? Everyone has been quick to point the finger and hide shame under guilt. When the tension between rejected love and trusted relationships erupts, the honey in the tea tastes like what we all have been through except for the one who has believed to live the given lie.

Exhale
Black Sheep

Strength To Live Again

1

If the Price is Right

The car stopped. Eve's coming heel to toe heel to toe, and he watched as she, the alter ego of Snowfall, paved the way. In the silent steps of six-inch heels, the placing of one foot in front of the other and the power of her confidence made the very all-white name brand dress of Von Sha' ShaVon's she was wearing to hide behind the fabric of her presence. Her strong back, long hair, and soft bangs lay over the right eye as she entered the room to the sound of *Deborah Cox's* song "Nobody's Supposed To Be Here." Looking at her watch as she takes her seat, having excitement from within waiting to embrace the other women who're soon to join her here at Pandora's Lounge. The environment of members only and the right place where all money is free if you're in the game, but hard labor if you are not the ace on the table, that is; clean cut, smelling fresh, muscular necks, broad shoulders, muscles cut up in tailored suits, alligators walking, and cash clips with all about the Benjamins on top. Liquid money in the middle, ready to make a deposit on the black card in the back; hello somebody they are here. The grown men are out tonight.

Whispers of *who is she, and is she here alone?* Suddenly a tall glass of red wine is laid to the right of my classic one of a kind St. Berla leather clutch. With a message written on the napkin underneath that says…*Who are you?* Glancing at the glass without turning around to see… who is the gentleman attempting to open me up? Thinking to myself, *I don't know if he really wants me to respond because this will cost him later.*

I was laughing as we were leaving Pandora's at two a.m. myself, Lauren, and Olivia. Kayla, who couldn't wait for all of us to get back to my house, just so she could address the fact that Mr. Carter was sitting with his nephew Evan, at the bar who appeared to be candied. Mr. Carter tried all night to get my attention. I had all of us laughing at how I kissed the napkin—leaving the impression of my lips from my new custom line Such A Lady red lipstick. Color Loving You number ten-fifteen, and a fifty-dollar bill with the answer to his question written on it.

I...Am Eve, the mother of all living.

Eve just couldn't stop relishing on how she sent the drink back by the waitress of the bar with the message and left the building.

Screaming and laughing with each of their heads tilt back. "Eve, you are a mess! Said Kayla. The man was trying to get to know you, and you shot him down like he had no intentions."

"Listen, Kayla; you ladies are laughing, but I've had my share, and right now, men are not the focus of my view." Them not knowing it wasn't Eve who was addressing old man Mr. Carter but Snowfall. The side of her, her friends, would only be invited to have a glimpse of. Mr. Carter can't do anything for me but give me a brown paper bag. Besides, I'm not interested in playing with the rich but awaiting the investor who has no problem controlling the wealth of my future.

"Eve, Kayla said, who was trying to figure it all out. Why should he give you a brown paper bag? And what do you suppose he put in it?" Asked Lauren.

"Lauren," Eve responded, "we've been raised in two different households with the view of two different worlds, and the only thing I can share with you right now is that you're too nosey to understand and too slow to believe me if I told you anyway. Just know that the bag can't come empty."Seeing everyone out, Eve said.

"Drive safe, and please text me and let me know that all of you have arrived home safe," hugging each of them as they turned around to walk out the door. Olivia, who we right out of the gate, teased and nicknamed Livia years ago when we first met her on the block of GrandChester Place. All of us, as her friends gathered that she has an old soul and have been here before perhaps living the life of one of her great aunties or somebody's auntie. We all agreed that her parents the Johnson's named her, the old lady named Olivia. That she would never get a man, and we had to take it upon ourselves to help her live the best young, attended life, and to come out of her shy shell. So, Livia, it is.

Livia slowly touches Eve on the shoulder, causing an energy surge and says.

"Hey, girl, I hope that this doesn't get you upset, but when was the last time you heard from Jay?" Jayden, that is, but his male friends call him JOC short for Jayden O'Connor; the man that has held my heart on lockdown for seven and a half years.

"Livia Jayden O'Connor is not the last thing I care to go to bed thinking about," Eve said.

"Why?" Livia asked.

"Because he's never here, and I don't care to dream any more vacant dreams about Jayden O'Connor. He's a busy man and obviously, there are other things, and people who come first. As long as he's okay with the decisions that he's making and understand that later this will alter his future one day,"Eve said. Livia turns and walks away, looking back to say. "I love you, girl, and I'm here for you, anything whenever you need me."

"Thanks, Liv, goodnight."

Taking a deep breath while preparing for bed.

With the thoughts of why I didn't drink that tall glass of red wine to calm my nerves.

Oh! How I should've kept that fifty dollar bill in my purse, trying to impress Mr. Carter, the old man with a wink in his eye, knowing that I needed some gas in that white Panamera Porsche parked in the garage with the red light one. God knows as soon as I start it up, the voice control operator whom I've taken the pleasure of naming Faith; Faith because it's only by faith that I'm able to afford to push the paddle and go. I can hear her now with a prophetic word for me in the morning.

"Good morning, Eve, in case you didn't know your gas light is on, and your fuel is way too low. Please make a decision soon, goodbye."

The night was well spent; I am looking forward to getting in this hot steamy shower and crawling in those white sheets on my bed. They are calling my name, listening to the smooth voice of *Luther Van-dross* singing "If Only For One Night." Between Luther, Livia, and all these memories are making me want to pick up the phone just to say hello, Jay, but my body is saying it's been a fast day and long night can we please just go to bed.

Finally, yes, climbing under the covers ready to pray the same ole prayer I've prayed for seven and a half years. God...I said, staring up at the ceiling as if I'm looking God right in the face.

"I believe you are God, and you hear prayers of even the sinful. After all, you died on the cross for all of our sins...well, your son Jesus did anyway, so just let me take this time to say, I have never claimed to be perfect or the best for that matter. And sometimes my body just wants to be held. You know, like held by some muscles, biceps, and triceps that you've created men to have and women to desire. I just want to know, do you care that I have no one to hold me tonight? You said in the big book and don't quote me cause I don't have the scripture in front of me right now."

Rolling over in the bed, still praying but feeling my sleep coming down on me.

"Dear God, you said I have not because I've asked not, perhaps I'm asking at the wrong times well anyway I'm asking again just for the night. Please, Jesus. I'll repent in the morning, but for right now, send Jayden O'Connor to forty-three thirty-two Eastwood Dr. and let him put my fire out. Ahh, Livia asking about the last time I've heard from Jay was like reminding me of the last time he laid in these sheets, and I had to call into work for work the next day was not an option. It was like rubbing two sticks together until they were a spark and a fire. You guessed it, the only fan that was fanning our flames was the ceiling fan. Cause all I remember was calling Jay daddy and him kissing my clavicle bone and saying daddy home good night."

It's four thirty-five in the morning, and my eyes are blurred by the look of my alarm clock in the center of my nightstand. I'm wondering who's ringing my phone when I wouldn't dare call anyone at this time of the morning. Whoever this is has got to be crazy, I mean straight outta their mind. With my head under the pillows and my body feeling chilled, I already know this silk scarf is somewhere at the bottom of the bed and is no longer wrapped around my head. Unless this is an emergency, go away honestly. I just got in a good position of my sleep, and really I don't want to come out of this place. Great, it stopped ringing and rolling over to find that warm spot in the middle of the bed where I had first started dreaming about Jay. There it is again my cell phone is ringing back to back.

"Hello?"Bringing the cell from underneath the pillows with me.

"Hello?" I yelled.

"Hello?" Taking a glance around the room and making sure I was all alone.

And this better be good cause whoever you are, I want you to know that my beauty sleep has just been interrupted because of you. As I was listening on the other end, there was a long period of silence. Lifting my head, and stopping to take a look at the phone and the contact picture of Kayla dancing was stirring me in the face.

"Kayla, hey girl, you there?" Eve said.

"Hello? Kayla, say something I'm here. What is it?" Eve said.

The sound of sobbing and long breaths were coming across the airways.

"Kayla baby, why are you crying? Please talk to me while I'm listening," Eve said.

"Eve… she's gone, she's gone, she left me. Why? Why Eve? She left me," Kayla said.

The phone drops, and all Eve could hear were the sounds of screaming and long whaling in the background. Throwing the covers back and jumping on her feet, pulling the string and turning the lamp on.

"Hey Kayla, where are you? Pick up the phone. I'm here for you." Chanting of long sounds of whaling.

"No, No! How Am I going to make it? God no I need her, please give her back to me she's all I have in this world, and I can't live without her."

"Kayla, Are you home? Hello…? I'm on my way, honey. I'm here for you just keep talking to me until I get there," Eve said.

"Eve, Kayla said, I can't breathe. It's hard; I can't believe she's gone, help me please."

"Is it your mother? Kayla, where is your mother? Kaysie, is it her?" Asked Eve.
Grabbing my sweat pants with my hair all over my head, Flip-flops on a baseball cap in one hand and keys in the other. Wait I need a bra on; I can't go like this. Rushing back into the house, up the stairs, take a right, snatched my bra out of the top dresser drawer, okay, I'll put this on at the stoplight. Let's go.

Eve said, "Kayla, can you hear me? I'm coming, baby." By this time, all I was hearing was arguing in the background as if someone's there, and she was not alone.

"Kayla, listen, please talk to me. Who are you arguing with?" Asked Eve.
As soon as I heard the very words of;

"You better get out; get the hell out, you killer!"
"You killed her!" Kayla said, "Everything you do and has done has always been for your benefit. Get out of my house. You are not my mother, and you will never be my mother. You killed my mother with your hateful ass. Get out of here. I hate you! You ain't no good, and you ain't never been any good!" said Kayla. "If you don't get out now. It's going to cost you your life, and you won't ever make it out! Ever!"

2

Sleeping Beauty

Pulling up in front of the Greater Spirit of God Missionary Baptist Church; this is where Kayla's Grandmother, Sweet Lady Mrs. Hannah Mae Williams, was one of the Charter members for over Seventy-four years.

All I know is that the people of this church are one of the best dressing church-going people in the city of Chicago. Now don't get me wrong, the pastor show nuff can preach; he was David, that is King David out of the Bible of his family with all those fine brothers. That one person who they always looked over cause he didn't have the beauty or stature of one who was tall, dark, and handsome. Shaking my head back and forth. Oh! But did he ever have the voice that'll make you cry? He had an anointing that will cause any sinner to take a stroll down the center aisle and not just to say I do but say I will Jesus!

One thing for sure is that the people of the Greater Spirit of God Church don't mind cutting a step either. Still, I'm yet to witness an upper room experience; I can't say that I have heard other people tongues-speaking in there that's for sure.

Looking in the rearview mirror to check this face one last time, and talking to myself, get yourself together, girl. I hope this lipstick is not too bright cause it's either red or burgundy in my purse, and at this point, I really don't think Sweet Lady Hannah Mae Williams would have two cents to say about it, cause today her lips are sealed. That's not right, Eve, now you know that's not right, chuckling, sometimes I have to laugh at myself. Okay, here I go. I have to get out of this car and go in and be strong for my girl Kayla, she out of all people needs me more than ever right now.

"Eve, you are absolutely right; the arrival time expired three minutes ago; you are now late. Should I activate the snooze button? I'm waiting for a response?"

"Faith! Hush up, not now! Hold your peace, or I'm going to silence you with the deactivation button. What do you think about that?"

"Have a good day, Eve and goodbye!"

"Wait, I'm tripping; is this who I really see in this mirror? Is this who I think it is getting ready to cross the street and heading into the same funeral I'm about to go in? Is this Sebastian? Sebastian Lamont Clemons goes to church…No way. I've got to see this up close we haven't seen him in years, the last I heard, he had gotten into some trouble."

The car door closes. As I head up the stairs with my curls cascading down the center of the nakedness of my back, the straight black line that runs up the middle of my legs and my gold pencil heels makes me stand tall and own my she power. By the way, I believe I'm kinda feeling myself right about now, only because I'm wearing one of my favorite dresses, which shows off my neck. The one part of my body I just adore, and of course, it is black, okay well it's a little black dress size six that is, and I've only recently been able to get back into it. I sure don't own a small house on the prairie skirt, not at all.

"So when I get in here, I don't want to hear anybody! I mean nobody, from the Greater Spirit of God Church or the Missionary Baptist rolling eyes side. Not one word, from Pastor Henry in the pulpit, the sleepy willows mothers board, wearing the feather and rhinestone box hats, and the deacons who take quick peeks and are always looking out the corner of their eye over those dirty glasses hanging off their noses. I can't forget the hellions at the back door, either called Ushers."

"Excuse me," tapping me on my shoulder as if I can't feel her.

"Excuse me, dear welcome to Greater Spirit of God Missionary Baptist Church, where Dr. Henry and First Lady Madeline Rose Mason are our Pastors. I have a seat for you in the back, honey," the Usher said.

I can't believe I'm talking to the same ole mean-looking, usher, every time I come up in here to visit with Kayla, batting both of my eyes.

"No! Thank you, but I'm here with the family, thanks again for offering," I responded, shaking my head like gone somewhere today, woman.

"Well, the usher said, you were late, and the family is up viewing the body. So what are you going to do? I'll wait."

See, that's what I'm talking about, that right there every time I come up here, it seems to be a bad taste in everyone's mouth on this back door—inhaling for about the third time. Now I see why the Greater Spirit of God Missionary Baptist Church calls Kayla's Grandmother Sweet Lady Mrs. Hannah Mae Williams. Because it seems everyone is a sourpuss outside of the youth and the cleanup committee with the three faces, I see no evil, hear no evil, and speak no evil. Only because of them being the first ones in the ladies' room, getting in on all of the church member's business. Like who's sleeping with who in the Aaron's Army Male Choir, you didn't hear me. The First Lady, whom the women of the church don't find friendly at all. Now that's just my observation, and I'm not the cleaning crew cause I'm not taking no one's dirty trash out. This is too good for everybody's church.

"Thank you, but no thank you," I said, preparing to walk off, giving her a nod and a wink from the left eye. I leaned into her right ear and whispered, *I'll just find my way from here, Sista,*"

As soon as I turned around from getting ready to swing to knock her butt clean-out, you didn't hear me. Salvation was delivering me once again, as I see Lauren waving me down to come to the front where all of them were in line to view the body of Mrs. Hannah Mae Williams, known as Honey, to all the grandchildren.

"*Hey, ladies,* I said. Whispering, *how is she?*"

"It's bad Eve," Livia says,

"I'm sure Livia, this has to be one of the hardest days of Kayla's life."

"Yes, Lauren said. She's taking it very hard." And I agreed.

Livia said, "Well, I have been staying over at her house for the past week, and when I say she barely comes out of her bedroom," leaning her head to the side to finish talking; she only comes out to use the bathroom and get something to drink, holding one finger up to put us on pause. "*It's not water that she's drinking. If you can feel me.*" Tilting her head to the right for the last time and says *yeah that.* What I was hearing puzzled me.

"Really, ladies, she hasn't eaten, and it's going on two weeks," Livia continued to say.

"You do know her grandmother raised her, and she's all that Kayla knows as a mother. Her mother, Kaysie, gave Kayla up at five years old," I took my time to share with them, being careful not to say too much.

"What?" Livia said.

"Eve, Kayla never shared that with me, she told me that her mother was sickly and she had to move to GranChester Place in the house with her grandmother at six."

"What happened, and why?" Lauren asked.

"Hold on, Livia," I said as I reached out to touch Lauren's hand.

Lauren asked, "Speaking of her mother, is she here? Did Kaysie show up?"

"Yes, I would believe so, Mrs. Hannah Mae Williams is her mother. Why would she not show up to her own mother's home going?" I asked, not trying to be funny.

"I can't say that I've never met her. What does she look like, and have any of you met her?" Lauren asked, looking back over her shoulders.

"No, says Livia,"I'm keeping my silence as if I'm not even in the conversation."

"Why, Livia? What's up? What do you know?"

"All I know is somebody killed Sweet Lady Mrs. Hannah Mae Williams, and it wasn't me."
Soon after speaking, Livia popped her neck and took her fingers and sealed up her lips.

But, I see she has not said two words to her Aunt Julia at all. I mean nothing at all. Look at my lips; *"Nothing, but something is going on,"* Lauren said.

There are three family members between Kayla and us, and the voice of one Madison Greer standing in the choir stand surrounded by the *God's Glory Praise Team* that is beginning to sing, "I'm Going Up A Yonder;" One of the most traditional black funeral songs that sends everyone over the edge at any home going male or female.

Seeing a small view of Mrs. Hannah Mae Williams laying there, all dressed in white with a one of a kind feathers and white rhinestone hat centered in the corner of the casket. Salt pepper hair slicked straight made into one classy side bun. Diamonds about her neck and single stud diamond earrings in her ears with soft pearly polish laying smooth on those nails with both hands holding one single red rose.

She's beautiful, I thought... *It's as if she's sleeping.*

And there it was, the loudest scream coming from the front of the church that caused everyone to gasp. It was her, Kayla was breaking her silence of pain, shouting.

"Mama, I need you here with me, no mom, wait! Come back; I'm not ready for all of this...what Am I going to do without you in my life! No daddy, and no mama, I can't go on without you."

Everyone ran over to console her. The look of handheld funeral home fans was like that of a sea as I glanced back, taking a glimpse of all the family and friends that came out to show their love and support to the family of Mrs. Hannah Mae Williams.

"Eve, Go get her, said Livia. They can't handle her hurry; go, she's on the floor."
Breaking the circle of ushers around her, and before I knew it, I was holding her in my arms, and her weak body rested back in my chest. I began to wipe her tears away as she wept while fighting the tears streaming down my own face because of Kayla's hurt. It was unbearable. I felt it like a thick cloud. It was the depth of pain at its lowest peak, resting on all of us. Various outbreaks began to take place all over the church. Grown men were wiping their faces, women having to embrace others, and holding them in their arms. As the grandchildren were rubbing their eyes looking as stiff broads wondering, is it okay to ask if Honey was ever going to get up out of that box.

"*Kayla,*" I whispered as I silently began to speak in her inner ear, rocking her back and forth, saying,…"*There are no words to help you feel better. There's nothing in the imagination that any of us here today could do to bring you to a place of healing. Only God can do this. Trust me; I know this to be true. Your Mother is here,*" placing my hand over her heart.

"She's love within you, and she will never leave you. Every day you can have her in your thoughts, and every time you look in the mirror, you will see her, for you will find her in your smile, your eyes, and the sound of your laughter. Even the very scent of her, trust me, you will know when she's near. Remember the life lessons and experiences you've learned along the way from gleaning her fields of life. They will be present in your tomorrows, and they will somehow lead you through your very own life circumstances."

Struggling to speak and to bring her head to my attention, she said.

"Eve, with her nose running, tears traced down her face and lapped under her chin, making a sound just below a whisper. *I don't know if I can make it past this one. She just told me it was true after hearing all these years, Kaysie was really my mother and to come by the house on Sunday after church. It was time that I knew the truth and met my father, and now she's gone. My heart no longer has a beat, and will my soul ever have a life?"*

With everything within me, I tried to encourage her.

"Kayla, rise up and believe with me that you will never lose sight of her." Strength in her legs came as she began to stand. Kayla started to walk in the hope that her one and only mother was waiting to live through her.

"Let us close our eyes and bow our heads to pray, the Greater Spirit of God's family and friends," Dr. Henry Mason stepped forward to the podium.

As soon as Pastor Mason started praying, what'll you know the light on my cell phone started flashing. This is the wrong time for phone calls. I bent all the way down, trying not to be noticed and be disrespectful during prayer to check my cell phone. I have two missed messages.

Let's see here, and I don't recognize this number. Who is this from?

14

The message read…"Be in the house by eight I'm coming home, and I'll be ready for dinner; loaded baked potato with extra cheese, please. You know how I like my steak; you can pick the choice of side. Oh! You can take dessert off me, and this is my new number, Daddy."

Oh No! He didn't! What smh… Jayden has a new number and didn't tell me. Who does Jayden O'Connor think he is? Eight o'clock, and I don't have any steak! He will mess around and get served two eggs over easy, a can of tuna and an oops upside the head fooling with me!
And I'm not kissing anything off of him. I refuse to be the other woman. It is over; It's been over, he can't just keep coming in and out of my life like I'm the one with no directions.
Wrong-way Jayden O'Connor and your GPS have sent you off, all the way off! Find another route for this road is closed. Lips curled up with a crick in my neck looking at my phone, wait this other message is from Livia I turned to lift my hand showing her my cell phone and whisper to her.
    "Why are you texting me at a funeral and you're sitting right next to me?"
Well, in-between me and Lauren were these untamed kids. I don't get it for the life of me. Why would you bring not one, not two, but three kids to a funeral, and one of them has to be breastfeed and burped?
Like I could read her lips, she pointed at her cell and said.
    "Read the message."
    Opening her text message, that was forwarded from Sebastian, and it read.
    "Olivia, what's up? It's good seeing you these days. If you don't mind me asking you first, before putting my foot in my mouth. How old are Kayla's twins?"
    "Good seeing you to Sebastian, yes it's been quite some time.

15

However, I'm sorry to say, Sebastian, but Kayla doesn't have any twins."

"Are you sure? Wasn't she pregnant with twins?" Sebastian asked. My eyes looked to jump outta their sockets, looking at Livia whispering and pointing for her to read my lips. *"What twins, and where did Sebastian get this news from?"* I dropped the cell phone on the floor, being clumsy. At the same time, everyone's eyes were closed, and their heads bowed.

The two old ladies sitting in the row in front of me leans in, one had a message to share with the other. I couldn't believe what my ears were hearing; the secret that was just passed has taken my focus.

"Joyce,...you know First Lady Madeline Rose brother Deacon Charles Larson? The one who is trying to take the church off from under Pastor Mason."
Joyce shook her head and looked out the corner of her eye.

"Well, it's said he's the father of Hannah Mae Williams's grandchild. You ain't heard it from me. But it's out there, Chile."

" Shut yo mouth, girl. Sho nuff?" The other lady asked.
Putting her hand up over her mouth, trying not to be heard.

"Yes, ma'am, that thang up there, cutting up with all that bad blood in her is too grown for all that. She knows her granny in a better place," the other lady said, "rumor has it that the little bastard child just found out Sweet Lady Hannah Mae Williams ain't even her mama."

"Whhhat?"

"Yep, one of the children of hers gave that child up and didn't want her because of who the daddy was."

"Well, Chile, it's bound to come out. And Deacon Charles is a married man with four kids of his own. Got all kinds of jealousy and hatred in his heart; he can't pastor me!"

16

The other lady said, who is the nosey board member sister Shirley Ann Stevenson who wasn't shy about speaking her truth at all.

"Shhh... Be in prayer about Chile," Shirley spoke up and said.

"Shirley, you know I will. Let me know what you find out now," Joyce, who is first in charge of all the holiday decorations and celebrations, spoke up and said.

Pastor Mason entering into the third gear, was still praying. *Yes, we are in a true Baptist church,* I thought. Lifting my head up to see if anyone recognized that it's me making all this noise. And what do I see?

Pastor Mason, while holding the mic in his left hand, praying, but tapping his watch with the right side as if to say you know what time it is and then suddenly blows a kiss. And my head followed this airborne kiss that's directed to the lady standing in the back of the church dressed in all black.

I mean sexy jet black lace even the veil over her eyes that fell from the top of her wide brim hat was lace— standing five-eight with a Diana Ross figure. She was so classy that I felt like I was looking at myself, having a strong urge to go back there to introduce who I was and see the face behind the veil. Her she power was in control of all questions that wanted to be asked. Observing that she caught the kiss with the grace of her black lace glove, she laid it right in the front of her two legs with a soft pity-pat. Whom I call the kitty girl because every lady has one and you can believe every now and then that she will rise up and purr.

I'm all out of place right now. My emotions are everywhere, and I don't know what to think up here at the Greater Spirit of God Missionary Baptist Church. Because the spirit is high all right, and it's not the right spirit over Sweet Lady Mrs. Hannah Mae's dead body. Did I just see that? Or is my equilibrium off? Because I'm really far from a balance right now. *Okay,* just my thoughts. *Slow down, Eve. Breathe in and breathe out. Take a few moments to try to figure all of this out.*

Okay, here it is, Jayden O'Connor has a new number. He would like a steak I don't have and wants me home by eight. I'm sitting in a blind church cause everybody has their head bowed, and eyes closed. An ex-boyfriend suddenly appears in search of some hidden twins that are yet to be discovered. I have no clue where to find Kayla's unknown babies, not to mention the kissing pastor over the pulpit to the classy lady in the back laced in jet black.

All of this over the dead body that's laid to rest Sweet Lady Hannah Mae Williams. So long, honey. However, eight o'clock is soon to come as we began to walk out of Greater Spirit of God Missionary Baptist Church behind the casket of Sweet Lady Mrs. Hannah Mae Williams weeping and sobbing from the family and friends yet remained.

Hearing the fantastic sound coming from behind us the God's Glory Praise Team singing the song from *Richard Smallwood & Vision* "The Sound of Healing."

Smh…every now, and then death shows up letting life know that even death has space in the time of life to live. I have questions? One is, does heaven have anybody in attendance? Because this body of people is sharp but sleep.

3

The Longest Ride Ever

Flying around the house multitasking like I am the fairy wonder of the world, hoping and praying that I can say everything that I need to speak to Jayden O'Connor. This is it! The last day he will see my face. He's never going to commit, what was I thinking to be caught up in this man's charade? I am so mad at me, myself, and I. Come on Eve, you're stronger than this and not to mention you're a better woman than the woman who you have tried to be. This is the only way I could describe how I feel right about now.

All this time, I wasted seven and a half years has been too long, but he keeps telling me that he needs time to work things out, to just know that his love is real. He reminds me of how I'm not going anywhere and, to stop mentally playing with myself cause I know that forever is my last name, and never will it change.

Taking the time to spray some Windex on the bathroom mirror to clean it. I'm having healthy thoughts of how I need to encourage myself. That part of me that likes to live over on the fleshy side of my body and not the spirit where God keeps calling me. I keep saying you got this. You can do this! Eight o'clock come on here, I'm ready for you Jayden O'Connor!

Oh, Lord! My heart is racing like the fastest horse getting ready to jump out the gate at the Kentucky Derby. If I know Jayden O'Connor as well as I do, he always catches me when I'm not ready. So to help me when it comes to dealing with this man lol lol all of my I's have to have eyes and all my T's will have to be capitalized.

Laughing and grinning all at the same time. It does not matter to me! This man is all of the above, and every area of my temptation. I cannot lie; a part of me can't wait to see him.

Walking down the hallway to enter my bedroom, twirling my cleaning towel in the air with Windex and holding pages of newspaper in the other hand. Let's be honest, Eve, okay in my Jackay voice. I want to smell his aura and feel his hand laid on the small part of my back when he grabs me to come close, for he always picks me up. All of my friends think this is the craziest thing about him picking me up and being a lot older than me. Yep, he looks me straight in the eyes. Like she's been waiting for me to ask if she's ready to be Mrs. Jayden O'Connor? I melt in those big arms of his. It's something about laying back in his chest, wrapped and embraced in all those muscles. I love him, I do.

Inhaling, twirling my hair and taking in this quiet moment of steering out my bedroom window. Reminiscing about the black velvet box I once dreamt about and how it felt so real. It took everything out of me to share with the other ladies. I shared it so I can have a witness and how part of the dream really did manifest.

There I was standing in the door frame of Jayden's secretary Greg's office. My body was wrapped in a simple red pencil skirt, nude five, inch pointed toe patent leather heels and an open crispy crisp white button-down. It represented a power move but soft on the landing. He meant Mr. O'Connor, like all the others, would take a good look and watch me move and work my magic to empower the team.

"Hello, Gregory. I'm here for the nine am Hospitality Management team meeting with Mr. O'Connor."

"Yes, Ms. Eve, how are you today?"

He asked. "I've been expecting you. Mr. O'Connor will be running behind for the meeting today; however, allow me to go ahead and get you started."
Handing me the black management binder with the gold logo letters that read body JOC TOWERS. Now I can say this, even though Jayden stays busy creating new endeavors of wealth for himself. He trusts me to handle all of the motivating, tier building, pieces of customer service training, hiring, and even all the bye byes.

Swerving around in his high back leather chair turning to his computer, asking me for dates, dates that would be suitable for me, and Mr. O'Connor's wedding date—taken by surprise if the other women were in the room like the flies on the wall to watch me say very softly.

"I'm sorry, Greg thinking too myself this is not what Mr. O'Connor and I are meeting about," I shared—speaking out once again.

"Today's meeting will cover all the Hospitality Management teams, as well as the expansion of the East and west new locations of the JOC Towers Hotels."
Sliding his right hand down his cherry wood desk and avoiding what I had just said. As he kept typing, he asked me not only to set a date for the wedding but to choose a ring from the black velvet box standing in front of the Jeweler. Who was dressed in the most pressed out, the blackest suit with the cleanest white shirt and tie I've ever seen on any white man.
 Not to mention how my lips instantly took shape as if I was sipping some hot green tea, and my eyes were fixed on the white gloves.

Slowly the Jeweler opened the black velvet box with, taking his time very gently sharing with me the three different diamond weights, styles, and cuts represented by Jewelry Eddie B's.

21

My Lord! Wiping my forehead,

"Gregory, what did you say the temperature was in the room? And Am I the only one out of breath from skipping? I'm really feeling a little faint if you care to know."

"By all means, Ms. Eve, please sit, take a seat. Maybe this is more than you've expected out of the meeting today, and I am sure you, Mr. O'Connor, will take pleasure in explaining his actions in place today."

Not even looking at Greg's face, all I see with excitement is this long black velvet four and a half-inch ladies jewelry box. One that she would find herself placing all of her favorite showpieces in. Pressing up on my tippy toes gazing in the box.

Seeing the reflection of so many hues shining from every angle that I may have tilt my head, examining three of the most beautiful rings that a woman has ever laid eyes on. Having no doubt in my mind that the middle ring that set up high shaped in the princess cut was for me.

Still reminiscing about the black velvet box, I can see it on my finger even now. Asking myself, is this moment real? Am I really in the moment of loving the man that has challenged my thinking about me being the only woman to love him? Jayden O'Connor watched me grow up in my teens, raised me in my twenties, and built a foundation within me in my thirties. He took care of my family from a secret place, held me in my pain, and laughed with me in my gain.

Jayden O'Connor paid for my house. It's fully furnished! Not to mention the white on white Road Ranger with peanut butter trimming around my white leather seats. Wait a minute I ain't done...the Panama Porsche that fits perfectly in the two in half car garage every night all of the three hundred and sixty-five days of the year. There is no limit on the love he says and gives me a black Bank of America credit card with travel rewards paid in advance that said happy birthday with a red bow! I'm over myself with Jayden's love. Smiling within the moment from ear to ear, the man that has kissed my body on the floor of the shower, under the dining room table, and behind the last dress that he ripped off my body in the back seat of the limo, leaving the grand opening of the first JOC Towers in New York City. Jay has loved and touched me with every measure of love except one condition.

"Wait!"

Smh…wait, wait a minute, stretching my hands far apart with a puzzled look on my face.

"How does this work? I'm here choosing a wedding ring with no Mr. Jayden O'Connor here to ask me for my hand in marriage?"

Suddenly without me even turning my frozen body to stare in the eyes of his voice, I hear coming from the entrance of the office door. In that split second, I knew that there is power in the moment of peace and a calmness in every waiting unanswered question. Slowly as I continued to reminisce about this moment, I turn to see the man that I will one day tell the world is my husband, Mr. Jayden O'Connor.

Bending on one knee, with his old ass, reaching for my hand addressing me with my full name

"Eve, Gracelyn Novae, why don't you pick out your ring and allow me to fulfill my part as your man."

And I woke up. Straight up out of the dream.

"No!"

Oh no, I was lying in my bed, whispering to *take me back*. I tried to get back into the dream, and it was too late, my eyes had already seen the street light on the corner through the side crack of the blinds in the windowpane. The last thing I remember after the dream I was sitting up laying pressed against my head broad, with my white sheets dressed around my legs inhaling and reaching over to grab a pen all at the same time to journal about the dream that I know will come to pass sooner than I think.

Two weeks later, after having the dream, Lauren called and asked.

"Would I like to go get a mani-pedi and stop in at the new Zendel's Boutique on Park Ave?" Pulling up in the front of my house, honking her horn like she was some crazy woman out of her mind yelling out of the window.

"Eve, come on! We're going to miss out on all the doorbuster sales," she said. Running out the house, I jumped in the passenger side of Lauren's Mercedes Benz, and I was getting ready to let her have it, and she pulled off so fast that we both couldn't stop laughing.

"Lauren, I said, you hear me," As she was cracking up laughing, ignoring me as I was calling her name. "Lauren!"

"What? Stop touching me, she said, pulling herself away from me as she laughed louder."

"Lauren, for the last time, and I'm making this clear to you again, girl, you better stop honking your horn in my neighborhood. We don't do that around here, sister girl. Maybe in your neighborhood with all those children running around, in and out of the street. But over here, we keep it in peace and in silence at forty-three thirty-two Eastwood Dr."

After getting our manicures and feet done, we were ready to shop and spend some money. The automatic doors open wide, and we walked into Zendel's where there was this vast gold Z with a glitter gold circle around it right on the entrance floor of the new boutique. Gold decorations were everywhere, in the windows, hanging from the ceiling, in the dressing rooms, and even on the mirrors behind the checkout counter.

Lauren was so excited as she turned and went down the first aisle, she said, "Eve, I'm looking for a dress to make Robert, her husband's mouth water and eyes buck out."

"What's the occasion?" I asked.

"No occasion, I just need him to remember what he has," she said,

By the time we met in the fifth aisle, everything that was in her shopping cart was for either him, Lauren's husband Robert, or their sixteen-year-old daughter Rachel. While she was trying on dresses, I continued to shop the shelves making eye contact with the little old grey-haired lady standing about four foot nine maybe.

"Would you be so kind as to reach the framed picture that's positioned on the top shelf right above me?"

"Sure, I can help you with that. What a beautiful picture this is." Handing it over, knocking over several books on the floor.

"Here," said Lauren. Coming around the corner, "Let me help you get those Eve."

Both of us placed the books on the lower shelf, and what do we see?

Turning afraid to look at each other, holding our breath scared to move. The little old lady was watching as if we were frozen.

"What is it, girls? Are you two stuck? Or do you ladies have bad knees?" She said, "You know, Dr. Jensen wants me to have surgery on my knees too." Pointing in the air just as she would say it to her Doctor face to face.

"No way, Dr. Jensen, I'm not going to do it!" Lauren and I were not able to move to answer her because of what we have zeroed in on. She decided to walk off, chuckling leaving us as-is.

"Eve."

Not even turning her head to look at my face saying softly.

"Do you see what I see?"

"Yes, Lauren, but is it what I'm really seeing?"

"Yes, Eve, it is."

She asked. "Are you going to pick it up?" Then she yelled out.

"Get it, hurry up, grab it!"

"Okay Lauren, hold on I'm trying to think!" I told her.

"Think about what Eve?"

Mustering up enough energy with my hands cause my legs were sho nuff weak.

"Lauren, look at the black velvet box that was in my dream, can you believe this?" Rubbing the velvet material on the box as if I was reliving the dream all over again.   "Lauren, my heartbeat is pounding fast. Tell me, what do you think this means for Jay and me?"

Walking to the cashier, this is the exact same box that was in my dream concerning Jay and me. I am so floored right now how could this be. My hair is standing up on the back of my neck and flipping the box around, standing here, scratching my head at the checkout counter and trying to figure out why there's no price tag?

"There's no price on it," Gasping up at the cashier man who was waiting to assist me.

"Well, then this is your lucky day to name your price." The cashier provoked me.

Immediately I spoke before I knew it.

"Seventy-five scent," and shoved the black velvet box into his hands.

"Sold!" He said, "Seventy-five cents." He chuckled and added the price to the total.

"Eve, why seventy-five scent where did that come from?"

"It's simply Lauren because of the number seven means complete, and the number five means grace. So I believe God has graced Mr. Jayden O'Connor and me to become one as husband and wife, and that completes it." Laughing together as the cashier began to say and grab a plastic bag to place the velvet box in.

"Your price is right, and the black velvet box belongs to the lovely lady in the Navy blue dress."

It had begun to rain outside, and we were rushing back to Lauren's car. Weaving in and out of the other vehicles, unlocking the doors to get in, and immediately we called the other ladies. Lauren and I were screaming through the car speakers and laughing about what had just happened at Zendel's. Everyone was so excited we couldn't even hear one another speaking.
Livia breaks in.

"Eve, are you and Lauren meeting up with Kayla and me? We are on our way to having dinner at Donavan's."

"That sounds good right about now, and I'm so hungry we are on our way."

The night was terrific roundtables, low lighting, white linen, laughter, champagne glasses of white, and sparkling red wine. Live jazz played by Mr. Paul Knight decked out in a white suit trimmed in a black lapel with a funky bow tie, accompanied by the Clements wearing gold dresses with white flowers on the right side of their hair. Seeing them, I was thinking, hellooo, ladies, swaying each of their hips from left to right while sliding their hands down the microphone pole. Bringing them up very slowly, popping their backs singing baby, baby, baby, fresh salad, candlelit centerpieces, and chattering of various conversations going on all around the room.

With no hesitation, I jumped right in, reminding the other ladies about the dream I once had about Mr. O'Connor and the black velvet box. Not leaving out how the day unfolded at the new boutique called Zendel's. All eyes were on me as I spoke with so much excitement, and then the questions began.

"All I would like to know is?" Taking the time to speak up and ask the question that the other women have been wanting to ask. Without being dared, she circled the table facing everyone one by one, with all the eye contact she had mustered up, she asked it.

"When do we get to meet this fine man Mr. Jayden O'Connor asked Kayla?"

"Kayla, please, Kayla, I do respect your boldness. However, Jayden O'Connor is not the man to keep much company. I do apologize" Circling the table in reverse of the direction, Kayla started from leaving the corner of my eye to her like she cast a spell of witchcraft with her head motions. It became so quiet at our table that if you listened very well, you could hear a rat in the corner licking ice.

"Eve, did you or did you not say that you were going to stop seeing Jayden for good?" Livia was asking, placing her face in her hand like I'll wait for you to respond.

"Now hold on Livia, there was a time or two that I tried to walk away from Jay, as a matter of fact, I knew fooling with him was going to cost me way too much when we first met. And If I would be honest with myself and all of you, my mama Evelyn G. Novae, the G, is short for Grace, hear me and hear me good Grace tried to call me out from the beginning. My own mama, shaking my head, she told me to my face."

"It's something about this man I don't like. He might look good, he might be a great businessman, and I can't put my finger on it right about now, but it's something about him that gets to the pit of my gut," she said. I'm not saying you shouldn't date him and that it won't work ever, but it's something about those eyes. It's in his eyes, she said.

Not to mention, I don't know if I like how he sprays his cologne on all the gifts that he buys you."

"Well, I told Evelyn Grace Novae that I thought it kept him in my mind, and It was a good jester to do so, so spray on my brother. What Grace doesn't know is that I'm not the only woman, nor is there room for another one. However, the benefits have been well deserved."

Leaning my right shoulder up against the wall and bringing myself out of daydreaming about Jayden O'Connor, the black velvet box, and the night being at Donavan's restaurant with the other women, realizing how relaxed I was. Rubbing my ring finger, thinking this is where a ring should have been by now from Mr. Jayden O'Connor. And how this was one day and night, I would never forget. I felt as though I needed some motivation right about now, and walking past the mirror, looking at myself, repeating my most potent affirmations that I know before Jay arrives at eight.

LOOK AT ME EVE

Anointing my head with some oil.

1. My mind belongs to me, and I'm free when it's just me.
2. I'm better to myself then Jayden O'Connor can ever be to me.
3. He who rejects you is not worthy of you.
4. Say no to the one who's telling you no. "No, Jay!"
5. Jayden O'Connor is not my focus nor my view.
6. I love myself more than I love you.

In slow motion in a downward position allowing my hands to be lowered on both sides of my head, okay… taking an intense breath, let me pour a glass of red wine and say a prayer so I can just calm all the way down. Reaching for my phone to see what time it was. Let's see where it's now seven-thirty. And the phone rings Omg! It's Jay calling to give me some type of excuse as always. I'm not answering; I need to see him face to face. No, you get over here.

That's what you can do! Empowering myself to speak with authority.

"Eve," Saying to myself, just answer the phone.

Say,…"Hello Jay."

"Hello Eve, I couldn't wait to hear your voice, how are you?"

"I'm well, Jay thanks for asking and you?"

"My day has been hectic from one staff meeting to the next since the time I got up this morning."
Okay, here it comes the excuse of why he's not able to come tonight.

"I can't wait to see you, and I was calling to say I'm on my way and to ask if you needed anything."

"Wow, I'm so surprised, not another meeting you must attend!"

"No, I'm free, I figured tonight will be the night that I'll make up for all those missed nights I could've been holding you."

"Well,… Jay, as a matter of fact, I do need to see you, and we need to, hesitating to say what I need to say and to be perfectly clear."

"Say it, Eve, what is it?" He's sounding like he is waiting to hear me say come home baby as usual.

"What are you trying to say you have my ear Eve, I'm listening I know it's something good cause there's never anything bad now is there?"

"I guess, I mean, I'm trying to figure out Jayden how I can help your night to become better than what your hectic day has been?" Holding my breath and rolling my eyes to the top of my head with my neck stuck out, murmuring underneath my breath, no Eve, that is not what you're trying to say!

"After dinner, you joining me in some hot bath water would be fine, he said."

This man is the life of me. Tall, dark, salt pepper and his beard and go-tee are my favorites out of them all to love when he kisses me. He takes me there all the way. The whitest teeth you can set your eyes on, his voice is as many beats of every drum in the heart of Jamaica, his skin is every bit of the spelling of healthy. Jay is immaculate. Cut about the face as if God drew the very facial hairs one strand at a time. He works out with a personal trainer at least three times a week.

When in meetings, he's always stitched in a tailor-made Brioni button-down suit, and the cufflinks are never dull. The smell of Clive Christian cologne is the wind that I smell before looking into his eyes; the lingering smell of it draws me to look away. Because the years of his life lived says it all from his soul as the colored rings of blueish-grey from around his pupil. In the back of my mind, I hear him saying, as always,... *I know you, and I'm here to meet your desires.* Clearing my voice to speak.

"Dinner should be ready soon. Bye, Jay, there's no need to bring anything. You have always been enough"

And here we go… Superwoman has just come alive. Out the shower in five, v-neck collar white babydoll dress laying on this body, just the way he likes it.
I'm confident he's going to kiss my neck, no panties at all, for Jay's favorite line is and I quote…*really Eve, they're not necessary.* Two curls in the top and four at the back. Fresh makeup, and just a little of "Black Out Load" perfume by *Joseph Turner* around the clavicle bone. The I-Robot is vacuuming the floor, dishwashing machine running on full

blast. Place a load of dirty clothes in, clean white sheets on the bed, pillows stacked, and fluffed. Candles lit in three different places; dining room, bathroom in the corner of the Jacuzzi, and in the bedroom directly over the headboard. I like it when he looks in my face and pleasures in the shadowed moments of making me feel good. The wine is chilled, the salad is tossed, garlic toast, fresh fruit chopped and dipped in chocolate—a variety of cheeses and Tollhouse original butter crackers on the side.

You can't get any better than this, Mr. O'Connor. Prancing around with the sound of *Teddy Pendergrass* in the air, "Close The Door" was playing through the intercom all over the house. Oven warming with seasoned asparagus and two baked potatoes with extra cheese, please. Just in case he's starving. Pulled the steaks out from marinating in the fridge ready for the grill, lights are low, fireplace burning real good. You can hear the crackling of the wood up in here pop, pop, popping. I'm so happy Jay is coming!

"No, Stop! Stop Eve, don't do this to yourself. How long are you going to be torn between two minds of making one decision? Jesus, please, I'm calling on you. I feel this man pulling on my spirit. Help me, my flesh is untamed, and this man is in my mind causing me to want to be wicked tonight."

I raised my voice, asking Atomie the computerized automated voice-controlled system that runs throughout the whole house.

"Atomie, please turn the music down." Hearing the sound from down the hall, I was focused on the foyer, the turning of the door handle, and then came to a knock. He's here touching my chest. Taking a look at the microwave time, it says seven forty-five he's early, and then comes another knock, I softly say.

"Jay, use your key, speaking out loud, the one I've never asked for back, but tonight I'm getting that key and my soul loosed from the pit of hell."

"Who Am I fooling? Lol, I'm In love with this man. I see it on paper now, Eve, Gracelyn O'Connor," Laughing at myself-putting these steaks on the grill. With some slithers of pineapple, mango saluted onions and mushrooms, sided with red, yellow, and green peppers topped with some A1 sauce on the side. I have my apron on with a towel over my right shoulder, spatula in the left hand, headed to the door to see what's the holdup.

Opening the door, all at the same time dropping the spatula.

"Oh, no!"

If I've ever looked like I may have been white, it's right about now. Standing to meet me below my waistline was five years old Nicholas as Lauren was getting out of her sixteen-year-old daughter Rachel's car. A beat-up powered blue1997 Cutlass Sierra with her son wrapped in a blanket seven-month-old baby boy Evan. Making her way to the door in a hurry, I can see it from here on her face, this is not going to be good but not now.

"Nooo, Lauren, you can't come. Not now," I said before I knew it.

"Eve, my marriage is over!"

"What are you talking about?" Ready to comfort her.

She was breaking down in my arms, leaving me to grab baby Evan out of her hands.

Broken and sobbing as I hugged her, standing in the frame of my door. Nicholas was grabbing the other side, shaking it, looking up at me to say.

"Auntie, Auntie Eve, my daddy says bye, bye to mommy and makes her cry really, really hard now mommy has on the sad face with the frown."

"Auntie Eve, I tried to make her laugh, but she says no, Nickolas not now mommy is hurting really bad." Patting, little Nicholas in the center of his back. Holding baby Evan as I looked over Lauren's shoulder as she cried her eyes out on my white babydoll dress. Just in a split second, I remembered I have no support of panties underneath at all.

While Atomie mistakenly heard the command to change the song, too, "Love Need and Want You Baby" by *Patti LaBelle*. And out of nowhere.

Suddenly, Jay's driver slowly drives bye in his white Phantom, also known as the Ghost, with the back window rolled down, never bringing his face to be present.

My bottom lip drops, and in my head, I'm trying to find the words to say on my tongue that couldn't come out. As my head and eyes followed in slow motion of the Ghost driving pass forty-three thirty-two Eastwood drive whispering. *It's been two months, Jay!*

4

Over Paid Retainers Fee

Pulling my hair behind my ears, "Please, Lauren, come in." Running in the house trying to turn the food off and to find my cell phone so I can send a message asking Jay to give me more time. Picking my phone up only to realize he had already left me a message.

"I see that you're busy, perhaps another time. Much love - JOC."

While handing Lauren some Kleenex and wanting to cry and go to sleep, and thinking about all of the preparation efforts that I had put into this night just to have a moment of truth with Jay, I really wanted to see how clever he would be to get me upstairs underneath those white sheets. I won't even lie to myself; I really wanted him to kiss my body, especially down below. Anyway, I have to focus because there are a thousand questions to ask Lauren right here and now.

"Lauren, why are you so torn up?"
She said nothing. Nodding my head in her face and lowering my voice again.

"What is going on with you?" I asked once more.

"And what in God's green earth are you doing driving your daughter Rachel's car and not your Mercedes?" She took a deep breath.

"Hold on, Lauren." Speaking softly,

"Sit down, Nickolas. Auntie Eve doesn't want you playing with that."

Grabbing from his grip, my one of a kind glass blown Vase made in Milan Italy purchased by Jay. He surprises me with a two-week paid vacation twice a year. In the first two weeks, Jay sends just my mother and me. He knows that Italy is one of our favorite places in the world to be. Jay also thinks so highly of his mother that the same love he has for his mother he has for mine. So his favorite saying is.

"To celebrate the women who've made all the difference in our lives. Not to mention Evelyn gave birth to you on her day of delivery, what's not to celebrate, he says?" So each time we travel, it's for our love for one another and the celebrations of our birthdays.

Whenever I take a flight for the second trip, it's just for me! Florence, Italy, here I come...Sicily, Assisi, Venice, Milan. And Rome, baby Rome! Jay believes in business people. His advice to me about being a woman of business is,

"Eve, we always need time alone to rest, think, review the old, strategically plan ahead, create new habits, and come back ready to walk out all new goals." It's the only time I can mix business with pleasure, according to Jay. At some time or another while on vacation, Jay always shows up. Whether the first week or the last, the excitement for me is not knowing when I will lay eyes on him. It reminds me of a husband in pursuit of his wife. So many times, he'll show up and catch me off guard, and he'll approach me as if this would be the first time of meeting me. Of course, I always play the role of hard to get. Because we all know that the dog is still after the kitty, according to my mother, Evelyn, she has always told the truth.

"Let the dog chase the cat! There's nothing wrong with the dog chasing the cat. The truth of the matter is knowing if the dog is calling you to just play or stay for another day. Some will call...here, kitty,

kitty, and only want to play. Others she said will play until they get hungry and realize they need you. Then they want you to stay so they can eat you up today and tomorrow! Now there's a cost for every meal attended, and don't forget your tip."

But one particular time, I had taken a boat from Venice over to the island of Milan, where sand from the shore was used to create some of the most expensive Vases ever. And if you have ever been to Venice, you will know that it's always and hear me when I say it's still raining on and off. Water is known to be everywhere. Here I was soaked and wet on a boat shoulder to shoulder full of people who I don't know trying to get somewhere. Ten minutes into the ride, I noticed a certain gentleman gets on the boat, but I couldn't make out his face at all because his rain hat covered the sides of his face and neck, he also kept his back towards everyone. Well, we were all trying to hold on and whether the raging waves.

Finally, we made it to the island of Milan, and my favorite store, Via Donte, in the Galleria Mall, was about to close. There were a few people there in the store still shopping. I just had to find that **one Vase that I would cherish forever**—a collector's item to remind me of my trip there to Italy for that particular year.

And there it was! So beautiful; standing alone on the top shelf, emerald green with traces of sparkled gold. An unusual piece and I asked with puppy eyes,

"This piece here, may I?"

Shortly after falling in love with it, another man from the back of the store simply states, Philip, that particular piece has already been purchased. I placed it there on purpose. I turned around to follow the voice speaking with the strong accent, and this short Italian man was adamant about the sold Vase, soon after hearing the man make his claims on the Vase that stole my heart.

Out of the corner of my eye, the strange gentleman that was on the boat trip over here to the island suddenly he had walked up the stairs and out of the store.

"Okay, something strange is going on," I said, holding the Vase with one hand very carefully while rubbing the texture of it with the other side. So I agreed to buy another piece; it was small and something to place on my vanity to hold my rings.

Later that afternoon, I decided to travel from my private Villa in Tuscany, Italy, walk the heart of Rome, and the streets of Monti, Via del Boschetto. You name it! Houses, Cafe's, an array of Vintage shops; some of the best smelling authentic Italian food you could ever breathe in seasoned with herbs and spices that captures the attention of the young and old anywhere. And it seemed as if everyone was out and about enjoying the night air. The streets and sidewalks were filled with people. Lights were hanging from the rooftop of buildings, name-brand shopping bags were seen in every color.

I wasn't afraid, but I actually thought that I was being followed which brings me to another truth you will get to experience while visiting Italy. The fact that the African American woman honey is considered to be one beautiful Goddess to the Italian men. Everywhere I turned, heads were spinning to embrace the blackness and beauty of my skin. The Italian men will walk up to you and kiss you from cheek to cheek and will try to kiss you on the lips if you let-'em. So to break the stare on one particular vacation, I decided to look busy and make a call to Kayla, but her phone went straight to voicemail. While trying to leave a message, I was getting an incoming call from Jayden.

"Hello, baby," with excitement, I said.
"Well, hello, lady. I hope you are enjoying your time away and getting some rest."
"As a matter of fact, I'm all caught up on rest. I'm out enjoying this lovely afternoon in Rome."
Jayden asks. "Have you had lunch yet?"
"Believe it or not, I'm actually walking into Margutta as we speak," one of my number one places to have a freshly made personal pan pizza.
"Since you didn't get to ride the last time you were there in Venice. He said, promise me when you leave Margutta; you'll make it over to St. Mark's to take a ride on one of the Gondolas. Oh! And make sure you ask for my great friend Francesco. He will take good care of you." So I did just that. I enjoyed my pizza with a nice chilled glass of red wine and made my way over to St. Mark's Square.
Francesco, who was wearing black pants with a black and white striped top, he was the young man who helped me in the Gondola and greeted me with one red rose.
As we pulled off from that loading station, Francesco explained to me that I was the only tourist in the boat that there was no other person here to wait on. On the way to the other site that he had to make it too. Perhaps there would be one or two more riders now, as we traveled in between streets and crossed under high rise bridges. Francesco began singing the love song "O'Sole Mio." Paddling with one hand and

pushing off the buildings with his feet. All while another man in the back of the Gondola played the accordion.

The sound of his voice made me want to be in the arms of my lover. I sat in the middle of the bench, took my time to fan out my midnight blue pleated maxi dress, and crossed my legs. I felt the breeze of the ocean. Even though I didn't know the words to the song, I followed the melody as Francesco was singing directly to me. Staring down, watching a few of the guppy fish in the ocean that came swimming by to the face of the water blowing kisses of love towards me, everything was so lovely.

As we approached another loading dock, my eyes followed the sound of men's shoes that were walking on the wooden plank toward the boat. Looking up from this man's pants suit only to realize that it was Jay standing there, clean cut with a smile on his face holding a bushel of fresh multi-colored flowers and a gold box with a red bow on it. I was so happy; I couldn't do anything but cover my face and rock back and forth with laughter.

"Jayden O'Connor, please get in this boat and kiss me," I said.

"What, did you think I wasn't coming?"

"Baby, I love you so much, I continued to say. You do it for me, and I'm so happy you're here, baby. Thank you for coming!"

He chuckled something crazy because once again, he caught me off guard. I was showered with his kind of love for his timing. He couldn't get in the Gondola fast enough for me because as soon as he sat down, I was all over him. I immediately sat in his lap, touching and rubbing him as I kissed all over his face. He never stops me; he just closes his eyes and lets me have my way. This moment will always be unforgettable for me.

"Quick open your gift," he said.

I removed the red bow and opened the gold box, and there it was, the sparkling gold emerald green one of a kind Vase I had fallen in love with at Via Donte's. My mouth was wide open. I couldn't do anything but laugh, give thanks, and ask.

"How did you do it, Jay?"

"Let's just say I have people who know how to follow to get me what I want so I can do what I need to get done," Jayden O'Connor said.

We both laughed so hard and enjoyed each other as Francesco continued to sing as we drifted into the sunset on the waters of Venice, Italy.

"Eve...Hello, waving her hand in my face, Eve, Are you listening? I'm dealing with abandonment issues here!"

"Yes, Lauren, now what were you saying?"

"Eve, it's true, Lauren said, Robert has been cheating. He has been cheating for the past four years."

"Hey, now wait, just one minute Lauren, are you sure?" I asked.

"Yes, I'm certain of it!" Nodding her head to make a believer outta me.

"How can you be so sure? Lauren, please, this is not the time to be losing a husband with three babies."

"I've talked with her face to face Eve. The nerve of this home-wrecking tramp. Well, the nerve of Robert with his two-timing. Ugh!" Covering her face to not show her shame.

She then says, "I'm not going to let them break me down like this. They cannot get the best of me."

"Lauren, I'm so proud of you for deciding to stand strong in all of this," I said.

"But wait! Girl, I know it's true because shortly after I had given birth to Nickolas, there was a large amount of money taken out of one of our accounts and several charges made on many of our credit cards. I remember it taking place as if it was an hour ago." Yelling as her nose began to run and tears fell from her eyes, making paths of streaks in her makeup.

"I asked Robert, I asked him, Eve, I said,

"Rob, honey, there's a large amount of money that has been withdrawn from one of our savings accounts. Lauren continued to explain. And Eve, you know how I am about saving money, and so does Robert."

"So, what was his explanation of the money?"

"He says Lauren, don't worry; I'll put it back, I'll put the money back. I'm investing in a small business deal, and I should have the money back in no time."

"I reminded him that we have children we need to put through college."

"Well, has he taken the time to put the money back at all or at least some of it?"

"Eve, this man has broken up our happy home. If Rob tries to fight me for what we have built together, I'm sorry to say, Eve, no matter the price, I will retain a Lawyer and fight the black off him?" She starts to cry uncontrollably. Both of my eyebrows were raised very high over what she just said. So as a committed man, you can love the black on him, and the color is not an issue, but as a black man with flaws, you want to take him for everything he has even the blackness of his skin no matter the price. Just as I was about to bring some clarity to the exposure of her heart, She spoke up.

"Rob has been all of my life, and there are times when I can't talk with him because he's always so irritable as if I'm his enemy. Don't get me wrong, Eve. It's not about the money right now, but we need all of what we have."

"Well, sure you do, there are children involved."

"I just need to know how to deal with this black man? If need be, I will get rid of his ass the best way I need to. All I need is a little help."

"He's a man Lauren, now wait a minute watch your tongue."
I listened carefully with my eyebrows raised this time even higher than the eyebrow pencil line that I had drawn on. It was both so much of what she said and the tone of how she said it. If we weren't best of friends, someone else could have easily mistaken her broken heart to a white woman always wanting to have what the black woman birthed out to later, either call the cops, holler rape, abuse, call the lawyer to take everything and run, or it's that time to set the trash out in a plastic bag somewhere in a cornfield to only claim later that he didn't come home last-night.

"Eve, he's so powerful over me, and every time I would ask him about the money, he gets mad and starts yelling as if I'm not adding to the balance. I'm being totally honest here. I don't know how to deal with this man. I need help before someone ends up dying."

"Okay, wait, slow down, Lauren, you are getting too upset. And you're going to make yourself sick, just take a breather."

"Let me do this," I said, reaching for Nickolas' hand to take him in the living room to watch television. So that he's out of the hearing of all of Lauren's hurt and pain, that he thinks is coming from his father.

"Sit here, Nickolas, until Auntie Eve comes back to get you," Eve said.

Patting me once again, he spoke up and said, "Auntie Eve, mommy wears really high heels and nasty clothes when she comes home at night."

"It's okay, nephew, rubbing his back; it's probably her nightgown she wears outside running to the mailbox under her housecoat."

Returning to the dining room to address Lauren and all of this madness in her life, I find her sitting on the couch

43

with her head tilt back pressed against my silver fur like pillows, her eyes were closed, and tears were running back off into her hair.

"So please, Lauren, take your time. Now share with me because this is not making any sense to me right now and saying things you can't take back, plus, I know Rob loves you."

"Eve, you're right, all of this is really beginning to make me sick to my stomach." Sitting up, trying to place her hands over her mouth as if she has to throw up.

Grabbing some paper towels from the kitchen and handing them to her just in case so she can take care of her sick feeling.

"Okay, Robert has removed money from your savings. Also, you've met a woman face to face who you believe is having an affair with your kid's father."

"Yes," Lauren raises her voice as if she's not only mad at Robert but at me just because I now know what's going on.

"How many times are you going to keep asking me to go over this. My head is swimming, and my stomach is in my back right now." As much as I can, I'm trying with everything I have within me to be sympathetic about how Lauren is feeling right now. Still, she's so emotional that she's not even aware that she's yelling at me, and I'm not the other woman who has divided her home and is sleeping with her man.

"Apparently, Rob has been lying to her and me."

"First of all, who is she? And where did she come from?"

"Elise, Elise Richards is who she is, and she comes from Charleston West Virginia. They met at one of Robs' construction job sites here in West Mi'Heir Estates. All I know is she moved here four years ago. Rob put a bid on building her house through the city of Charlotte N. Carolina. Eve, from the ground up, he built her a five-bedroom house, I am so mad right now! I'm angry every day! My heart says kill him, hide my kids, do time, and get on with my life. But my mind says I don't know if I dare to live without him,"

"Oh no, the hell he didn't!" I said, mad as hell.

"Yes, Eve, he did with a swimming pool and a three-car garage. Rachel walked in the other day we were going at it, and she overheard us arguing and swears that she hates daddy now."

He told her, "Our yard is not big enough for a swimming pool, just to be proud of the swings she still has." How many years has she outgrown swings? She's driving! After finding out, she often says,

"Something bad is going to happen to her cheating daddy for hurting her mom and abandoning the family that has always stuck by him."

She swears she wants to kill him with her bare hands. Two days ago, I found a note written to her best friend, Dana, from across the street. It was in her dirty clothes basket while I was doing laundry. Here's the strange thing about it, the note was wrapped in one of my laced bodysuit lingerie. And it said.

"He dies tonight!"

I don't know who else to share this with. I've been holding it in. My family is so divided right now. Promise me; Eve, you won't share any of this with the ladies.

I'm just not ready to face them right now. Plus, if Kayla gets a hold of it, she'll bury me six feet under with her bare hands.

"Now he knows we only live in a four-bedroom house with a raggedy Noah's Ark treehouse and an angry pit-bull in the backyard. I'm so broken." Lauren said as she began to cry out loud.

45

"Eve, I've lost my man." Lifting her head to look me in the face with bloodshot red eyes.

"No, Lauren, you need to hear me, first things first. Rachel is hurt by her father's actions, and she needs counseling to talk out her anger before she acts out loud. Robert loves you, and these children do you hear me?" Wiping her tears, shaking her head, she openly agrees with me.

"Yes, he does, and this heifer of a so-called woman can't have my husband!" Pointing her finger in the air as if she's looking the woman Elise right in the eyes.

"He's mine, and I love him. Plus, he's the only one who has ever loved me"—standing up on her feet, yelling to the top of her lungs as she took her time to walk around my couch.

"Eve, I never shared this with anyone, but Robert was my first."

"Are you kidding me? You have never told me that!"

"Yes, it's true I don't know another man's love, only Rob's. What Am I going to do without him?"

"You are going to make it with or without him, do you hear me?"

"He's the only man I have ever called big papa,

I have given this man all of me, from head to toe. I wouldn't even know how to kiss another man." I mean, how do you have sex with someone other than the man who has introduced you to it? On top of that, who can touch my body as Rob does? Omg! What if he has had oral sex with this woman Eve? Really I just can't believe this; I wonder If Robert loves on her body the same way he loves on me? He loves me, Eve, in such a way that I don't just climax, but we both cum at the same time. So we can share in one another's pleasure. My husband waits on me to get there just to hear me call him big papa. Eve, I yearn for him the morning he leaves the house after loving my whole body. Robert kisses every inch of me, and he's not afraid cause he knows that my body belongs to him. I just don't know if another man will love me the same way."

After having an extended breakdown, Lauren then adds.

"Robert is leaving me with these kids can never be an option. All we know is the way he has loved us as a family. Eve, does God hate me for marrying a black man outside of my race and having mixed kids?"

"Lauren stop, stop it, where are you getting all of this from? God is not mad at you, nor is Rob leaving you, rubbing her back as I tried to calm her down! We need to just think and speak more positively here."

"No! Eve, you are not getting it; Rob has brought Elise a ring. I saw it on her finger, and she told me Rob proposed to her. As much as I don't want to, I believe her because I have the receipt for the ring. From our monthly credit card statement, and that's not all. He put money down on her a brand new Cadillac CT6 not too long ago. Ask me, Eve, go ahead ask me how do I know? I'm glad you asked," Lauren said. Not giving me a chance to even ask, she started in as if my mouth was too dry to get the question out.

"Now wait a minute, Lauren, this is too much." Rubbing the sides of my head, pushing all of my hair to the back, "You need to sit down and talk with Robert because what you are telling me makes me think he has not only gone too far, but this has been premeditated for quite some time." Eve, dropping her head and her voice all at the same time.

"All I know right now is Robert's baby sister Danielle called and asked, were we at the house? Because she was going to stop by on her way to her son's basketball game and bring the plates for our new car. Danielle said she was mad;

we did not tell her or their parents, Mr. and Mrs. Thomas, that we had even gotten a new Cadillac."

"What? As I yelled out! No way, Lauren, this is disturbing to me, and you cannot tell me that all of this has been going on."

"Wait a minute, sit down there's more. I told Danielle. Don't waste your time coming because we have not purchased a new car. There must be some kind of mistake." In return, she sent me over a picture from her cell phone of the License plates with Elise house info but addressed to Robert V. Thomas. His name is on the paperwork Eve, and showing through the window of the envelope. I shared it with her.

"Bring them and hurry, but it must be some kind of a mistake, I'll check into it. So as any wife would, I began to entertain the thought that Rob was planning on surprising me with a new car. Now that I've opened the envelope and seen Rob's and Elise Richard's name on the paperwork, I know this for sure that this is one surprise from hell that has taken me by storm, and I need more than water to cool me off."

As difficult as it was, Lauren continued to explain how she met face to face with this other woman Elise. She hid the License plates in the bottom drawer of her vanity. Under her one of a kind lingerie created by *R.U.Ready For Take Off*. Until she found the right time to confront Robert and to tell him that she had the plates to Elise's brand new car. And he needed to explain with the truth and fast. Lauren also knew she had a matter of days to reveal the car plates to Robert before his sister, Danielle, or their parents brought it up.

"Eve, I hate to say it. I'm so jealous. She's five, five, and every bit of one hundred and ten pounds, hazel eyes and beautiful silky smooth hair combed straight back laying against her shoulders without a strand of hair out of place.

The doorbell chimed, and as I made my way to the door, I noticed the silhouette of her shapely body standing in four and a half-inch heels echoing from the wall in the foyer."

"Hello, may I help you?"
As I opened the door, I looked over at her as if she's the one lost and in need of directions.

"Hi, my name is Attorney Elise Richards. I'm looking for Robby."

"Who?" I asked her

"Rob," Thomas?" She asked again.

"You do mean Mr. Robert Rob Thomas, right?" I said as I continued to talk firmly, viewing her facial expression from the corner of my right eye. She also continued to stand there. Trying to help her, I said.

"I'm sorry to say there is no Robby here." Shaking my head back and forth as I began to ask with a chuckle. "How can I help you?"

"Well, my Robby and perhaps Rob to you. Again, my name is Elise. I live a few blocks over. And I understand that Robert is the head man in charge of the extension of the West. Bel'Heir Estates development project."

"Yes, the whole project is under the management of his Construction Company RVT's. This would be right, and again, how does this information involve you, Ms. or Mrs. Elise Richards?"

"Ms., for now, please soon be Mrs. Thomas, and thank you."

With a pleasant smile on her face looking away as if she's in total bliss.

"Well, to ease your mind of my unannounced visit, allow me to say I've called Mr. Thomas's cell phone several times. To inform him that he can't possibly work on another job without the tool belt that he left in the backyard laying up against the storage shed." Laughing out loud, looking at me as if I was to be laughing with her. But for some reason, she continued to say.

"My calls are going directly to voicemail. I find that very odd as he never goes without answering my calls after the second ring."

Clearing my throat as I asked in a very low but don't play with me tone from one woman to the next. Oh! And she picked up on it very well.

"I must ask." Taking the opportunity to address somebody, Ms. Elise.

"How did you end up at this address? And did you ever give the thought that perhaps the tool belt belongs to another man on the site?"

"You must be the nanny with all the questions he spoke so highly about?" she asked me. "Are you?" Persuasively speaking from the back of her voice.

"Eve, within this moment, I felt as though I was on the front line of a desert war with twelve sandstorms blowing all at the same time."

"My emotions were all over the place. I experienced being insecure and abandoned all at the same time. By a woman that was bold enough to knock on my door and talk to me about a man, I thought I had, and a husband I believed could never walk away. She made me feel as though I was fighting over some territory that already belonged to me. I'm standing here thinking to myself *this woman thinks I'm the nanny.* You better look again, woman. Where in the hell did she get this from? I have sixteen years under my belt with this man who she was so casually calling Robby. Robby, who in the hell is Robby? I wonder what other lies she has been given about me because I'm not the nanny, and I'm sho-nuff, not the maid."

Hearing the shakiness of Laurens' voice, she knew she had to give me the whole truth without holding anything back.

"As I looked down at her right hand and noticed there, it was. Eve, on her ring finger, was an engagement ring. A pear-shaped three and a half-carat ring. Sparkling as if it was freshly cut from the jeweler, cleaned, and placed on her right ring finger today."

"I'm so sorry, baby girl, you've had to endure all of this," I said.

"It silenced me, Eve." Sobbing as she let her head hit my shoulder. Lauren cried, boy, did she ever cry.

"Get it out, baby girl; I said just get it all out."

"What are people going to think when they find out that Robert left me for this black woman?"

I said, what? It's at the point now I'm starting to shake this black talk off and yell duck before you get jacked up.

"Can you believe Robert has all the nerve to leave me for a black woman! A pissy black woman," Lauren said.

"I would like to think that because you are hurt, you are lashing out. So I'll just ask that you tread lightly right about here, I told her. It really doesn't matter what anyone thinks, not even me. So take your time, for you and these babies. You need to be honest with yourself for the true measure of the depth of this situation is not known. Oh, and Lauren, be reminded to search your heart for the color of love. I'd like to know what you come up with."

"I'm sorry, Eve, did I somehow offend you?"

"I don't owe you that satisfaction of knowing, however, on another note, let's be honest, you may never get the truth fully." Turning her body to face me. I encouraged her to hold her head up.

"Lauren, you face me woman to woman. Whether you stay or go, you will need grace." Taking a deep breath, I gave her the truth.

"For change will be present. Do you hear me?" With tears streaming down her face. In her silence, she nodded her head, not once but twice.

"You will need grace for forgiveness and that much more of the beauty of grace to carry you and your family to a place of change. The fear of not knowing what that change would possibly be."

It caused her to be afraid to face me directly in the eyes, so in deep thought, she heard me but looked past me. I then took it upon myself to take one step to the right of her to be seen and to say these words in the pit of her soul.
Putting myself in her shoes as I watched the smoothness of the glossy glaze that covered her pupils, along with the blood vessel that was busted in the corner of her left eye. I asked her the most important question she will ever have to ask the man who has fathered her three children and promised to love you until death do you part.

"Where do we go from here?" She cried in my chest as I held her.

"I'm not ready to ask Rob that," she yelled as her voice became hoarse. Grabbing my shirt with such a tight grip, the whaling of pain wrecks her thought process, crying out loud.

"I'm afraid of his answer, simply because he has loved her beyond me, and my mind won't let me think of asking him something I'll have to remember for the rest of my life," she sobs.

"Eve, my hand slid down the inside frame of the door, resting so gently on the knob. Elise had no idea while I was stirring down at her ring. I was comparing her ring with mine. In my head, I was thinking. *Was I only worth one carat of a diamond that had to take him four years to pay off on layaway before I was able to even wear it?* It was so beautiful that I became silent instantly. It shut me down. I had nothing more to say because I knew this lovely young lady standing before me had stolen my husband's heart."

"If I may begin again, Robert was over yesterday late afternoon doing some last-minute work on our underground water sprinkler system. I don't believe he realized he left his tool belt. It was lying in the backyard up against the shed, she said. I also know the tool belt belongs to him because it seems as though he left his checkbook in the front pocket of the tool belt. So I took it upon myself to bring it to the address that's printed on the checks. Three blocks over make two rights down the street, house on the left you have arrived at your destination, Ms. Richards is what my GPS told me. And what do we have here? You, the nanny, are still working."

"I was actually cooking, preparing dinner for Mr. Thomas and his family. I would have invited you, but it seems as though your GPS has brought you way out of line. Bitch, I will walk you to the backyard and put dirt on you and a headstone that says buried less than fifteen minutes. I am not the nanny I would have you to know. I am the one and only wife as I reached and snatched the tool belt. Thank you for the delivery. I'm sure if you saw Robert's name on the checks, then you must have seen mine. Now get off my porch. And tell your raggedy GPS to take yo ass back three blocks over make two rights down the street to the house on the left and arrive at your dirt-digging underwater destination, Ms. Somebody Richards."

"Well, I'm glad you got the checkbook back," she replied.

"Yeah," I said with a funny smirk as I applauded her, and proceeded to close the door because I was done talking with this woman that had me feeling like I was in a battle of hardcore war over my own husband, and I didn't know why. She immediately put her foot in the door, Eve, and said.

"Wait, the wife, did you say you are his wife?" She repeated herself.

"Yes, and as a matter of fact, I am, and if you don't mind, please remove your foot. I have nothing more to say to you or anyone concerning my husband or where he keeps or leaves his tools," I told her.

"Hold on, I'm sorry, really, I thought you were the nasty nanny of Robby's three kids with a mean attitude. He shared with me that the mother of his kids was killed in a car accident by a drunk driver five years ago on October the nineteenth, approximately three-thirty in the afternoon."

"Killed in a car accident Eve, Rob will never say such a thing besides October the nineteenth is our anniversary date and the time of our wedding."

"Well, I do apologize, I'm sorry I didn't get your first name." She said.

"It's not necessary; I told her Mrs. Thomas is enough for you to know."

"Omg! Lauren, this had to have been terrible for you. Did you say anything else to her?"

"Then she comes up with this brilliant idea and runs back to her car and grabs her cell phone to prove to me some of the things that she had begun to share wasn't a lie, I was so in the state of denial about everything that was going on Eve. She went to her car, and I saw her put something in her pocket. But she came back to the front porch with her cell phone so fast that I didn't have time to say it's over,"

"Listen, Elise; I don't need to know any more. Now that you know the truth of who I am. Just go," I said to her.

"What? Girl, were you crazy? You didn't know this woman. She could have had a gun or even a knife."

"I know right, but she insisted on showing me pictures of them on dinner dates, and how all of them visited the Cincinnati Safari Children's Zoo with her eight-year-old daughter, Jessica." Huffing and puffing with the movement of her chest elevating up and down with as much anger that she could ask me.

"Do you really want to know Eve, when was the last time Robert took the children and me to the Zoo?" Taking my designer pillow from the back of her, Lauren then begins to slap it as if no one was watching her go through her hurt moment of pain.

"Eve, I can't believe this, Elise wasn't afraid to show me. She even had videos of them making out in her bedroom jacuzzi. That Robby as she calls him was sucking her toes in a rose petal bubble bath with candles lit everywhere, and I do mean everywhere."

"Everywhere, Lauren?" I asked.

"Everywhere, look at my lips everywhere, and he was the one who lit all the candles."

"No!"

"Yes!"

"Nooo, no way!"

"Oh! Yes, he did, and his punk ass is not right!" Which to say, this particular night was the night? She said pointing at her chest.

"My Robert, Yes! Her Robby," Lauren took a deep breath.

"He proposed to her with this gorgeous three and a half-carat pear-shaped diamond ring. Honestly, I could tell that she was very hesitant about showing me the proposal portion of the video. She tried, but then I couldn't do it. I couldn't watch it. I became a coward in the face of adultery; I'm so hurt, Eve."

As Lauren began to make a long wail out, beating her chest, her wail became silent as she leaned back against the back of the couch. She squeezed my pillow between her legs and found herself rocking back and forth.

"Lauren, I know you are hurt, and as much as it hurts me to see you like this. You don't have to continue trying to explain making yourself sick about all of this bad news." "But wait a minute, so what was it she had placed in her pocket you never said?"

"I don't know it made me feel a little uneasy, though. So I kept my distance between us. But I do know it was Rob in those pictures and Eve my heart is so broken. It was Rob with bubbles floating on top of his head. Like he was enjoying every bit of sucking and being underwater kissing another woman's toes that are not mine."

Sobbing to catch her breath, Lauren brokenly said,

"I didn't even have to ask her to leave. Tears began to stream down my face as I steered off in the far distance. And out of nowhere. I heard the wedding bells ringing. I heard the sound of his and my voice as we recited our wedding vows before God and man. It was the best day of my life. On that promise of a day, October the nineteenth."

The only thing I could do at this point was to just hold Lauren in my arms. Suddenly out of the corner of my eyes, I saw Nickolas trying to enter back into the room. Hence, with my right hand, I waved him off to go back into the other room as we laid back on the couch, and she wept and wept and wept some more, barely having any strength to mustard the words to say.

"Eve, this woman came to my house, my home is where my family dwells. The place where I'm raising our children. I get out of my bed early every morning, having prepared his hot breakfast. Two over-easy eggs on top of buttered whole-wheat toast with four strips of curd peppercorn bacon on the side."

Taking another deep breath, She continued, "Two cups of black coffee and one spoon of organic raw sugar stirred in the middle while he's reading the morning paper."

"You're better than me. Jayden O'Connor isn't getting no coffee."

"I thought it was me. When Robert was coming home late for months, he would be falling asleep on the couch and not coming to get in the bed, and those months have become four years. I was so ashamed of sharing that I was losing my husband to my friends that I was alone in this whole process feeling unloved by the one man whom I love so much. I was trying to figure out if Rob was still in love with me because he hasn't touched my body in months, and if I was to call it off the top, that was about seven months ago."

Rising on her feet picking up baby Evan she began to stroll around the room. With him in her arms rubbing the back of his sandy brown hair with streaks of blonde running throughout the crown of his head. And her voice dropped so ever softly sharing the last time she and Robert made love.

"Even in our distant but closeness. I knew it, taking a long pause, I saw all the signs I just couldn't believe Robert would cheat and have an affair with me. I've been here for him; it was nothing for me to put money in his pocket from my nursing checks. Name brand clothes on his back, I've paid to put him through college when his own mother said he would be nothing, but a low down dirty dog like his father, who was the neighborhood hoe. Speaking of his dad, Mr. Thomas put him out at the age of fourteen because of his drinking addiction, and when he would come home drunk, he would beat Rob and tell him to get his shit and get out because, in that house, there was only one real man sleeping with his mama. When I met Robert, he walked with his head down and a hump in his back. His self-esteem was so low that I called the man out of him and addressed the issues of his past. The men from my church invested so much time with him. It was their love for God and my love for my husband that I raised his head daily and spoke love to his heart and in his hearing. He was a broken man with no vision of life. I was there when Rob's teeth were missing, rotten, and the souls of his shoes were running over. There were no suits in his closet, and he didn't even know his shirt size and not to mention how to tie a tie. I might be white, but I'm his wife, and I will forever be!"

"Lauren, please allow me to share and interject another way of thinking that could open the possibility of change to take place in the space of healing. You are aware of some devastating news, and I know for sure that it has come and shaken your world. However, I have some questions you don't have to answer now, nor do you owe me any answers for this is not a quiz. All I ask for you is that you would consider being honest with yourself."

Steering her right in the eyes and nodding as she began to nod her head. The sound of the room became very silent and still. You could hear the pounding of her heart beating as I held both of her hands with the tightest hold. Very faint, she opened her mouth as tears streamed down both sides of her cheeks.

"I'm listening to you, Eve," she said.

And I asked the most critical questions that will shift not only her life but the lives of the whole family, including Robert. The man she now believes is a cheating husband.

"Do you love him enough to forgive him without blame?"

"Yes, Eve, I do, I love him," she said.

I said, "Wait a minute, putting up one finger while looking out of the corner of one eye, let me finish. Are you willing to forgive him? If so... perhaps this God the one who has revealed Himself to many souls. As the healer of relationships, in every wounded and injured place, is here to restore. Lauren, again I must ask you where do you go from here? Because life will not wait for you to decide to remain alive. Even if you stop living on purpose for the opportunity of this one moment in your marriage of unfaithfulness to exist."

Grabbing her by her face with my hands, Lauren didn't know I was praying from my heart on the inside, asking God what it is He will have me say to her, to help her move out of this dry valley. I took a deep breath in front of her, and I didn't want to show any signs of doubt that God, the Almighty, was powerful. Knowing God could heal her marriage. Taking my time, I began to speak, reassuring her.

"You will survive, and I need you to breathe in this experience of pain and have life because this pain was designed to sting, but not kill."

5

Dear Olivia

Wow, finally! Olivia, you are in the right place here at the Parker Joyner Workout Gym. It's hot and steamy in here just the way I like it, and I can't even see my legs. Taking a seat with a white towel wrapped around my naked body and one twisted around my red locks. Relaxing my back against the wall, thinking of how the night before was so long working the night shift.

At the Half Black Coffee Shop, was it ever busy? I love that place. I really do. Oh! How I love the owners, especially for what the business stands for.

They welcome the meeting grounds of all people of every culture you can think of, to the idea of interracial relationships.

The one reason I always like to share about the Half Black Coffee Shop is that the owners Montana's black and white, male on male.

For months they have met over lunch at Mama D's Soul Food Cafe while discussing a restaurant business deal. Which never got off the ground, because of the two different backgrounds of their own family favorite foods? That idea was never a happy middle. Trying to get both of them to decide the menu for customers, it was not good at all. So they both decided to continue to eat the fabulous Soul Food dishes you ever wanted to taste at Mama D's Soul Food Cafe.

Because they were one of Mama D's favorite love couples to see, she never made them wait in the long line just to be seated. The Montana's, one couple who was sho-nuff in her VIP Club of members. Who ate well and looked forward to having one of the best experiences while being there. Homemade chicken and dressing with two scoops of cranberry sauce, Big Ma's four-cheese Mac in its own separate hot pot, ground smothered pork chops, mixed greens, and cabbage, a side of Pecan mashed sweet potatoes with melted marshmallows on top, and a side plate of chopped onions with peppered tomatoes. Now one of the things she was famous for that everyone had to order with every meal was Linda's Green Sweet Tea. You just had to have it. It had mint leaves and floating strawberries and blackberries. The tea is so good Mama D bottled it up, and it's being sold in local corner stores even now. It was named after her daughter after surviving a nine-month coma who, for years, was in an abusive relationship who now runs her own battered and bruised women's shelter called HELP... Heal Every Lady's Pain.

One thing they both took notice of was whenever they met at Mama D's; after eating, both men ordered a half cup of black coffee and at the close of every meeting, all except for one time in particular when Chase left the table. Leaving a half cup after drinking the first round of coffee, but Troy never touched his coffee at all. This is the story Chase tells, and boy can he say it. He'll always remember how he asked Troy.

"Would you like me to get you a fresh cup of black coffee to go?"

"No, But I would like the bill," Troy said, placing the open palm of his left hand tracing it down the center of Chase's back.

Chase said it was at that moment when turning from what had his attention, the book Freedom of My Own Choice, written by Author Carmile Jones, which was on the new release bookshelf standing right in front of him. Slowly I placed the book back on the shelf and felt the warmth of his touch; his love called out to me. Chase reminds each of us over time while working on their forever black and white love story how this is where they can meet up with the name Half Black Coffee Shop meeting up at Mama D's Soul Food Cafe.

He shares how I was not trying to allow my mind to go there, but of course, how could I not? It was Troy, the epitome of every other woman's dream man. Tall dark and with all the handsome he could have it was there. I wanted my mind to go there, and with a shy look on my face as if I was scared. I followed the pearled glare on his white button-down shirt all the way up. Taking notice of the few hairs on his chest that I had never paid any attention to before. Not even the small mole that was in the corner on the left side of his bottom lip. And right there, our eyes locked, and he said he just knew that Troy was the one black man he had to have in his life. The one man who would give him orders and take excellent care of him.

Troy is black, and of course, Chase is all white, that's for sure. He's tall thin, reddish-blonde hair, wears name brand T-shirts under suit coats and loafers. They just recently celebrated three years of marriage, and for the last eight months have been going through the proper paperwork to adopt a two-month-old African American baby boy. I really hope this goes well for them because this will be the third attempt, and all the other ones have left both of them pretty devastated.

So that was the workflow of last night, and as far as I'm concerned, it really doesn't matter now at this point cause I'm here at Parker Joyner Workout Gym. This hot steam has been calling for my body all week, plus it's a bonus being in here alone. Any minute now, I could drop my towel and totally relax in the moment of peace. As the steam begins to fill the room, and sweat is just rolling off my body, I can feel it running down my neck. While taking my shower sandals off to allow my feet to touch the dampness of the wet floor, even though my feet were bare, the water felt useful to the souls of my feet.

Let me see how to work this plan to make my next move to get this Twenty-six thousand nine hundred and twenty-five-dollar Submariner Rolex watch. I can't wait until I get it, I have been so looking forward to wearing this watch as I swim my laps in the pool to train for the upcoming ten-lane swimming competition. The winner gets a Parker Joyner swim bag with all new swim gear, five hundred dollars, and a free membership to the gym for one year.

A lot of people may think I'm materialistic, rolling my eyes blowing out hot steam chucking, but I don't think so at all. I believe in getting what I want, and when I want it, I get it! I call it peek-a-boo hide and sneak. I see you, play the game and get paid. The deck is dealt out but, not always even. And when you draw, if you play the wrong card, you know me I'm gonna show my hand, and if that black heart shows up joker it is over! Lol, …now what!

Thumping my left arm in the air, snapping those fingers like hey pa-da, something my daddy LeRoy always told me, know when you're in and call it out when you bow. One day I will bow, and I know I will, as sure as I'm black, I need too. Simply because I do believe in God and I know He has better for me. However, today as far as I'm concerned, I don't look to be bowing down at no time soon. Smiling from ear to ear, this girl is about to boss out. I'm a winner even when the winners get short.

Okay, let me run over this game plan again, cause my head has taken off with many ideas. There are two ladies, Crystal, who is blonde and very dingy, and while laughing, makes a five-sec count complete circle and drops her head. Then there's Mrs. Julie who is very talkative, smells like

mothballs and babbles way too long, about most of the time
her eight-year soon to be nine-year-old granddaughter Sara.
Who's getting ready to visit her for the summer months.
Usually, it's nothing worth listening to; still, she looks at you
as if she's waiting for you to nod your head when she nods
anyway. And then there's Richard, who is this older
gentleman, who wears a toupee on the top of his head but is
very knowledgeable about any watch, especially the Rolex.
He's also reticent but observant of everything, and I do mean
everything. Richard looks through his hanging magnifying
glass as if he's the only and most exceptional flaw inspector.

But they all work the watch counter on Saturday
evenings at Roman's, and for the past six months, I've only
noticed the three of them working this shift. So my plan is to
stop by tonight and pay ole laughing Crystal a visit. If the
timing is right, I'll slide her a special love note. She'll read it,
and I'll make my move.

Looking at the light that hit the floor. As the door
from the steam room opens, and the voice behind the steam
says, "Hello, wow, it feels great in here."
Speaking out loud as she enters the steam room;

"Hi, I said yeah, it does feel really good here."
Even though I was not able to make out her face, her voice
sounds beautiful.

I asked, "How long do you normally stay in?"

She answered, "Probably five to seven minutes, and
you?"

"You should try staying in for twenty minutes; if you
really would like to get your best body detox twenty minutes
tops. But don't go any longer than that, or you'll be walking
out of here like a California raisin for real all dried up." We
both laughed.

"I'm sorry where my manners are. My name is Lynn,
and I'm one month new here at the Parker Joyner Workout

Gym. Normally I head to the gym when I need some alone time from my husband and kids." Never giving a space to share who I was, she continued on about how busy she was and how unhappy she has been being married to a Hispanic man.

A Hispanic man who knows nothing about being romantic and giving a woman quality time, but is more concerned with fixing any and everything in and out of their home.

"This is my second marriage, and I promise after four kids within this marriage, I will never marry again." Motioning back and forth, I can feel the steam pressing towards me as she began moving both of her arms. Hearing her voice, I could imagine she's shaking her head with a discussing look on her face as if she knows she's married to the wrong man.

"Every morning he's off to work, and when he comes home, he's off to work in the yard until the sun goes down he's working, working, working. I would be a happy wife today if he would take the time to work on me and my needs. I'm so frustrated with him right now. She continued on, and I wouldn't mind dancing on a stripper pole for someone to pay me some attention at this point just to fulfill all my neglected needs. My husband Xavier is either building a fence, planting trees, pouring concrete, pulling weeds, laying a roof, or sleeping on his back with his mouth wide open. I'm sick of it!"

As much as I could, I tried to comfort her. Moving over to the bench, she was sitting on and gently placing my arms around her shoulders after hearing her voice crack as if she was about to cry at any moment. And there it was the broken spirit of the other woman.

"Lynn, excuse me, Lynn, Lynn," cutting her off from talking so much. I'm thinking *really you came up in this steam room disturbing the peace in here.* That I was so having after making and serving coffee tables all last night, woman, please be quiet.

"Hey! Hey, hey Lynn, you should be counting the many blessings you have. By having a hard-working man who cares enough about the issues in your home. There's a lot of women who would love to be in your shoes."

"I am very thankful for Xavier, and he is a good man. But he pays me no attention, and we've been married now for twelve years, and the white man Tom on my job pays me more attention than my own husband."

Outcomes a prolonged sobbing of a cry, as she reaches up, and the body towel drops laying across her lap as she covers her face.

Embarrassed that she has shared all of her marriage business with a complete stranger and has no idea who I am in the steam room with her. Lynn begins to apologize, how sorry she was for uncontrollable crying and involving me in her life. And how she thought once she got in the steam room. It would just be her in here alone having an opportunity to blow off some neglected steam she's been carrying. Shaking my head as Lynn's face remains unnoticed. Still, I was able to make out the white of her skin and the silver charm bracelet that had a dangling hourglass with sand sifting to the bottom.

Somehow out of nowhere, I could hear the sound of my Aunt Chloe calling me as a little child to come and meet her best friend. I was trying to get the tone of her voice out of my mind, shaking my head back and forth.

She would call me over to her again and again. I was wearing a yellow dress, two ponytails, and white Barbie doll laced socks that wrapped around my ankles.

Aunt Chloe introduces me to her best friend, Trinity, at four years old. I don't know who has been worse in my life for me. The imaginary conversations with Trinity or my mother's sister Chloe that fucked me and blamed it on some bitch who I have never ever seen. She kissed me between my legs and gave me gifts, candy, and lots of money to keep it between me, her, and Trinity. Here they go.

Why are you so materialistic everyone asks? They think that's all my mind is on is things...cars, jewelry, top of the line name brands, fur coats, and sports gear. My answer to them is for all the hellfire and brimstone I've been through. It's a sin for me not to get rewarded. You heard me I'm gonna get paid!

The sound of the steam came bursting out of the steam pipes once more to fill the steam room, and even though she had covered her face, she jumped, and before I knew it, I had already had her wrapped up in my arms, trying to make a bad situation better for the time being. Realizing that her naked breast was pressed against mine and I touched her.

"Trinity wanted to contact me," just like Aunt Chloe said.
 I felt her breasts, caressing her in the time of want as I waited for a response, and there was none, so I proceeded to bring her to a place of pleasure where she's been longing for and the place where Trinity became my best friend. The vapor was thick, and sweat ran off my forehead as I kissed between the crease of both her breasts; the taste of salt was on my tongue. She uncovered her face and began to kiss me from my shoulder to the lips; I laid her back on the bench slowly, her legs opened and relaxed. Again I felt the weight of her damp towel land on the top of my right foot. She took notice of my nails and wanted to know the meaning.

"Why are your nails fluorescent underneath? They're glowing in the dark," she asked. I never answered her but felt her body give in to the moment of release.

Just what I was looking for, her body was relaxed, and Lynn's head tilted back as her legs opened wider.

With a still small voice, she whispered, "*Give me that.*"

"Only if you cum for me, and let me take you where you want to go."

"I will, for you, I will," she said.

And there it was three small yeses' while pushing me away as if she can't take anymore was the release her body has been longing for and her mind wanted to embrace.

She was all mine, "Hello, Lynn, meet Trinity she's six, and she wants to be your best friend, but it's going to cost you for the rest of your life."

Opening the door to make my exit seeing me from the backside, and she whispered.

"Wait…excuse me. What's your name, and will I ever see you again?" Never turning to show my face or to make known my name I left. Two ladies walked by heading to the showers as I joined them in the conversation of taking a cruise to the Bahamas for their next girl trip vacation.

"Hello…hey Eve, what's going on?"

"All is well."

"Where have you been? I've been trying to reach you all morning Livia?"

"Well, Eve, believe it or not, It's complicated. I'm beginning to love going to the Parker Joyner workout gym on Saturdays. I'm walking out right now, heading to the post office to retrieve my mail."

"What's so complicated and special about going to the gym other than seeing all the nice gentlemen walking around with a chest full of muscles," she asked?

I couldn't help myself from chuckling. Thinking and laughing at the same time, you know me, but you really don't know me. As a matter of fact, none of my friends really know the real me. The real me who I want to be. I'm not only in the closet but, I'm in the back of the closet like old clothes, nobody remembers to wear. Your true original self holds the most value. *Men, what men,* I thought? Men are the furthest from my mind. You can have these men I'm tossing ladies, mumbling under my breath.

"Excuse me, Livia, I missed that. Did you say something?"

"Well, if you must know the best part of Saturday mornings at Parker Joyner is the steam room, you should try it sometimes. It's a great way to detox and blow off some overrated steam." Then immediately, Eve asked.

"Livia, I was wondering if you and Kayla wanted to meet me at Pandora's for a glass of wine tonight?"

"Sure, why not, what about Lauren?" I asked.

"No, Lauren is going through something right now, plus baby Evan is not feeling well at all," she replied.

"Lauren is always going through. When is she not? And little Evan's nose is always running. Okay, well, what time? I'm in, I can sure use a glass of white wine right about now," I said.

Pulling my mail out of my security deposit box, all the while, my mind kept drifting to what just happened, not even one hour ago. Questioning myself, did that just happen? Like did I just make love to a crying white woman who's unhappily married to a Hispanic man with four kids? Wearing a silver bracelet with an hourglass charm hanging from it, who knows for what?
It's been so many years now since something like this has happened with me, and I'm so disappointed within myself because I promised myself. I told myself that I would never allow this to happen again. For three hundred and sixty-five days, I said to myself that God created me to love a man, at least this is what my father LeRoy Johnson would always

say. When he would catch me kissing the lips on the girl doll, my Auntie Chloe gave me as a little girl because I was the best little niece that knew how to keep secrets; our secrets. This is what auntie used to tell me;

"God blast it, Olivia, didn't I tell you to stop kissing that damn doll in the lips; you are a girl, and girls don't kiss girls in the mouth. Keep your damn lips off that doll," this is what LeRoy Johnson would say.

I remember running away from him, with my doll Christie tight to my chest, for he would be drunk and would always try to snatch my toy, Christie. My mother, Sherry Ann, would ever come to my aid and say.

"LeRoy Johnson, she's just a baby. Let her have the baby doll; she's not harming anybody. Plus, we don't want to upset Olivia before the caseworker makes her way over here. And you know how Olivia can get cranky, just like you're old mammy cranky, Frankie."

"I don't know who gave her permission to come over my house and reheat my food. Talking about my turkey isn't fully done. My turkey was good! I've been cooking as long as that ole left eye of hers has been out. Next time keep your mama at home or at least outta my kitchen. I don't need no-one's help."

Little did I know, I thought the caseworker was someone coming from the hospital. Because she always asked questions concerning my weight and eating habits. I just wanted my dad to know I earned it. I received the right to keep my doll. This is what Auntie Chloe would say. She didn't want me to tell anybody that we were kissing on the lips and gave me my baby Christie and made me Cris-cross and hope to die over my heart. And I promised it would be just between me, her and Trinity.

Daddy would go fishing, and Sherry Ann would be right at Bingo until the lights were turned out. My parents would always ask Auntie Chloe, my daddy's sister, would she come over to babysit while they went out. We played all kinds of games whenever she wasn't mad with me.

Because sometimes I just didn't want to play. I didn't feel good all the time. Mama didn't have to remind me that it wasn't a play day. Some days I just didn't feel right. I was a sick child way too much. I couldn't do anything but lay there in pain.

"I would always ask, but why?"

"Because you have a disease," My mother said it was from birth. All she knows is that I got it from birth, but God was going to heal me. She told me to keep believing and not to worry. Auntie and I played follow the leader, how long can you make me feel it, oh, and I can't forget about just the three of us, me, auntie, and Trinity.

Most of the time, auntie and I would play this game in the upstairs guest bedroom—all the way in the back of the back closet on the floor. No one could find out about Trinity here. We had to hide her. But we had to do everything Trinity said, or I didn't get to get my snack mama would leave me. And auntie would punish me with a whooping and make me take a nap with the covers over my head while she ate my treat.

Auntie Chloe would press up against me from the front while holding my butt cheeks far apart from the back. She would sometimes rub both of my nipples with her hands wide open. Then there were those times when she would show me how to make my chest bumps bigger by smudging a butter stick over both of them.

"Some kind of way, I will always make you feel better, now stop crying," she would say. Staring at me in the face with those bold eyes making me look the other way, cause she wouldn't back down until I closed my eyes or dropped my head.

Tears were streaming down my face, putting one leg in the car after the other and taking notice of how low I feel at this point, hearing the voice of Trinity in my head speaking from the sound of my Auntie Chloe.

"Look at me in the rearview mirror, Olivia open your eyes and look at me! I want to tell you that I love you and how much you make me feel good."

"No, Trinity, I can't. I'm not strong enough to face you. Why do you want me to love another woman, Trinity? I just want to love my real friends and me!" Yelling out as I slammed the car door.

"I hate you, Auntie Chloe, you and your fucking best friend Trinity that's not here, both of you can go to hell!"

Stuffing my mail in between the seat and the console, and dropping some on the floorboard, and the passenger seat of the car. Looking down and realizing three of the sealed envelopes were letters from her: Chloe, my father's LeRoy sister.

Out of the corner of my eyes, I saw them lying there on the passenger seat, with my top lip twitching with distaste. There were three of them. All the letters have large shaded black hearts with a hole in the center of them surrounding my name.

"Olivia please forgive me across the back of the envelope."

Back and forth, shaking my head like open the letters, you'll never know what she wants to say. No, I don't want to open the letters. She can't control me anymore. And even though she's been writing to me for years now, I've never dared to read any of her letters. One reason is that it was another parent that called the police on auntie, not mine. When it hit the paper, my dad was sick. He didn't know what to do with himself. For days he walked around the house saying he was going to kill 'em; everybody that locked up his

72

little sister Chloe. He became so depressed that he had stopped drinking but, that's an understatement. He drinks for breakfast, lunch, and dinner now. I can't tell him that his only baby sister Chloe is the child monster that the paper named her to be. He's so little now that he weighs under a hundred pounds. My mom even stopped him from driving because he would fall asleep at the wheel. Once one parent can forward with her daughter's story. The braveness of the other parents and their child also came to the frontline. Not my mom! Because they don't know and I guess I'm still having a hard time with not breaking our bond. I'm afraid to tell my mom and dad because of how silly I was to have followed the lead of someone I could not see. It's like people saying they serve this God that they cannot see. Oh! And I'm not going to even have words about believing in whether there is a devil: heaven or hell. Cause my minds so messed up. For years I have believed in a nobody. I have allowed someone else's addiction to create one for me.

I never wanted girls, I just wanted my snacks. My mom left me for being good while she was gone and now I want girls and pretend to like men. It reminds me of a book I read last summer about breaking soul ties. I don't know, do I have a soul tie? The words on the pages said that the fear of facing any truth would cause you to put this book down, and the cycle would continue. At that time, I wasn't strong enough to meet my reality. My daddy's only little sister has been molesting other little girls and me for years. She loved me forever in a day did Auntie Chloe drill it in my head to cross my heart and hope to die if I did not keep our secret. I never wanted to die! I never wanted to leave and abandoned my mommy and daddy. She's been in the penitentiary now going on six years, and she claims to have found God. I don't know, and fuck, I don't care. Cause where was God when she was raping the four other girls she's behind bars serving time for and me? What could she possibly say to the parents of the young girl, who committed suicide? Even though she was brave enough to confess to the pastor at church. She didn't have the boldness to share with her perfect Christian family that she desired pretty shy girls who helped her have the ability to be someone she wasn't raised to be. So, I just wanted to have enough courage to face my truth of knowing I'm not alone. This has happened to more people than just me.

So I opened one of the letters, only because I heard on the radio that the Prophetess named Susan her last name started with an L something.

"For every wrong God has a measure of grace," On my way to work. I would hear her say it with boldness.

And so it read…, "Dear Olivia, I never meant to hurt you."

That was enough for me. Cause guess what Chloe, I'm hurt! This is all that I can stand of your lying sad story—bawling up the letters as tight as I can with both hands throwing them to the back of the car. They landed behind the back seat in the trunk while tears lapped under my chin. Hitting the front of my light grey shirt created a cold, wet spot that says, hey, you Olivia Ann Marie Johnson feel every moment of where you are right now—taking a few swings in the air as if I'm looking her right in the face, and reaching out to hurt her and make her feel how I've been feeling at the bottom of hurt. The grip of the steering wheel caused my fingers to become numb, and hands turned red as blood from any dying animal laying in the street.

It's because of you I live my struggle every fucking moment of the day, and I hope you rot in prison with your bitch ass. I yelled, you deserve to rot, die and never live again; just die!

I cross my heart and hope you die; you touched me. Why did you kiss me? Yelling to the top of my lungs, I don't love you, and I never will, you raped me, you bitch! Hitting the steering wheel with my open fists, as a matter of fact, you can no longer be known as my aunt. Fuck that you're only my daddy's little sister. You don't even have a name! I hate you! I was crying uncontrollably.

Seeing flashbacks of Lynn's body lying there in the steam room, holding my face in my hands as my body slid down in the seat of the car, trying not to be noticed by the people who are walking by. Wiping my runny nose with the cuff of the sleeve of my shirt, turning the ignition on and starting the car suddenly, I hear Eve.

"Hello? Olivia, who are you talking to, and are you crying?"

"No, Eve, what are you talking about?"

"It sounded like you were crying and yelling at someone."

I became silent because I really don't know how much of my madness Eve really did hear. I thought she had hung up already.

"Hello, Livia," she called out to me.

"Yes, Eve, I'm here."

"Are you listening to me?" Eve yelled, and it came bursting in the car surround sound speakers and trying to sit up to answer her.

"Yes, I heard you, Eve, I heard everything you said," clearing my thoughts.

"What did you hear me say, Livia since you are listening cause it sounds like to me you're in a storm and yelling at somebody for a life jacket?"

"No! Eve," I said.

"Are you sure cause you know my love can reach and cover you wherever you are right now! I love you that much, my friend."

Wiping my face, as I repositioned myself in the driver seat, and looking around outside, cracking the window to get some fresh air in, I took a deep breath.

"No, for real, I heard you; you were rambling on about how you can't wait to wear this bad white dress that has flowers all over it with the back out. I heard you now get off the phone and make ready for tonight so I can see you in this badass dress."

I was trying to find a genuine laugh to laugh back at her, cause she was so caught up about this white dress and which shoes to wear.

"Really, Eve, the shoes are not going to be the problem. The problem is going to be if old man Mr. Carter is going to be there and who's going to drink all of those drinks he'll be sending over to the table tonight?" I said as I found a fake laugh.

"Hush up, girl, I'll see you tonight about ten," she said as we laughed out loud.

"Bye, my friend," I said, as I turned up the radio station WCLR FM hearing the smooth sounds of *New Edition* "Can You Stand the Rain." Driving off, I glanced in the rearview mirror speeding off, leaving how I felt in the puddle as I was about to drown in.

6

Saturday Night

Hey Baby! Singing the song "Juicy Fruit" by the *Mtume band*, I even had the nerve to mix it in with "Mary Jane" by the legend himself *Rick James.*

Sitting at the vanity applying my makeup and I was feeling sexy with a smile from one ear to the other. Smelling so good with some *Tom Ford* "Mandarino Di Amalfi" around my neck, two squirts on the wrist, one on the right, and don't forget, the left. Wave your hands in the air, wave 'em like you just don't care. Singing out loud while bobbing my neck;

"You know very well what you are,

You're my sugar thang, my chocolate star.

I've had a few but not that many,

But you're the only one that gives me good and plenty.

Juicy!"

Standing face to face with myself in my three mirrored vanity, with my legs crossed. Okay, wait a minute here I go! Both arms straight up, moving all ten fingers in the air over her head. Eve was all geeked up, moving her body while streaming her hands down about this part of the song.

"Candy rain coming down,

Last in my mind, and spread you all around.

Here I am, oh, this loves for you.

Hey Baby! Sweet as morning dew.

Close my eyes oh what fantasy and you're right here with me.

JUICY Hey Baby...

Mary Jane....

And when I'm feeling low
She comes as no surprise
Turns me on with her love
Takes me to paradise
Do you love me, Mary Jane?
Yeah. Whoa-oh-oh
Do ya? Do ya? Do ya?
Now, do you think you love me, Mary Jane?
"Don't you play no games."

I'm tickled lol lol. Eve girl, you're a mess! Laughing at myself wondering what the night has to offer, I hope for a full deck so I can play any card in my hand. Brushing my curls down the center of my back, I always feel so good when it's time to step out for the night and catch up with the other ladies.

Standing up, stepping into one six inches pointed toe gold heel one at a time. High waist black lace thong panties with matching Bre'el Chic La Rae is my Secret Demi Bra. Pushing my girls up like. Sit up. And act right now, ladies, we are dancing tonight and turning around, looking at my speakers and sitting on my Love Seat that's positioned in the middle of my room.

I'm about ten feet from the nightstand as my Sade Pandora station changes songs to another one of my favorites. Swinging my right arm in the air with my index finger pointing out as if I'm talking to the whole world, and they are right here in my dressing room listening to me sing the song "In My Mind" by Artist *Heather Headley.* Oh! How I love this song, placing my hands over my heart to feel all the love I have to give. But it often reminds me of Mr... Mr. Jayden O'Connor, that is.

I walked over to my dresser and picked up my Triple Berry Sangria, a half glass of refreshing blend of red wine and berries, from one of the top Austrian wineries in the world, *John Lukes Winery*. I love it when Jayden O'Connor takes me there; it's one of the most amazing trips. I'll never ever forget. By the way, *John Lukes Winery* consistently ranks as one of the top-rated activities in Australia for over the past forty-nine years, and every year there's something new to look forward to. Picking up the next line of the song yelling at the top of my lungs as if I'm *Heather Headley* herself.

"I don't care what they say; I'll always be your lady..., in my mind."

The first year Jayden O'Connor had taken me to *John Lukes Winery* for our first ever wine tasting together. Everything was beautiful as always, this man he will always make sure I'm taking care of. Our three-day weekend was so intimate and unforgettable. Of course, large groups had the same tour, but you know Jayden O'Connor, he has to have me all to himself. He takes care of me so well that he makes sure he leaves no room for competition for his time with me or no other man.

So we had our very own experienced and well-informed tour guide Mr. Frank Costello, and he was the most helpful guy. Jayden O'Connor requests him every year upon our return. Frank always set up our very own personal tasty picnic lunch on the top floor in the center of the balcony. The table was set for just him and me; white tablecloth, fresh flowers, and a crisp garden salad with candles and fresh fruit for dessert overlooking the long fields of ripe grapes ready to be pressed and poured. The sun is always soft and beaming down into the sunset as we looked out. Others were holding glasses of some of the best-tasting wine in the world. Walking around as couples or in groups while posing and taking pictures, the sound of laughter was in the air.

I had to take a moment to inhale and take in the deepest breath of all the beauty that was around me. I loved this day that I had never seen before, seeing members of companies raise their wine glasses and make a toast to one another while tour buses were coming and going.

The shared togetherness between Jayden O'Connor and I was altogether lovely. He always knows the right time to pull me close or to hold my hand and make me want a kiss right at that moment. That moment when he turns and looks me in the eyes.

"And says no more for you, lady, you've had enough," he takes my wine glass and carries me off to a hot bubble bath and white sheets for the night. There's nothing in the world better than being in the presence of a great man who has come to appreciate and enjoy the more beautiful things in life. It was one of our first dates here years ago that he taught me how to hold a wine glass correctly, also to know my wines; light, medium, or full-bodied and to sleep well on one thousand count sheets or above after a long night of making some of the best-rated love ever.

Jayden O'Connor can make love to me anywhere. The room was spinning with a cold temperature, and the sun was burnt orange set in its own shadow, the sound of night animals was in the air. Blowing from the high beam canopy bed was bold white sheets in the wind that had no direction.

As I handled Jay's body with the claw of my hands, and he engulfed himself in mine. I was thinking, *why is this man's love for me so full?* He gave me all of him, and somehow my head was leaning off the bottom of the bed, I had no choice but to take notice of the soft red uplighting that was placed all around the room. Very smoothly, as he positioned me in the next position, I started singing one of *Maxwell's* songs. You know I did. Stop playing; smile.

"Whenever, Wherever, Whatever" baby... just give it, don't hold back, I want it.

Entering the kitchen in my heels to pour me another glass of Triple Berry Sangria from the stock that I brought home from our last trip to Austria. Jay goes every year to choose new wines for the restaurants at the JOC Towers Hotels he owns.

Every year on our last day there, you guessed it; laughing out loud, Jayden O'Connor usually carries me to the black tinted windows, unmarked SUV with all of my shopping bags, gifts, and memories of a lifetime. Because of the one hour ride back to the airport from the Winery. I always find myself sleeping in the small of his chest wrapped in his arms for the whole trip back.

"I love you, Jay baby," I said, wanting him to know how much I'm missing him right now. Playing with the diamond pendant on my necklace Jayden O'Connor I'll always be your lady as the song fades out.

At this point, even though I still have to finish getting dressed, I'm feeling myself and this wine, laughing, singing, and dancing all at the same time got me feeling right on top of my game. Picking up the phone, getting my lips curled up, I'm about to call my baby; Putting in my security code to unlock the screen saver. And here we go pressing the picture with my baby's face on it. That says the husband in my favorite category. Two rings, and I don't care how busy you are. Pick up the phone, baby, pickup. Playing with the curls in my hair and waiting for him to answer.

"Hello," he said.

Holding the phone up to my mouth, and singing in his ears like.

"Do what you want, I don't care, I'll be your lollipop. You can lick me everywhere Juicy Fruit…you's so juicy, Juicy."

"Hello, Eve… there she is the woman who adds value to me and keeps a smile on my face." Hearing the sound of my baby's voice always makes me melt. Deep dark chocolate, bald head, six two salt pepper goatee just the way I like it.

"Why haven't I heard from you Eve in the past three weeks?"
In his stern voice, like I needed a spanking for being wrong, I'll take it lol, lol.

"Jayden, stop, you know I love it when you handle me this way."
Placing my hand over my mouth and trying not to let him know that I'm smiling from ear to ear.

"Hi Daddy," I said with all the excitement I could muster up. While lying back on the bed looking at the ceiling and waiting to hear his voice, my heart is pounding like we just met two hours ago and called one another when we had only made it home from our first date.

"Say hi to me, love, and tell me you miss me."

"Eve"

"Yes, baby, talk to me."

"You already know that I miss you and I love you more than you know."

"Jayden O'Connor!"

Putting up with me and my ways, he always gives in to me.
He said, "I love you, Eve, and I can see right now where this is going. Just say you need some, one on one with Mr. businessman himself. Is that what this is all about? Are you playing the stay away from the O'Connor game? Until I have to come and find you?"
"And how many times do I have to tell you, Eve, you can run, but you can't hide, you will be mine forever. It doesn't matter who I'm with; you belong to me."

"Bye Jayden I didn't call you for this. To hear you talk about who you are with. I was getting ready to go to

Pandora's with the ladies. And I was feeling pretty good. Really I just needed to hear your voice; that's all, and you're beginning to disturb my groove right about now."

"Have you been drinking baby," he asked?

"Yes, I've had a few glasses of wine, but I'm well."

"Well, how about I send you over a driver?"

"Bye, Jay, I'm hanging up."

"No, you're not, unless you want to see me and trust me you won't be seeing the other women at all tonight or for a while, Is this where you want to take this?"

"Jayden, why do you always have to throw this up in my face. That you're with this other woman?"

"With whom Eve, I am a busy man. Where would I find the time Eve please not to tonight?"

"Stop Jay! Sitting up in the bed, don't do that to me. Morgan, you know who I'm talking about."

"For the last time, Morgan is my business partner Eve and only my business partner."

Right away, from his background, I heard the sound of the computerized voice say floor one eighteen, and the bell of the elevator made a chime noise, and the doors opened.

"Where are you," I asked?

Avoiding my question, as if what I heard was only by mistake;

"She was here even when I was down, and for me, there was no way out until I met Morgan. Do you hear me? How do you ask me to get rid of this woman? When she was there when the woman I loved with every fiber of my being, gave birth to my only three children cheated on me and walked out of our marriage with?"

"With whom? Whom? Whom? Jayden O'Connor, I asked you a question."

"Never mind, Eve, I told you before you wouldn't understand. Anyway, my ex-wife, Blair, has nothing to do with my future. She is my past for a reason, and my past has no bearings on my next move to create history."

"You know what Eve, I don't like the way this conversation is heading, and you will never get it if I told you it all anyway."

"Jay, I'll never know where you're hurt lies if you don't trust me enough to know where the sores are."

"Listen, woman, I am a man, and I have been a man all of my life. Since I was nine years old, watching my mother sleep in a broken-down truck with no tires in the junkyard. The back windows busted out, no engine with only the driver side door on. And as soon as she fell asleep, I climbed out of the truck and ran to Bradley's Fast Foods, the twenty-four-hour convenience store four and a half blocks, and stole my mother some lunch to take to work with her the next day." "Do you know how hard it was to take two pieces of white bread out of a whole loaf, a can of Vienna sausages, and a Kit Kat bar?" "I've never asked anybody for anything. Not even to spare my life because I had to learn how to make a way out of no way. Even when I didn't know, if I would make it back to that ole broke down truck smelling like cat piss every night, running from the owner of the store Mr. Tom Bradley. You know what Eve, no one knows this to this day, but one night after dropping a glass bottle of seven-up pop and dodging the bullets, he was shouting at me. It was by the grace of God; somehow, the man upstairs knew I had to make it back to my mother. And make sure she was all right, and while she slept, I stayed awake, making sure she got her rest, and no one came to harass us, not even my ole dope feen daddy Jake. So when the men who were in my life said that they will always have my back, they left me in the gutter with a broken bottle in my hand, Eve, lying in a pool of blood with a dead body lying next to me with no answers.

This woman Morgan, who you don't seem to care for, was there."

"When I didn't have money to hold a lawyer's attention for fifteen minutes, she sacrificed her time, body and two pairs of ran over heels, holding down four corners on two blocks. Warming backseats of stopped cars she had no idea she would get out of. When I was too scared to look over my shoulders to see if any family members were in the courtroom. Or had they left after hearing and seeing all of the evidence. She was still there waiting in the wings for me after hearing Judge Lawson say, do you understand that you're facing a sentence sixty years to life in prison. Eve Morgan was there!"

My cell phone began to vibrate as I looked down. I was afraid to release my breath or even blink for that matter, after listening to Jay and all the tension on the phone. It was a text message from Kayla saying.

"I should be arriving at Pandora's in exactly twelve minutes. Girl, I can't wait to share with you ladies all the good news and to show off my new hairdo. Eve, I hope you like it."

Quickly I responded back.

"I'm leaving the house in five minutes, and it should only take me ten to get there. I'm always excited to hear some good news, and I'm sure your hair is becoming on you, for you have a face that can wow any new haircut."

"And for the last time, keep this in your mind and not the back of it," he said.

Hearing Jay continues on, he said, "Whatever we are working on is just that; a work in progress. To better us, me and you, whether you want it or not, I asked you for a commitment, and you gave me one, so there are no reneges. Therefore, you and I will never hold this conversation again. Do you hear me, and have I made myself very clear?"

In my silence, I stood up with my back against the closet door, dropping the diamond pendant on my necklace against my chest, feeling the vibration of the weight of it as it laid against my skin. I was waiting to breathe out.

"Answer me, Eve!"

"Why, because you take care of me, Jay? Is that why? Hold on a minute, let's get this understood. I make enough money to pay my own car note and to lay the foundation of my own home."

"I know Eve, and this is true, but you want me because I'm useful to you. Say no more. Now answer me for the last time because I won't ask again. Have I made myself clear?"

"Yes, baby, yes, you've made yourself very clear."

"Enjoy yourself, your driver Mr. Cox has arrived, goodbye."

"Eve," he said.

"Yes," submissively, I answered.

"Don't keep him waiting."

Thinking to myself…the moment, we've all been waiting for reciting the television host. Alex Tomas from the Name Your Price Game Show that is for me to throw my damn phone.

Walking and overlooking down from my bathroom window and sure enough, just like Jayden O'Connor said, Mr. Cox was waiting and allowing myself to take a moment of silence to find peace in the room. To calm down and make light of a difficult situation with Jay and me. Typically, it's only when I want more from him about his past life; this is when we seem to always go to the left of getting an understanding of things that he and I have ever needed an understanding of. Even the *Bible* tells you to do that, you haven't heard it from me, but I do believe it says.

"Thou shalt always trust and call on God in everything and get an understanding of all things pertaining to life that He so freely gave each of us."

Head just a shaking, let me step into this white dress so I can wow the brothers and make the sisters clutch their men tight tonight. Okay, girlfriend, we see you. Perfect it's laying just right on the curve of these hips, the best part of this dress is the fact that I love having my back out and revealing this ole sexy smooth back. Of course, the beautiful flowers so elegantly detail the hell out of the front of it. Believe it or not, I'm wearing this dress tonight. I wish somebody would say something crazy.

Rubbing down the right side of my thigh while holding my waistline with my own warm embrace and thinking how it would be nice just to be held tonight on the dance floor next to some good ole smelling dark chocolate, it wouldn't hurt to feel a little almond joy either. I had to take my time to laugh at that lol lol holla back at me if anybody understands. Two snaps with the wrist, and I rolled both my eyes.

Looking in the body length mirror hanging on the wall in the foyer of the house, so ready to walk out and enjoy the night to prove to Mr. Jayden O'Connor that there's more than himself. Who would like to be with this fine, as old Chinese China in Beijing, shaped like a tasty piece of pear dipped in white chocolate, and all these blooming rose petals I'm wearing tonight? I'll mess around and catch another love up in Pandora's Lounge when the clock strikes midnight, and It'll be a secret that can't be told.

One last time, turning around and looking how pleased I was at how the glow of my skin is from the Alpha & Omega exfoliating body scrub. The best treatments are called Skin Deep Be Who You Are Black & Beautiful. I've been treating myself to these treatments for the past four weeks now.

I'm going to have to call and share with Ty how I love the skin I'm in and how well my skin is looking fabulous. I needed this organic treatment, and she introduced me too if only Jayden was home to rub the inside of these thighs, honey. Stepping out the front door and encouraging myself.

"Eve, the night is fresh, and all about you and the other woman, step out and be the best you inside of you."

"Hello Cox, it's been a while," as he opened the back door.

"Indeed, it has Ms. Novae," Mr. Cox said.
While holding my hand as I slid in on the air condition blowing softly and these black leather heated seats just the way I like them—a little of this and a little of that.

I said with a chuckle, "Cox, you remember the seats."

"How can I forget, you are Mr. O'Connor's favorite lady, everything has to be right!"
We laughed, and slowly the back door shut.

"Thank you, Cox, for picking up the flowers; there are beautifully arranged."

"Special delivery from Mr. Jayden O'Connor himself, he said to make sure you get out of the truck with a smile." I reached over to smell the flowers and to read the card as always Jayden knows how to make me smile from ear to ear.

It read, "Eve, if the heart could only hold one love, mine would be full because of you."

- JOC

Resting my head back on the headrest, feeling the warmth of these heated seats while hearing the speakers release the mellow sounds of *Bhoe Hudson* the song "Good Loving is Looking For You." Placing my card next to my heart and waiting to feel the pulse of my own heartbeat. I love this man and how he takes the time to love on me, only if he would take the time out with me to spend better days. The light from my cell phone lit up in my purse, checking to see who's calling, but it was a text from Kayla.

She said, "Where are you, girl! Pandora's Lounge is packed, and they have a new live band playing tonight, hurry I have us a VIP table down front."

"I responded, I'm actually pulling up right now. Has Livia arrived there yet?"

"No, not yet, but hurry, come on in so you can hear this band and see my new hairdo!"

"I'm getting out now."

Mr. Cox pulled in front of Pandora's Lounge as the line is wrapped around the corner of the building with people waiting to get in.

"Wow, this must be some hot band in there, Kayla was right, people are everywhere."

Just then, the back door swung open, and the reach from Mr. Cox was very warm and secure.

"Allow me," he said.

Handing the strength of his hand and assisting me out of the black SUV with tinted windows as we stood inside the frame of the door.

"Thanks, Cox once again I appreciate you for all that you do."

"Not a problem, Ms. Eve, enjoy your evening. I'll be here when you return, he said, oh, and here is a little something for you to enjoy yourself," placing in my right hand, an envelope that was sealed, and he continues to say softly leaning in to make sure he was heard.

"This should be enough to take care of all your expenses for the night. Even your purchases you've made before enhancing all your beauty needs."

Mr. Cox moved my hand left to right as to say no, no, no, no, no.

"Thank you, but no thanks. Please return Jay his money and send him my love. For everything is well, I'm not broke; I have my own money."

"I do understand," he replied.

"Ms. Eve, however, allowing Mr. O'Connor to make provision for the night makes my job a whole lot smoother. For you, yourself, know that it's not easy returning allowances back to Mr. O'Connor. Please, without troubling you, as he cleared his throat. How would you like to explain yourself to Mr. O'Connor for I have accomplished my job?" With an award smirk seen on both of our faces, neither of us knew what to say at this point. Because, sadly, to say Jayden O'Connor does not like the refusal of any kind, I mean at all, for he sees them as negative energy and rejection. I was really being stubborn and set in my own way.

Immediately Cox began to share.

"It's not about you showing Mr. O'Connor that you can take care of yourself; it has everything to do with him showing you he can take care of you alone."
Taking in a deep breath all at the same time dropping the envelope into my mocha leathered snakeskin clutch.

"For you Cox, the job is well done, please send my thank you's with a kind message if you don't mind," I said. He tilts his head because he knows I'm about to blow off some steam, being fully aware of the snow that's about to fall but very ladylike. I was still in my feelings about me and Jayden's conversation prior to Cox arriving back at the house. Nonetheless, the residue of the argument was yet on me.

Cox said, "I'm listening."
Checking my cleavage and pushing my clutch up under my left arm softly with a subtle but nasty tone, I shared with Cox a delivery message for Mr. Jayden O'Connor.

"As I said before, the ride was safe, flowers are beautiful, affection is always known, the package will get spent, but be mindful...Eve has no ring on."

Cox said, "Eve. Be nice," the famous words of Mr. Jayden O'Connor himself, as I continued to say very gently.

"And never ever forget, your presence would be more needed on any given day!"

Mr. Cox winked out of his left eye and escorted me to the front of the line, just when the doors to the VIP had just opened.

7

Celebrate the Secret

The door opened, and wherever Eve showed up, Snowfall walked out her poise and beauty she revealed. With all of her essence, Eve was here in the building, and everyone there knew. She was a different caliber of a woman. And Snowfall had just embraced them all. Eve had no problem allowing her inner beauty to be known.

All the other women began to whisper.

"She's gorgeous, and she walks with so much confidence, wow!"

With eyebrows raised and necks cocked, "This woman looks like a money bag all by herself."

"I wonder what the name brand dress she's wearing is? My gosh, that dress is bad on her ass! Or hey! It might be the right bra and girdle she's wearing because she's not jiggling anywhere, and her lady bumps are sitting all together lovely in the right places."

"I believe that she is the businesswoman, who is known as the top giver here at Pandora's Lounge as far as women givers."

"Yeah, I think it is, girls. That woman has blessed so many people in life."

"Well, does anyone know what she does for a living?"

"I've heard so many great things about her, and her experience speaks well for her."

"Is that all her hair?"

Hearing laughs and finger-popping, if it is, she got it together with honey, nor is she dragging her feet. Her back is secure and tall, she must be from out of town, or is she from here? They asked one another.

"Hello Eve, I believe there's a VIP table for you down in the front. Enjoy yourself."

"Thanks, Paul, good looking out, I appreciate you, Sir."

This was one of the many security men named Paul, who is black, muscular and buffed on the outside, but every bit of a caramel milk chocolate teddy bear in the heart. He is always in keeping with the dress code; I must say black suit and all, he is up in here.

Out of all of the security men, he would take the time to address her, for he remembers Eve from frequenting Pandora's Lounge from time to time with the other women. He notices how they would hang around all night with wine glasses, talking, dancing, sometimes with each other, laughing, making a toast to the trust of the girlfriend's circle, and enjoying good music.

As she made her way through the crowd, even before she made it to her seat, a waitress approached her with her favorite. A tall glass of Sangria, and a glass of red wine with a variety of mixed berries, citrus, and lime. A side garnish of one fresh orange slice with a green leaf hanging off the side rim of the wine glass.

"Greetings Eve, from the gentlemen seated at Box Seat number one," the waitress Re-Re said. Snowfall did not bring any attention to the gentlemen at all, and she thought every moment had its own time. Eve joined Kayla as she slid in her seat, excited as she reached over and embraced her with a warm girlfriend's hug and complimented her on this new look, she's been raving to everyone about.

"I love it! I love your new look Kayla; I absolutely love it!" Eve said, waving her hands gently. With her hands over her mouth giggling.

Kayla asked, "Eve, do you really like it?"

"Yes, I do, I don't like it, I love it Kayla it's becoming on you, I feel like I'm looking at the other woman."

Kayla smiled, then paused and asked, "What other woman?"

"The other woman who's been waiting to get to the surface of you and your new life."
We both started laughing at one another.

"Stop Eve, stop, please, you don't have to go that far. You're too funny, girl."

"Naw, I'm telling the truth with your stuck butt!"

"Was I a girl?"

"All the way to the left, but you got it right now, lady."

"Yep! I'm feeling it."

"Wait a minute, give me five more minutes to talk about this new haircut, placing both my hands upon my hips, and laughing so hard at Kayla. Yeah! Miss cutie pie, you didn't tell me you were going to cut it so short," Eve said to Kayla.

Rubbing the back of her neck, she went on explaining about her new haircut, while trying to talk over the *Black Onyx Band* that had everyone jamming on the dance floor. A total of five of them, two fine brothers and three bad sisters. You didn't hear me. These sisters in this band are bad, dressed in gold silk dresses with a middle part down the center of their heads as they were singing and dancing, throwing eighteen inches of bone straight Malaysian hair. The *Black Onyx Band* were singing, "Tonight, Is The Night I Need To Love You Right."

"I really didn't have a choice, but to cut it, Eve, after my mama Hannah Mae died, I lost thirty-nine pounds and all my hair" Kayla started to get choked up. Being in agreement with her, I shook my head.

"Yeah, I know, it got pretty bad for you Kayla, and it seemed to have all happened so fast." Kayla became very quiet, and a frozen look came to the front of her face. Wanting to break her stare,

"I know you miss her girl; she was one of a kind, ole Sweet Lady Mrs. Hannah Mae Williams." I tried to sing it to take Kayla's mind off of losing her.

All of a sudden, out of nowhere,

"Okay!" Kayla said, Feeling the groove of the next song, Kayla jumped up, landing on her feet.

"Hey, *Black Onyx*, hold on now that's my song, they're really about to sing now, I hear it just about every day on the R & B station eighty-eight point nine on my way to work," Kayla cheered the band on.

"Get It, Get It Baby, It Belongs to You!"
Kayla was standing up slowly, swaying her body from left to right, throwing her head back with her arms wrapped around her waist smiling from ear to ear. I watched her.
She was in the moment of feeling her inner soul, that called her out of being that bottled up angry black woman. I can tell Kayla is allowing healing to be present in her life and for it to be her strength since the death of her grandmother, who raised her like a mother. She has found her place of joy once again.

"I see you," I said, and as soon as she went to reach for her wine glass. A gentleman was standing on the side of her touching her by the hand and whispering in her ear.

He asked, *"May I have this dance, pretty lady?"*

Placing a two-hundred-dollar Black card in her hand and taking a quick glance at it immediately. She made eye contact with me. Not knowing that at the time of the offer, the Black card give away had just gone up in price on the blackboard to five hundred dollars. Everyone was listening for the whistle sound to take in the true moment to celebrate one another. Once again, Snowfall surfaced and nodded her head towards Kayla like; you already know what time it is precious. Be about it. A valuable time comes with a price. Flipping the Black card over, she laid it on the table as he escorted her to the dance floor.

Waving towards the back door watching with excitement as Livia was making her way to the VIP section to join us. You see, a lot of people wanted to have access to the private Lounge. Even though they had the money to pay the yearly dues, they still weren't prepared to bring the blessings in the house that was needed to gift one another with a Pandora's black-owned business gift card.

You must be informed that the gentlemen who frequent Pandora's private Lounge were truly intentional about approaching the successful black woman. Time was never wasted in Pandora's. And Aleena, the owner, wouldn't have it any other way but to allow nothing but the Class A woman in the house. Aleena did not believe in having a room full of women as her guest with nothing to offer the gentlemen who were mature, responsible, and hunting. There is no room for slack. You have to have excellent credit, not just good credit. If it's just good, you're not getting in, not even through the back door. It won't happen! But, wait just one minute now, when you get that credit right. You're more than welcome and invite a friend. The staff will know you and your full name.

You see, Pandora's Lounge is all about the true essence and high value of the colored culture, the owners that are two highly educated black women. Upfront and never in the back, Aleena McBride and the woman behind the scenes are her mother, Tola X. Aleena inherited millions from her great grandmother Mayella. For years, Tola X raised hell about the purchase of the boarded-up private night club.

Aleena's grandmother Sara and great grandmother Mayella were slaves. Great grandmama was the slave to the wife and family of old man Nelson. He was white, wealthy, and used to be wrong in his heart toward colored people until he met and fell in love with black gal Mayella Ida-LeeAnn Lounge.

Mayella was a poor country child scared for her life. She was a runaway slave from her mother, Estelle, and father James, burning house. She was beautiful inside and out, even from beneath all that dust and sweat of running in the bushes and dirt roads under the black skies of any night given over to screams of shots, murder, and death.

Well, in the days of 1878 in the backwoods of Hawthorne, Virginia. One well-known slave owner burnt James and Estelle Louis' family's house up in flames. Because of his anger toward Mayella's father, James. Who ran for his life? He ran away from a slave auction house located on one hundred forty-eight Second Street, Johns Bury County, Alabama. Colored slave, James Louis, is formerly known as James L.C. Lounge. He got away and changed his name to James L. C. Louis. He was among one hundred Negros who were for sale at the price of twenty to forty pounds for field hands, cooks, washers, ironers, carpenters, and engineers.

When Paul G. Dowthard realized riding by in his 1876 powered blue Fast Track four-door Ford Mustang, he notices the movement of the bushes. Cautiously in his heart, the known slave then bowed down his head to the ground. There it was with no doubt, the face of the twenty-five-dollar award out for colored slave James L. C. Lounge on the eighth day of December. The reward read and described him as a colored slave, James Lounge, aka James Louis. Being about the age of twenty-three, pleasing countenance, oval-shaped face, quick spoken, and can tell many pleasurable stories. He is shiny black and stout built, large limbs, long fingers, and large feet. The toe next to his two big toes is mashed off, on both feet. The above reward will be paid on his delivery to me, Mr. Curtis L. Whit-More, or at any jail in Johns Bury County, Alabama.

He chased and followed James Louis all the way home. Because of the chase, other whites soon we're well aware that a runaway colored slave had just got caught, and they all came ready and willing to kill. They called colored slave James Louis outta the house, or they threatened to burn it down, with him, his mother Louise Day, his wife Estelle, and three kids. Mayella and her siblings, older brother James, Jr., and baby sister Ida all headed for the back door under the instruction of their father, James.

"Outback everybody now!" He yelled!

The white men yelled back, "We got you now, colored boy!"

"Yeah, come on outta their negro, so we can hang you. And let the day birds eat your flesh and the night dogs eat your bones."

While he detained them in the front yard, he gave his family time to escape the burning house from handmade firebombs. So he thought as the front door closed.

Mayella's mother, Estelle, ran back through the house to stop her husband, James Louis, for she wasn't ready to meet the day of his death. Now Mayella's brother James Jr, jumped through the flames of the back door that spread and made a way through the house from the front porch. Short of breathing, James Jr, ran around the house to search for their father's mother, Louise, at no prevail, he fought hard through the smoke and tried to carry out his mother, Estelle, and never made it.

The sound of faint drum beats echoed in the far distance as Mayella laid in the bushes and weeds outback. The sky she viewed became very small. Even to blink became a challenge of life or death. While bugs and insects swarmed over her face and body, she dares not move or make the littlest sound, for death was upon her, in the heart of white men who carried a hatred for the created skin color opposite of white. For hours the white men raped, spit on, and torched her ten-year-old baby sister Ida to death. One by one, they beat and tormented the only man she had ever known as her father. Mayelle heard the cold-hearted white men whipping him and calling him to the lowest of all names, other than the man she had known him to be.

For he was her only hero. They degraded her father, Mr. James L. C. Lounge, until the bodies of them, both. Ten-year-old baby sister Ida and the man that had kissed her goodnight and prayed with their family before he would leave out in pursuit of work every morning leaned up against the old wooden shed in the back of the house. With a black X in the bottom right corner of the foundation of the dirt floor and the worn-out wood planks. The place where other runaway slaves would pass through on their nights of nothing but grace and hope.

They would crawl under the spot that marked the X for safety and confidence—the promise of making it to another safe house once they got in the shed. The first thing the slaves sought out was the message to freedom written as a note out of *Bible* pages stuffed under the inner lining in one of the chairs left for resting. Of course, there was food left like dry beans and rice left in socks—raisins for energy to be on the run.

The message was visible. You see, all the runaway slaves that occupied safe houses either had biblical names or had changed their names to reference someone out of the *Bible*. Whenever a slave came to James shed, the message of freedom, as outlined in the *Bible*, was simply mapped out from the book of James to help them get to the next safe house. If chapter eight was circled, they knew they had eight more miles to go. Then there was a series of a number that depicts a verse. The circled number or numbers indicated that either the name of X marked sheds to look for to arrive at the right safe house and not a trap house, or how many days they had to rest in that particular safe house before another slave or family was seeking safety and rest. The slaves knew where they were at all times except for the ones who didn't follow the hidden messages that were designed to save them and to bring them to a means of escape. To just make it there and stay on their journey to freedom was most of the desires anyway. Then some had nothing else to live for and gave up because all of their family had been taken far, far away, or killed.

The two bodies left there for Mayella to later identify without anyone knowing she was present was to be a reminder that slaves were not to be free but always owned. Dazed out of her mind in pissy clothes, and hearing screams from a burning mother and her brother Jr. Yelling;

"Help! Help us! Free us."
The repeated high pitch of James shouted warnings.

"Nooo. Don't go out there. Baby, come back, James, and be with your family. Please come back; I love you, James Louis," ringing all from her mother, Estelle.

After Mayella was able to get away in the middle of the night, she came to the back of this white house that was marked with the same black X in the bottom right corner her parents taught her about, and in her mind, she was led to believe that she was free. Three knocks with two pauses and four more beats to follow, she was breathless to do it. But she did it. The door opened, her eyes were wide open without a word she turned and began to take off.

"Wait! May I help you?" With her two fingers placed over her mouth, whispering to Mayella.

"No, gal! Don't go; you're at the right house, we are here to help you escape." The wife of Mr. John C. Nelson stood at the back door of their five-bedroom home and embraced the colored gal of Mayella Ida-LeeAnn Lounge.

"John C. Nelson, get in here, you best to get in right now! We have work on our hands." She called out, holding up the fainted fourteen-year-old Mayelle Ida-LeeAnn Lounge.

John C. Nelson came running from the back room.

"By golly, what in the blood-red dickens do we have here, Sue Ann?"

"Get her to me, let me get her downstairs quick," Mr. Nelson said with his hands shaking and heart racing.

"Hurry John, before the neighbors notice something wrong here." Sun Ann warned him.

This was the story of Aleena Mcbride's great, great grandmother, Mayella Ida-LeeAnn Lounge. For years she was the hidden runaway slave who lived with the family of the Nelson's. She nursed their two children Molly and Johnathan, while having the duties of a wife under the sickly care of Sue Ann Nelson. For days at a time, Sue Ann would lay in the bed from the pain of a rare disease called Dysentery; an illness that struck Sweden in the 1800s, where Sue Ann was initially birthed and raised until she met Mr. John C. Nelson traveling with her father to purchase colored slaves. From this disease, Sue Ann's life and marriage went downhill very fast; it was an excessive flow of discharge or fluid, in most cases. It was pinpointed as hemorrhaging very regularly and reoccurring.

The late, Mayella Alee Lounge became more helpful than she realized to the Nelson family. She would sing and was the only one who had this songbird voice from her family. Songs of the heart would fill the air in the rooms of the whole house as she was cleaning daily, and Mr. Nelson would watch from the bedroom down the hall how she cared for his wife. Encouraging her, to get up and try to do something,

"Come on, Mam, Sue Ann; you can do it, let's walk today."
He has seen Mayella, speaking oh so firm, but also soft to her as well.

"Sue Ann, you are needed as a mother and a wife today," she would always say, looking at her in the dim of her eyes. However, the fight was just not there many days for Sue Ann to be the woman Mr. John C. Nelson had married. The woman of his dreams, he would always share it with the other men of the little old town of Crosby they lived in.

And one chilly morning, in the middle of summer, Mayella had prepared breakfast. Oh, how she could cook and clean just like her mother, Estelle. She had already sent the children off to school. Mr. John C. Nelson came in from morning farming and looked upon Mayella's beauty and acknowledged her strength.

"Mayella, your one mighty fine colored gal, and you're going to make some good ole man lucky to have you one day," he dared to share the truth.
Not knowing how to respond, she giggled, continued to wipe off the stove, and look away.
For she has never had the pleasure of being in the company of any man other than Mr. John C. Nelson and the man in her

dreams, she wishes he could see her as a woman now, her father James, Louis.

He said, "Now, don't go getting yourself in a twist, it'll be years from now, gal."
There was a pause from Mr. John C. Nelson, and nothing said in return.

"Mayella, if there was one wish, what would that be?" Staring at the ceiling, he asked.

She replied, "To have my own private junk joint, so I could sing all night and make colored people feel good again and think of good memories, nothing but good ole memories," She was happy to share about the hidden dream of her heart Pandora's Lounge. He grabbed her and pulled her close, he said.

"Mayella, you just might have that one day!"

"Yes, Sir," Mayella said.

"Do you hear me, gal?"
With a grin resting on the left side of his mouth
Feeling a bit uncomfortable that close in the face and the arms of Mr. Nelson, she repeated herself once more.

"Yes, Sir, looking away, I do understand all dreams are possible If I only believe."

Then there was a call from Sue Ann upstairs; she was coughing and gagging. She needed to sit up to catch her breath and to have a sip of room temperature water.

"Thank you, Mayella, you've been so kind, coughing… you've been kind to me down through the years, you know," She held tight to her arm while taking a small sip of water.

"Mrs. Sue Ann, Mam, now don't go starting that, cause you and Mr. John C. Nelson have saved my life, and I owe you both as well as the dear children of yours everything within me to give."

John C. Nelson called Mayella from the bedroom down the hall, and this time the sound of his voice was something different from any other time. She went to the door of Mrs. Sue Ann's bedroom and responded,

"Mr. Nelson, I'll be right there, Sir," she said.
Taking a second look all the way down to the other end of the hallway, Mr. Nelson was stark whitewashed naked, and she turned and looked away quickly, slamming the bedroom door she rested her back to not look upon the nakedness of her slave owner.

"What is it, gal?" Sue Ann asked, looking toward the door.
With her mouth wide open, but nothing came out.

"Mayella!" He called.
From across the room, Mayella and Mrs. Sue Ann made eye contact.

"Mayella!" As his voice got louder, he called once again.

"Sir, Mr. Nelson Sir, I'll be right there."
Trying to catch her breath, breathing heavily in her chest, She was afraid to release the knob on the bedroom door.

"Go on, Mayella," Sue Ann reached out to her in thin air from her sickbed.

"Mrs. Sue Ann, no, not out of any of my lived years. I can't."

"Listen to me, gal, Mr. John Nelson needs you!"
She whispered, out of all that she had and said.

"Mayella, Go…get on in there and love Mr. John C. Nelson for me."

"Mam, I can't, I've never been alone with a man before."

"Awe…Mayella John C. Nelson wouldn't dare harm you."
Mr. Nelson said once more,

"Mayella! I require you! Must I come in there after you, gal?"

"No, Sir, Right away!"

"He'll take his time, go on gal, no one will know, I promise you Mayella, I promise."

Eyes bigger than headlights, on a dark night of midnight skies, slowly she opened the door, and the house was soundless, but you could feel the wind coming through the bedroom window all the way down the hall from where Mr. John C. Nelson was waiting.

Walking backward out of the bedroom door with tears streaming down her face, Mrs. Sue Ann nodded towards her and said.

"No one will know MayElla; you have my permission." Shaking her head with a yes, she then said, "It's our family secret."

Nine months later, the private birth of Pandora's Lounge was in the great loins of Aleena. Aleena Mcbride's mother, who was Tola X. Ruling from the sideline Tola X was combative like her mother Hope, and Hope's mother was Mayella Ida LeeAnn Lounge whose mother was Estelle Mary Jean Lounge.

Although Aleena, being the new owner of a slave master's wealth, she is not racist, her vision for the private country club was a catered place.

That of only affluent colored people, a place where colored people felt that the private members of the club were free, free to celebrate and be celebrated. For their hard-earned status, they had obtained through the acknowledgment of many struggles of oppression, by the fortitude of the forefathers of those who came before them and paved the way.

The upheld culture of this elite colored people inspires one another within a certain age sec. Holding true to their own value by gifting one another with shared prosperity of business, to further education, and build self-worth as an honored people. It's there in the social environment where the men and women maintain the respect of one another's rights as great people of change.

"Hey Lady, you are sparkling tonight, my love," Livia said as she approached our girlfriend's VIP table.

"I know, don't hate," I said as I blew Livia a kiss and laughed out loud with both arms up and open wide-reaching to hug me.
Livia was singing as she reached out for me on the other side of the table.

"Your lover boy, old man, Mr. Carter and his gay nephew want to know, what's your phone number?" Embracing her back with a loving hug, and the other line to the song created by the Time "Seven, Seven, Seven, Ninety-Three Eleven. I already have some age-old cheese, Mr. Jayden O'Connor. We laughed, boy, did we ever laugh.

"What's up baby, whatcha got brewing?" She said, hugging me back as we rocked back and forth, showing all my whites.

I said to Livia, "A whole lotta ham hocks, black-eyed peas and cornbread on the side, please." Smacking her hips while chuckling it off, we both sat down as everyone watched how we spread the love toward one another.

Then the music dropped down low, and everyone began to grab their bottles and wine glasses, and all we heard was.

"Ladies and gentlemen, please help me welcome to the stage, two-time millionaire and private owner of Pandora's Lounge, the lovely Mrs. Aleena Mcbride."

The lead singer of *The Black Onyx Band* welcomed Aleena to the stage as if she was the next act to follow. Aleena welcomed all of her guests for the evening as always; the men within the club would still walk around and greet all the beautiful ladies with a gold bottle of Aleena's signature wine created just for *Pandora's Lounge* called "Fizz Up."

The ladies would all be sitting with their hand out, ready for the men to fill up all empty glasses with fizz from the pouring. Once the glasses were filled, the women would stand and greet them with taps of love kisses from cheek to cheek, the music would be bumping, and excitement would be floating in the air. Sometimes, on any given night, you might leave out of there with three to four of Pandora's black gift cards, totaling up to seven to eight thousand dollars. All from wealthy blacks wanting to see one another make it and to maintain their level of greatness they have achieved. The adrenaline pushes you to be in a better position to give back to the people you love and the ones who don't mind showing you love. This is one time in the night being at Pandora's private Lounge that if you were in the bathroom, you were coming out for this celebration. No one ever wants to miss the filling of wine glasses and the interchanging of Pandora's Black business gift cards. Dancing women take the stage with fancy costumes from head to toe, confetti and a whole lot of balloons are dropped from the ceiling. The men and women are reminded as if it was the birth of a new year, with handshakes, kisses, hugs, and gifts of all kinds, of outright nothing but 'pure de' love.

8

The Blacker the Berry

Sitting straight up in the chair, and holding my posture not allowing my back to rest, while both of my arms were folded, my left hand was supporting my chin, and I began making my countdown for the gentlemen to approach me on hunt and demand. Five… four…three… two… and…

He has a very clever look about him; however, he was kind enough to greet me by waitress with a chilled glass of rich red wine. As Snowfall, I paused, looking over my right shoulder and lifted up my head with my eyes to the ground I raised them. As I was making out the frame of his face, he glanced at me. Real slow, he didn't miss it. I blinked, and he stood up.

Turning away, "He's coming," I said.

I opened my clutch, and with my lighted mirror, I began to refresh the gloss on my lips from left to right, I applied it. They shined, and there he stood.

In the back of me but facing me from the mirror being reminded that my mother, Evelyn G. Short, for Grace, Novae would always say.

"Wait until he comes, for he will show up. If he's truly a gentleman, give him the space to show his hand. Believe me. Providing if he was raised right, he wouldn't come empty-handed."

"So give him the honor of knowing the other woman he's about to meet," she schooled me like the back of her hand was the open side and laid it all out.

Licking his lips, "Good evening," he said.

I turned and looked away. This gentleman dropped one five thousand dollars black card in my open clutch that I had laying on the table right in front of me. I viewed it. Yes, I did. You know I did. Somebody has to deal with the Snowfall when the forecast calls for it. I also took the opportunity of stirring him in the eyes, by way of my lighted mirror, and did not speak a mumbling word. With his right hand, he flipped another five thousand dollars black card right in front of my mirror covering my face; all except my eyes.
He had all of my attention immediately as I felt the backlash of a blizzard all over my body.

"My name is Eve, who do I have the pleasure of seeing in my view?"
He dropped the black card, and at the same beat of the drummer in *The Black Onyx Band*. The card fell in my clutch. Boom! Right between the allowance package, Mr. Cox gave me from Jayden O'Connor and my very own personal designer, lip gloss, called Kiss Me Right. I had the pleasure of creating this lip-gloss, not even three months ago. I closed my clutch only because I play for keeps, but the light from the mirror was still on. And the silence between him and I was there.

"What does your silence mean?" With a smirk on my face, I asked.
Without speaking a word, this time, he laid a receipt on the table, placing it right in front of me. Making sure I was able to read it, he pushed it close to me as I leaned in. It read the date, his name CEO Mekhi, the store number, one fourteen at ten twenty-three p.m. For the time the food was ordered at the SkyLoft Club from cage suite number nine eleven.

Taking my back posture from before. I said, "You are a bold man Mr. Henderson."
"Please call me Mekhi, all my friends do."

"Friends are earned in my circle," I said. Quickly Mekhi jumped in.

"We are beyond friends, anytime I can identify your body at a crime scene."

"Never in a million years will you be able to, and furthermore, what evidence do you have, and it better be good?" Snowfall was talking with her slick self.

"With a scar, on the back of your left leg about the size of your total hamstring."

"Did you have a valid search warrant, Mr. Henderson?" I questioned him.

"A written tattoo that says Breathe in the center of the lower part of your back."

"I am innocent until proven guilty Mr. CEO!"

"Just about where the crease of the Coccyx bone ends and the meeting arrangement of several multi-colored belly beads that wraps around your body so smoothly."

"Not to mention the dangling diamond that hangs from one of the belly strands falling right in the crease of..."

"Hey! I plead the fifth Mr. Mekhi. Henderson," I said. Standing up on my feet, turning towards Mekhi to place my finger over his lips, desiring for him not to speak, not... one more word.

"Everything is coming to me now, and I remember your face all so well. I mean, I remember traveling and having to stay at the Sky Loft Club, but what do you have to do with any of it? And out of all this time, why have you saved this receipt?" I asked.

"Do you?" he asked

"Yes," I said, catching the side view of his face.

"I just figured out who you are."

And amid my turn, my feet get tangled in the leg of the chair. No need to worry my fall was very soft and intimate. I landed in the arms of Mr. Mekhi Henderson, the handsome young CEO himself. Who entered in my overnight suite, in the SkyLoft Club at the Lega C. Airport. Cage room number, nine eleven.

It was as if he had just spent me out and dipped me in the middle of my own wonderland.

"I'm sorry, and thank you so much," I said, trying to catch my breath and relax in my fall.

"No apologies needed my treasure, just allow me to…"

Resting back in his arms, looking at the fullness of his lips,

"Just allow you to what? And why are you calling me treasure? My name is Eve, better known as Snowfall."

Mekhi spoke up, "I'm just saying you're priceless and valuable in every way whether you have been known to be cold and heavy with all your truth or viewed as a precious gem in the hearts and eyes of those who know how to manage the value of another being a great asset." I closed my eyes and him...Mr. Mekhi Henderson was still there, holding me. I was in very much need of his touch.

"Plus, I've paid for my right tonight, right, he asked?" Waiting for an answer while yet holding my naked back in the break of my fall;

"Right?" With a very stern voice, he asked once more.

With the softness of all of my vocal cords submitted, I answered, "Yes... Mekhi, yes, you're right."

He lifted me and pulled me close real fast, taking me away in the beat of the song that the guest band *Black Onyx* was singing, "This Love Will Last A Lifetime."

For the first time ever in my life, I no longer had the desire to be cold and much too heavy to deal with; Snowfall just left the building. He tamed her and put her in the fourth quarter of the game, outta there. He is about to win me over.

After listening to Mekhi, I suddenly had an aha moment. The only purpose to be known as Snowfall. Evelyn G. Novae taught me how to protect your true self so that others will not know how to deal with you.

I was wounded; let's be honest for a long time, my heart has been broken, and I have never had the need to deal with the shattered pieces because it was a lost love, I was still in love with. Even though it was no longer my own and in one day belonged to another. After the love, I wanted to keep used me and walked out. It was easy for me to walk as Snowfall. It was after this experience that I became less of me in my very own thoughts. So I dealt with men in my past life who didn't understand my worth, nor did they know how to manage all of me mentally, socially, nor spiritually. But...Grandma Tilly used to remind my papa.

She said, "God knew what He was doing. He created the woman for the man. It's in the *Bible*, look it up, Sir."

And in reality, somehow, the script was flipped. Instead of them having the need of me being an asset, I became cold on the inside because I was dealing with the poor management of men either not knowing they too were an asset and had more to offer within any relationship or they too themselves only identified as being a strong liability, nothing more, nothing less. So a lot of those throwaways became nothing but physical, sexual encounters of wasted space, time, and caused me short moments of pleasure and a whole lot of missed currency I could have had.

You see, as Snowfall, I am used to dealing with men who walk with Green Seals in their pockets. The game is higher at this point. Years ago, I was exposed to another caliber of men. I didn't meet Jayden O'Connor by my good looks alone. Although it was a snare, whether clean or dirty, they had 'em. She saw it all and enjoyed what came with it from being spread across the beds laid on worn sheets or simply counted out of suitcases, guarded by security men holding guns under the sight of one eye and scarred faces. Marked on green tables, dark rooms, and smoke infested air with shots of pool sticks making a strike and sounded out background music. She was there. The money that has the one comma and three zero's following in all four corners; the faces on the thousand-dollar Green Seal are that of two-time President Grover Cleveland. He was famed to be the twenty-second and twenty-fourth president of the United States. He earned the right to lead with two non-consecutive terms. Now there you have it. I have earned, the right such as the president, to come face to face with the men who possess nothing but Green Seals. Twice over if they got it, I get it too. If you see it and believe you can have it. And if you get it, you can get it again.

Whispering in my ear;

He said, *"Eve, my treasure, I really do mean business. Check the balance on both of your black cards and be so kind as to give a brother a friendship pass."*

I looked away to play hard, and sometimes it's not easy to walk away from leftover residue on you.

"Look at me!" Mekhi raised the sound of his voice. Everyone was watching us, so I thought.

My body was cold all over with chills. This man just rescued me in a matter of thirty-seconds and demanded me to look him in both his eyes, with his black all-out chocolate self. My mind was thinking. *Heaven is sharing all the black love tonight.*

Stop! You know I looked at him. Stop it now! His eyes were amber gingerbread brown.

"I am your emergency man," he said.
I submitted myself like somebody wet a poodle named Dallas as he looked upon all of the facial expressions that I gave; simply, I trust you, Mekhi.

He said, "I'm not saying that you need to be rescued, but every game needs a catcher to win." I couldn't do anything but lay my head in the middle of his chest. Smell the earthy essence of his cologne and let him continue to lead me in the most extended slow dance I have ever danced in my life, but you know it was every bit of three to five minutes long.
Within the moment, so many things were running through my head. I wanted to tell him. Just take me away. Don't get me wrong, as much as I needed to have gotten jazzy up in here earlier. The other woman in me couldn't do a thing but chuckle, submit, lay, and look the other way.

To the God of Abraham, Isaac, and Jacob, in the heaven's above, everything is coming back to me now the night I met this man!

"Mr. Henderson, I remember it all so clear now!" I said, sighing.

"Be free to call me Mekhi. Mr. Henderson is way too old for me. I'm a General from another open field, but you don't see any old scars on me, although for others, Lord Khiruss is necessary."

Raising my eyebrows, "Yes, Mekhi, it is." I said, correcting myself.

"Thank you for following the rules." He responded back.

"Okay, smh, right. Rules are to be followed." I said, giving him a look out of the corner of my right eye.

"Forgive me, did you say Lord?" I asked Mekhi with a puzzled look on my face.

Mekhi said, "No, I didn't."

"Oh! I'm sorry I do apologize I must have misunderstood you over all this music." Exhaling as I continued to speak. I thought I heard you say, "Lord Khi-russ," I said hesitantly.

"You did, he said, and for others, I said, my rank preferred is Lord Khi-russ."

He reached over and touched the lower part of my neck and said, "Carry on beautiful; I'm listening." Trying to snap out of the fact that this man just told me that some people address him as Lord. Who? What people? And why in the hell are they calling you Lord? With your left hand touching all down my neck. This is what I was thinking but wasn't daring enough to ask.

With a serious look, he said, "Leave that conversation alone, Eve. Perhaps for another day and time."

I turned away to smile.

"I'm listening," he said.

"Mekhi, you have seen my whole body." I shared.

"Yep! I'm pretty sure I did. I could identify your body if you were wrapped in a mummy suit buried in a pyramid from the rock of ages." He said.

Laughing and pointing my finger towards his eyes, "I told you don't look!" I said, being shy.

"Okay, but I'm a man-baby. I looked, and then I asked you can I help you get up," Mekhi said, laughing so hard.

I couldn't do anything about it but join the joy of his laughter.

"Mekhi, so Do you remember everything that really happened that night?"

"I do!"

"No, really come on, do you?" I appeased at him.

"Nah ladies, first you tell me what you remember; he gave me my space and listened.

"Now let me see, I remember getting to the Lega C. Airport searching for the SkyLoft, which was in an unusual hidden place within the airport and you would miss it if you didn't know what you were looking for.

There were no waiting lines. So when I walked in, I placed my left hand to my chest and my right side toward heaven. I was like, thank you, God!

"Hello, Ms. Novae, and welcome to the SkyLoft Club here in the Lega C. Airport," the hostess greeted me.

"Thank you," I said.
Nodding my head and giving a smile, even though I was feeling a bit overwhelmed and tired in my body. However, I still had the strength and know-how to be the woman of all manners.

Showing my members-only card to the hostess who was greeting everyone at the front sliding doors and there it was a sudden peace came over me as I entered what was known as the Grand VIP Clubs of all airports around the world. The one and only SkyLoft Club without any hesitation, it was my first time here.

Side note. After being added as a family member under the account of Mr. Jayden O'Connor. Jayden flies so much that he has accumulated so many frequent flyer miles, and indeed, he would always take the time to share.

"Eve, whenever you have a need or a desire to just take a quick trip somewhere; it's nothing to it. Just arrange it and make it happen under my name," he has always said that to me, and in that order. He will be pleased to know once again that I am flying to New York for three days by way of him.

Tired but grinning from ear to ear. I had to take my flashing Star moment of being here at the SkyLoft Club, which offers you the delicacies of flying without running the hallways here at the Lega C. Airport from gate to gate or trying to find a comfort place in an upright chair, just to get a few hours of sleep. How about when you no longer have to lay on your luggage just to make sure, you wake up with a toothbrush and a clean pair of clothes to change into. Well, the SkyLoft is that members-only club. It takes you away from all of that, also let me mention the company also offers overnight stays on stormy nights like tonight. So here I was, canceled flight, and happy to be here holding my own SkyLoft Club members only card.

Written in all gold in the top right corner was my name Eve G. Novae with a five star-studded diamond following which meant everything was covered. Personal driver, to my cage suite, meals with unlimited drinks, all access to the workout gym, the business center, lite shopping according to any, and all available club members. Triple points earned with cash-back. Don't let me leave out the offer includes travel back to the Lega C. Airport, just in time to catch any and all flights. No questions asked, of who you are, or whose family you are with? Not even the company you may be there as a representative.

Placing my green card on top of the red ultraviolet light, waiting to hear the sound of my name called in the overhead p. a. system. Who would listen to it? I'm glad you care enough to know. Doctors, lawyers, television stars, pilots, chefs, contractors, scientists, preachers, judges, those who played sports, and some internationally known as the wealthiest businessmen and women from every country and continent you could possibly think of.

Keep in mind that your name also appears on the digital marque placed in the center of the room. It had an array of bold exotic flowers flowing out of this fantastic water fountain filled with huge Coy fish and Chinese designed umbrellas hanging upside down under the plaque in memory of Dr. Stanley L. Garrison.

"Thank you for joining us, Ms. Novae," said Bryan, the front desk clerk, who was kind enough to give me detailed instructions as he handed me my cage room key. Just as he handed me the cage key, another worker from behind bumped into me. Turning with only seeing the side view of his face, I said, "Excuse you, that was rather rude."

"Excuse me, Ms. Lady, I don't mean any harm. Is there anything I can do for you?" Placing his hand on my back, he said.
Rolling my eyes too fast to see who was speaking,
I said no, "Can't you see I'm being helped."

Bryan continued to speak, "Ms. Novae, I do apologize for the slight interruption. If you would please, take the first left at the end of this hall, one quick right, through the open doors, and your driver Mr. Sanchez will be there to greet you with a welcome sign. Please know, Mr. Sanchez should get you safely to your suite, cage number nine-eleven for the night,"
"Also, for your returning flight first thing in the morning at four forty-five, you will receive a wake-up call to prepare you for your morning travel back to Lega C. Airport. Gate G2 Flight 1054, please take readily to board at six-fifty a.m. departing Lega C. Airport at seven twenty. If you should have any questions in the meantime, don't hesitate to give the front desk a call, we're just a reach away. Enjoy your stay, and thank you again for joining us here at SkyLoft Club, the best place where everyone is pleasant, and everything is taken care of."

Leaving the receptionist's desk, following all the instructions, that was right down to the tee, Bryan was right. I landed right at the front door of nine-eleven; that was an actual cage to get into the suite. It was beautiful. The Cage itself was very tall—jet black iron bars with double doors shaped like a king-size butterfly. The covered ceiling of the Cage was gracefully decorated with white hanging Peonies. I was captivated by the smell of the freshness of all the flowers. It was a small entrance of a garden, with two chairs and one small table, but very welcoming.

As Mr. Sanchez retrieved my luggage, I waited for him. There you are, Ms. Novae, placing my Cage key in the awning-covered gate. The double doors opened up as we walked toward this frosted screen door with no handles. It slid to the left, and the actual glass door lowered from the top of the door frame, disappearing right into the floor.

"Ms. Novae, is everything all right?" Standing there watching, as I stood in pure silence, he asked.

I stood there with the thought. *Have I really been living grand? Apparently, not at all,*

"Yes,…yes, Mr. Sanchez, all is well," taking a quick view of this well-dressed caged suite.

White walls, engineered natural oak hardwood floors, with hints of various shades of grey and gold, were all throughout the place. Reaching into my purse to offer Mr. Sanchez a tip and immediately, he refused. By putting his hand out, he stopped me, nodded his head, and then stated.

"That wouldn't be necessary," he said. And that I should receive a call within the next five minutes to confirm my stay.

Mr. Sanchez said, turning to walk out, "Ms. Novae, everything has already been taken care of, good night, and, I look forward to my return in the morning."

He soon walked across the threshold, and the glass door lifted back up out of the floor on its own. The frosted screen returned to its proper place, and the caged gates closed automatically. I'm done; somebody needs to marry me today! Lol

There I was left in this glamorous room to embrace it all. I must be honest with you. It's kind of not my everyday living. Taking in a deep breath, I just want a hot steamy shower to relax my body and calm all the way down. It's been such an exhausting day; last-minute packing, the hustle, and bustle of highway seventy-two and the hunger panes off only, half a bowl of Blueberry Almond Crunch cereal. My watch was forty-three minutes after eleven p.m., And I had exactly five hours and forty-five minutes before my wake up call. Board my plane to fall all the way back to sleep. And rest as the plane peel itself off that runway.

From when we left the airport, it had started to rain, and the thunder and lightning were showing out outside. Now I can hear it hitting against the windows. My hair is a mess, and there's not one curl left in my head, I mean it's straight like a wet mop hung out to dry in the Arizona desert. And these shoes of mine are soaked just look at me, brushing all of the wetness off of my dress. I'm just going to shower, order me something light to drink, perhaps a small salad and lay my head down, now that I've made it to the Lega C. Airport in this terrible thunderstorm.

Behind me, the telephone on the nightstand started ringing from across the other side of the room as I made my way to answer it. I took notice that this whole other side of the room was full of different arrangements of my favorite flowers. All over was placed pink and white Peonies. My heart was flooded, and my breath was still, with my hands held out wide. Why are all of these flowers here?

I laid across the bed as I reached for the ringing phone. Kicking my heels off, I said, with a mouth full of held back sighs and tears at any moment was ready to fall.

"Hello?"

And there was nothing.

"Hello… Are you there?"

"I miss you, can you tell?" He said.

Rolling over to lay on my back, grabbing the white sheets on the bed with my one free hand and began to laugh as an arch formed in my back with a whole lot of love.

"Baby, you miss me?" I was happy all of the moment.

"I do, he said."

I couldn't stop smiling and rubbing my right hand down the front of my chest and across my breast.

"Thank you for all the beautiful flowers, baby; I know you did this."

Because he's a man of very few words, he didn't respond. He would never say.

"I don't know how could I ever doubt that you love, you spoil me so much," I said as I began to twirl and play in my hair.

"Why would you doubt? Spoiling you is the best part of loving you, he said to me?" He teased me.

"Does this mean that I get to see you tonight, by way of a surprise visit, since you love to spoil me so much?"
He said, "Eve."
And I waited.
Gazing up at the chandelier as it sparkled, making many patterns of lighted triangles on all four walls, fidgeting each of my toes one by one, I was taking in every moment of how I was experiencing so many mixed feelings right now.
Jayden said as if he has already checked his calendar.

"Tonight would not be a good night, darling. I have a critical meeting in the morning I must attend."

Being a little upset but sassy, I said. "Handle your business, Mr. O'Connor."

"Now Eve," he said.

"No, Jayden, we are all good, I just have to realize that, this is how it's always going to be. Right? Give her all that she wants! All but no time!"

"No, Eve! Come on now."

"No, Jayden, I get it...your surprise visits are only on your time. When I want to be mad and get over you, I can't because you always seem to amaze me." Slapping the air as if he was right in front of me. Because I'm so fed up with allowing him to be a bully of my love for him, push any way he wants, as long as he gives a gift, put a red bow on it, and catch up to me later.

"This is what love is about, helping you realize there's only one man's love you'll ever need, as far as I am concerned. Now tell me… you won't leave me?"

I said, "Jayden O'Connor, I won't, so there you have it, again I'm not going anywhere."

"Good enough darling, I won't hold you, I know that your flight has been canceled because of the storm, and I'm sure it's been a long day, I'll let you prepare for tomorrow, sleep well and think of me," he said.

"Good night Jay!" As I slammed the phone down.

"Thank you for joining us at the best place where everyone is pleasant and everything
Is taken care of here at the SkyLoft Club; my name is Shirley, Operator number four zero six one three, how may I help you?"The sound of her voice was soothing.

"Hello operator, would you be so kind as to connect me with the kitchen, I would like to place an order?"
Rising up from the bed, I unbutton my dress, to step out of it while on hold, I headed to the bathroom to turn the shower on.

"Yes, Ms. Novae, not a problem, is there anything else I can help you with?" She asked.

I said, "No, not at this time, but thanks for asking." The operator said,

"Please hold, and enjoy your stay here with us at The Sky Loft."

Ring, ring…kitchen! A loud voice from the other end.

"Oh! Well, hi to you too," I said. Staring at the phone as he sounded like he's ready to punch out.

"Hello?" "Kitchen, what can I do for you?" He said with a foreign accent.

"Yes, I would like to place an order," I said.

"Sorry, de Kitchen will be closed in ten minutes, okay, do you know your order?" He asked. I can make it for you in ten minutes; please Mam one order for you, okay. He continued saying because de' time, I'm sorry one order until in de morning for breakfast, okay."

Trying to get one word in, "Excuse me! Excuse me, Sir, I just would like to order a tall glass of red wine, and a small Summer Berry Salad, Arugula greens, with vinegar dressing on the side okay."

"Okay, okay, I do for you ten minutes, okay, we bring to you, not a problem, okay. You come in de morning, and I make a whole lot for you, okay," he said, hanging up the phone about to cry because I'm thinking to myself that I'm going to need the entire bottle of wine. Between the thunderstorm, Jayden O'Connor's wicked calendar, and now him. The ten-minute man with all these okay's! I'm afraid to call back. Ten minutes I do for you okay, okay, okay, okay, holding my neck laughing out loud, to keep from crying making fun of my whole day.

When it rains it pours in the thunderstorm, I can't get any time from the old man who loves to spoil me, and de'ten-minute kitchen Cook, who can't speak English very well, okay, okay, okay.

Making my way over to turn the music on as loud as I can get it so I can make my soul happy, and gazing in the mirror, knowing that I need some happy mood up in here. So I can relax and sleep well before this flight in the morning, with a whole lot of de breakfast okay, okay, okay as soon as the music came on. I began to strip and twirl around like I was in an open field dancing under the brightest rainbow with the biggest pot of gold my eyes could ever lay hold of. I ended up in the bathroom, and even though I was upset, I was showering with Jayden O'Connor on my mind. Steam had filled the glass shower walls, and I wish he was standing under this hot water with me, holding my body tight in his arms, making love to me from behind as the water would continue to beat our bodies with all these mirrors in here. The first thing he would say is to turn around because he likes to watch my facial expressions in the mirror and how the artwork of two bodies can become one with so much passion. Somehow he remembers to say we are making history in the moment of now just you and me. This is a moment you will never forget, nor will I.

Fifteen minutes later, there was a chime ringing in the back of all the music.
And another chime was coming; it was from the doorbell. Yelling to the top of my lungs, trying to speak over the music,

"Hold on!"
Chime. Chime.
"Hold on; I'm coming! Hold on; please give me one minute."
Chime.
"Hello? Wait, please, I can't hear you the music is on, and I have suds all in my hair. Don't go anywhere I need that food, I'm so hungry, and I didn't think you would come this fast." White suds in my hair, running down the sides of my

face, and getting all into my eyes, they began to burn, and I couldn't see a thing. Water dripped on the floor as I jumped out of the shower, grabbing my bathrobe and headed for the door. Charles Bolton was singing the song, I'm A Better Man Because of You, in the background from the R & B station eighty-eight point nine. With the most talked-about host on the radio Billy D who's called Rock With It; hyping all the listeners up as they called in one by one.

Feeling the coolness from the air shivering and shaking, I dashed out of the bathroom, and I heard the caller say, "Dj, can you play my song?"
Making a quick left, and before I knew it, I was sliding. I fell and slid right in front of the glass door, which immediately retrieved out of the top door frame. The automatic frosted sliding door became open. To my shame, there I was on my stomach. The bathrobe that I never got a chance to put on was wrapped between my legs, and my hair had fallen out of my wet beehive, with bubbly suds covering my whole face. Slowly, I turned but was too embarrassed to ask for help. I laid there at the feet of one of the workers from the Sky Loft Club. Naked black butt and all.

"Don't look at me! Sir, do not look at me! I mean it!" I said.

"Are you okay? Ms. Novae, here allow me to help you up!" He said.
Easing to give me his hand while trying to look the other way to not look upon my nakedness, I was out of it, and my body was sore instantly. I remembered hearing the sound of his voice from somewhere, but when I made the food order, I knew for a fact that it wasn't the Chef's voice from the telephone call.

"No, Sir, please turn around, and don't touch me!" Lowering my voice, I said.

Embarrassed, I then said, "Don't even look at me."

Clearing my eyes as fast as I could and wrapped my robe around my cold and wet body. He placed my food tray on the table in the front foyer. Once again, he had completely turned away from me.

And he said, "I promise not to look."

"Thank you, Sir, now go, just go and don't try to help me."

"Oh! But wait! Waiter," I said.
Now being able to see him from the back, and that he was a sexy black buff in all the right places, of a young man. Turning his head to the side to be even with his right shoulder.

He said to me, "No, I'm not the waiter, and because I'm on my job, Mr. Henderson would be excellent as a proper address, Ms. Novae. Unfortunately, your order was placed at a time that the kitchen was closing. I do apologize the chef has left for the night. With that being understood and if you don't mind me saying regretfully once more, I do apologize for bumping into you earlier so therefore, as the leading overseer, here at the Sky Loft Club. I personally made sure that you got all that you asked for. Ms. Novae, please take note. I have given you a complimentary gift certificate of one to three nights staying here with us at the Sky Loft Club, for you, any family member or friend of your choice."

With both of my eyebrows raised,

"May I ask one more request of you, Mr. Henderson?" Laughing under my breath,

Is there any way I could get the whole bottle of red wine? I'm going to need it? I asked. Trying so hard not to laugh as he walked out, Mr. Henderson turned and walked away, shaking his head while placing the bottle down with a tall empty glass.

He said to me, "Ms. Novae, please place the locks on your doors, it's the two buttons on the inside wall to your right. A copy of your receipt is here, go easy on the red wine. It's one of our specialties here called Sangria. It's light, but it will sneak up on you, and your summer berry salad is fresh. I hope you like your dressing, and it's not too sweet for your taste, for I squeezed the juice from the berry's myself. Take good care of yourself. And once again Thank you, for being an honored guest of Sky Loft, the best place where everyone is pleasant, and all things are taken care of!"

The night was well spent, and Mekhi, aka Lord Khi, and I had much to talk about. He would share, and I would share. As we handled the rest of the night laughing on and off, I suddenly noticed this young man Mekhi had me wrapped in the midst of his arms, and I was one giggling sister. Well, the other ladies were enjoying themselves as well, with dancing and sharing in conversations around the room. They each would send me a text message being funny as we always do with each other. Woman overboard, woman down, have you seen her, tell me, have you seen her? Come through mayday, mayday, I believe we lost her. They laughed, boy, did they ever laugh at me. I gazed down at my phone from time to time and saw that they were teasing at me all in the group text. And I laughed even harder from Mekhi being so funny.

However, the island that I was on, I can tell you this... I wasn't alone. I felt safe, and I didn't have a care in the world. I knew something was different. For the first time ever in my life, I felt that I belong here, and it had nothing to do with my control of wanting a man to hold, have, and love me. I promised myself in Jayden O'Connor's face that I would not give this position to another man. But, there I was in my favorite place that I usually share with the one and only Mr. Jaden O'Connor. I was nestled back in the chest of Mekhi Henderson for hours, as we both took the time to share memories and photos from our gallery. Okay, so when we weren't sharing pictures. This man made me feel as though I was the only woman in the room, on lockdown in the boxcar or following the lead on the dance floor. It was very strange to me because not once while being in his presence did I ever think of Jayden O'Connor, his gain, power, or his money.

As Mekhi walked me back to our VIP table, meeting the other ladies there.

He asked me right out in the open, "Shall I see you home safe?"

"Mekhi, you're much too kind," I said. And I smiled from within.

In return, he said to me right in front of the ladies, "Once again, follow the rules and answer my question." Kayla was taken aback, and she had started to get smart, rocking back on one leg. I had to cut her off because I knew she didn't understand the man that I was just exposed to. So I helped her before she ruined a perfectly good night. You see, Kayla is not as submissive as I am. I just simply believe in letting a man lead. It's nothing like the leadership of a great man, honey.
So I answered his question and said, with a simple answer no more than this.

"Thank you for asking. However, I do have a driver, and I believe I will make it home safe. Because you have extended yourself, that lets me know that I'll be on your mind. Would that be right Mr. Henderson?" I asked.
Livia following the conversation from one mouth to the next, holding her breath to keep from saying one peeping word.

Mekhi pulled me close whispers in my left ear and spoke, *"If I've seen you once, I'll see you again,"* he then simply took me by the right hand, kissed it, and departed out of my presence.

Livia asked, "Did you give him your number, Eve?"
Missing him as he walked away, "He didn't ask."

Kayla being unlearned and full of wine, says, "What? Mr., I don't know who you think is young blood, but I smell a fat rat, and he didn't come out of my neighborhood."

Walking Out of Pandora's being ushered by Mr. Cox, I said, "Goodnight to Kayla and Livia with a hug and a kiss."

Kayla said, "Good night, ladies."

Livia last but said, "good night, Kayla, good night Eve as always it's been a wonderful night to celebrate."

9

Naked & Not Ashamed

Rubbing my stomach, I'm hungry and don't know what I have a taste for.

"Hold on; I'm coming." Beep, beep, beep. Reaching down into my work bag to answer my cell phone;

"I'm coming just a minute."

"Hello? Hello, this is Eve."

"Well, hello, lady, how is your day going?" Mekhi asked.

"Mekhi? Is this Mekhi?" I asked, wanting it to be him.

"Yes, It's Mekhi," he said.

Smiling, I asked, "Hi, thanks for calling my day has been well, and how about you?"

I asked, "Wait, how did you get my number? I don't seem to remember you asking me for it?"

"Do I need your permission to pursue you?" He asked, being the chaser.

Not knowing what to say, so I said nothing. However, I was so turned on by this man's manliness. My gosh, Mr. Mekhi Henderson baby, turns me all the way on. Mr. The CEO himself takes me to the fifth floor, where I have to ask grace to keep me. Jesus Christ, somebody, Please!

He responded, "My day has been spent, but there's only one person who could save my night."

Nervous and anxious all at the same time. I asked, "And who might that be young man?"

"You, of course," he said.

"Mekhi, you always seem to find a way to bring a smile to my face," I added.

"Is that so?" He asked.

"Yes, every time, so may I ask what you are up to tonight? Since you need me to be your night saver suck-a." We both laughed.

Then Mekhi answered, "I'm parked outside of Suma Yaki Asian Bistro on state street. Wondering if a lovely lady such as yourself wouldn't mind joining me for dinner and a lite glass of wine?"

As soon as he began to ask, I started running upstairs to my bedroom closet, faster than a bolt of lightning as he continued speaking.

"Yes, catching my balance from falling into my walk-in closet. I mean, of course, I would love to join you. Would a pair of jeans be okay with a little naked shoulder?"

"No! Not with me, a dress would be great. Silk; do not be ashamed. Nothing underneath, wear heels. Oh! And Eve," Mekhi was challenging as he continued to say.

"Yes," lowering my voice as I replied.

Placing his demand on me. He said, "Make sure your hair is down."

I inhaled as my chin fell in the center part of my chest.

"Are you there?" He asked.

"Yes, Mekhi, I'm sorry, taking all kinds of baby breaths, did I misunderstand you? I know that you said a dress would be lovely...clearing my throat. Silk, of course, and I can handle that Mekhi but, did you mean to say nothing underneath? Continuing to speak, I said, and please forgive me because I'm just asking... to make sure I didn't misunderstand you," chuckling to play it off.

"No, there is no misunderstanding you heard me— nothing tight, preferably lose. I'll see you in forty-five minutes. Don't keep me waiting, eating without you would be a tragedy," he said.

"Hello?...Mekhi ... Mekhi, I'm still here. Are you there?" I asked, stirring down at the phone. This man is a mystery. The screen read call ended.

Walking up to get in my white Panamera Porsche as the doors on their own unlocked and I was greeted by Faith the voice control.

"You look mighty fine tonight, Eve. I'm curious; what are you wearing?" Faith asked hyping me up even more than I needed to be.

"Well, thank you, Faith," tossing my black leather clutch on the passenger seat.

"If you insist on me sharing, I'm wearing barely there."

"Faith laughed and responded...I understand, say no more."

And I bagged that baby up and took off and left smoke in the garage. Zoom, she was gone.

Driving talking to Olivia;

"Eve, Are you serious?" She asked.

"Yes, I'm showing up with no panties on. Watch me, girl, watch me!" I said, cracking up to Olivia.

"Eve, this man has you all the way outta the box!" Olivia said.

"I know Olivia, and I like it simply because I just never know with Mekhi, it's always something new and fresh, plus he draws me into him. Olivia, I feel as if I could do life with him. Hear me out; with Mekhi, every moment is a moment to live in. He's teaching me how to live in the moment but, more importantly, how to take a risk at love with no rules and even though he's young and I'm going to be truthful here, Livia. I was and still is a little afraid of entertaining the thought that this young punk has me wide open."

"Girl!" Livia called my name and laughed at the same dog on time, laughing but very serious, Livia continued to listen.

"I want to be open because he's pouring into me, and I'm breathing on my own."

Livia said, laughing hysterically, "Eve, I'm so happy for you! This man is on you so tight I can hear your cat purring all the way over here. Shit!"

"Livia, stop it, please! Don't shake me up before I get over there in this man's face; I'm already nervous," I said.

"You should be. You don't have on no damn panties or a bra on. Eve, I believe you have gotten yourself a freak!" Livia said.

"Eve, excuse me and pardon me for butting in," Faith said, interrupting.

Olivia said, "No, But Eve all jokes aside. This young man Mekhi. If I'm not mistaken, thinking back over the relationship details that you've shared with me thus far, for real, this young man is everything you've wanted Jayden O'Connor to be to and for you. Attentive, a gift-giver because you were on his mind and not a gift-giver to makeup because he messed up. He knows how to balance his time even though he's a busy man, and not to mention Mekhi is showing you that he wants to love you and only you." She added but then turned around and asked, "Who wants to share their man these days?"

"Excuse me, Eve," Faith said, butting in once again.

"Not now, Faith, can't you see I'm on the phone!" As I took the time to outline my lips with lipstick and reposition my hair while waiting on the green light, I notice a message running across the screen of the GPS. It read…"Look heifer; you are about to be late, just saying," - Faith.

"Faith, cut it out!" I yelled.

Faith said back, "Why do you call me Faith and believe not the words that I say? Eve, now is not the time to stiffen your heart. There will come a day you will say faith, faith, and my doors will be shut. Don't get locked out, my sista. Ignoring Faith, I said, feeling all sexy and stuff with my naked bareback, "Olivia, you are so right Mekhi is everything that Jayden O'Connor is not. He paid so much attention to me when we were at Pandora's Lounge that I can't tell you the last time I've even asked Jayden for any quality time.

As a matter of fact, Jayden O'Connor has been calling me, and all of a sudden, my time has become so limited.

I asked him, "Don't you have something to do with Morgan?"

"In two minutes, you will arrive at your destination," said Faith.

"Thanks, Faith."

"Allow me to give you a suggestion," Faith responds once again, butting in sarcastically.

"Faith, not now, I'm on the phone with Olivia! Shut off!" Sending a demand to my owner's control panel.

Faith says immediately,"Eve, I know who you're talking to I'm not stupid. But, in two minutes you will be looking stupid because you will be late. Now about that suggestion, you probably should hang up now.

Have a great night, and Eve, close your legs upon getting back in the car it seems as though you've forgotten your panties, goodbye."Faith said in a hurry.

"Faith, I'm shutting you down for two days!" I said, upset.

"Okay, Olivia, I'm going to have to let you go," hurrying up, trying to get out of the car. Bye Olivia bye, I'll call you later and share with you how everything went,"I said.

Olivia said, laughing out loud, "Okay, Eve, hurry up, go, get in there and stroll, so your booty won't be jiggling."

The restaurant was full. Every square table was occupied, and the walls were all brick. Bamboo plants and Asian artwork of dragons, flowers, and trees accented the place. I scanned the room, noticing Mekhi seated all the way in the back at the red leather circular booth next to the bar. The lighting was dimmed shallow, and soft oriental music was playing.
Asian candleholders were arranged in the center of each table wrapped in white linen, making a reflection upon the ceiling.

"How many will be joining you tonight?" The female hostess asked. Afraid to look me in the eye because my titties was standing at attention as the cool breeze was blowing from the vent just above me.

I said, "Thank you for asking; I'll be joining the handsome young man in the back."
As she stepped aside and allowed me to find my own way, swaying as I walked softly from the souls of my feet, noticing all eyes on me with my Vonsha'Sha'Von's Casper cream v-neck silk dress on, I never missed a beat. Mr. Henderson watched me as I watched him. I wanted to see him because he wanted to see me. The closer I got, the more I wanted to be next to him. Mekhi dipped his garnish in his glass of wine, whisked it around, took a small drink, and stood to greet me. My belt was tied in the front. It dangled and slid in between the split that ran up my inner thigh.

"Hello, darling," he said. As I took notice that his embrace was warm.

"Thank you for having me."

"Come on now, you must know the pleasure is all mine," he said as he made eye contact with me. I felt his right hand run down the center of my spin and crossed over my belly beads.

I reached back and caught his hand and asked, "Must you?"
He looked down at me with these glossed over eyes and sucked in his bottom lip to bite down on it.

"I am a lady," I said, making eye contact with him once more.
Still, in his grip and out of everyone's sight, he reached up and caressed my left breast, squeezing it until he reached the firmness of my nipple. My head dropped, trying to bear the honesty of his touch.

"May I?" Pointing to the booth to have a seat. I asked.

"Please, join me," he said, taking me by the right hand.

"Eve," he called.

"Yes," I answered.

"I want you to know that this is my favorite dress I've seen on you. I love it! Most importantly, I love that you aim to please," Mekhi said.
I was silent, but I watched him gaze at my nakedness with no shame.
So we ate, and he played in my hair. As we talked from one conversation to the other, he smiled at me as I smiled back. There was definitely a connected vibe between us. He couldn't keep his eyes off me nor his hands.
Times I would share stories about the photos within my cell, and he would gently move my hair to the side and kiss the back of my neck. Every time he did it, it made my right leg extend out from under the table. "You already know I felt giddy inside. Girl Stop!" Lol, and Mekhi would rub my inner thigh. Yes, he did, rolling my eyes.

I asked him, "You love touching my body?"

He said with the biggest grin on his face, "I do."
Having the desire to get to know more about him more seriously, I asked for more pressing questions.

"So tell me about how you became this great Sky Loft Club CEO of a man?"

"He said, " Ah, here we go."
Pushing him off to the edge of the booth and trying not to bust my side from laughing so hard.

"Mekhi, Stop! Please. Really I'm asking because I really want to know why anyone would call you Lord Khi-russ? I'm curious," so I'm asking.

"Eve, my lady, touching my face, I don't know if you are ready to hear about the old man I used to be," he said.

"Why wouldn't I? It was the old man that brought me to meet the new one. I'm listening," I said.
"I have been on the streets since I was twelve years old. Early on, I became known for being in the game and the weight of my notoriety of drug dealing," he said, beginning to explain easily.

"You sold drugs, Mekhi? I can't see it. Even though in your manliness, your heart seems to be gold," I said

"Gold it was. True that but, gold I had to get!" Mekhi said.

"So share please," I said.

"There were three men among sixteen people named in an indictment, which was held on charges involving an alleged scheme to distribute substantial packages of Cocaine and Heroin. From eight different states. In the first count, these three men were accused of conspiracy to possess and distribute nine hundred pounds of marijuana. They were also charged with transporting millions of dollars from the same eight states."

"Out of the three, one of them is accused in four counts of traveling in interstate commerce to distribute a large sum of a mixture containing cocaine," he said.

"I asked... okay, so what does all of this have to do with you?"

"Well, the Commercial Appeal in all eight of these states reported that the Drug Enforcement Administration agents had a search warrant to search all eight of my nightclubs in these eight different states in connection with the investigation," he continued to say.

"Okay," I said softly, glancing over my wine glass.

"And because of who I was and had become in such a short period of time, my investments in the game covered me more than the hits and investigations that were out on me. My mentor was a Master in weight, so I moved up the ranks so fast that the streets called me Lord Khi-russ which means forever Lord, rise and rule. That's it, that's all," he said, taking his time to explain.

"So, what part of this story is still a part of your life today?" I inquired.

"None of it! The complications of the birth of my daughter led me to sell all eight of my O'Malley's nightclubs named after my mothers brother. And I invested in available space for the private Sky Loft Club within twelve major airports from around the world."
He was confident in sharing that he was a man of vision, even against the odds.

"Wow! Your idea of changing one plan to a master plan was great! I don't know anyone who has ever thought of that," I shared.

Mekhi said, "Well, I'm a hands-on person and always have been. So right now, I work for my daughter, who, by the way, is six years old," he looked at me and smiled.

"Really?" I asked.

"Indeed she is, and by the way, she's my one and only. Who looks just like me."

His smile became bigger as he leaned back.

"On my father's side of my family, we all call her Jr," he said, wearing the proud father look.

"Oh, how cute is that! And her birth name is?" I asked.

"Makaila Shanell Henderson," he shared as he thought about her.

"Hopefully, one day, I'll get to meet Makaila?" I squeezed it in very passively. Out of concern, I asked Mekhi.

"Are you afraid that perhaps one day, these men or their families will try to retaliate?"

"Not at all, my future is secure. Don't worry; I'll be around for you and Jr. for a long time," he said, planting a kiss on the right side of my cheek.

"Is that right?" I asked.

"As long as you would have me," he said.

Watching my lips as I shared a few things concerning my past life, dreams, and future goals. Interrupting me as I spoke, Mekhi, this time planted one of the juiciest kisses a woman could have ever wanted to be planted on her lips.

"I should see to it that you make it in at a reasonable hour Ms. lady. Let's go," he said as he rubbed down the side of my chin. Taking notice as the time had passed that after eating, he and I were the only two people left in the restaurant. Other than the workers who had decided to sit down in a half-lit room at the bar to have a late-night drink, and of course, those of whom were cleaning and prepping for the next day as I walked out on the balls of my feet. Taking short baby breaths, silk laying next to my body, with an exposed bareback, and nothing underneath. The man that wanted me naked for the night. Mr. Mekhi Henderson, honey, walked behind me, and I let-'em.

10

Bonding

One year is here! Mekhi and I had spent so much time together. We have gone to the Kentucky Derby twice already. Mekhi loves to race and bet on his horse, Blaze. Blaze is an all-black well-trained horse and has the shiniest mane; he's a stallion, all right. Not to brag but, Blaze is the number one in the highest bid race and has maintained that position for the last six years. So if you haven't made a note about my man, don't be so slow with the pen. Write home to your daddy and tell your mama. My baby is a headliner. Rolling in all kinds of dough, this man is one of the best businessmen I've ever known. I don't know how he does it, but managing seven streams of income, all I can say is if he's got it, I got it!

I noticed that when we are there, there's not much conversation between Mekhi and I unless we're in between leaving or approaching the next conversation. So I've learned to know my place. The woman of silence when need be. I only ask questions during the intermission and always come with my best lady on; attitude and all. Every so often, Mekhi gets a taste of Snowfall, and he makes remarks.

He would say, "Hot diggity dog give me more of her. Who is that again?"
Make no mistake; he is all man in our relationship; however, now he does like it when I bring about a little check on him every now and then. Try it sometimes it works. You ain't heard it from me—wink wink.

Whenever we go, I still wear the color sea-foam. It's soft, ladylike, and it stands down from being the power woman that I am. Plus, it allows Mekhi to walk in his boss hood without any competition from me as being his crown. He likes to show me off, and I let him. I have to work out before I attend the derby with Mekhi because the men are always looking and comparing the trophy of a woman you show up with to the scank of a Lil girl they shouldn't have brought.

I had no idea that he's such a great cook and I've enjoyed cooking with him. When it's my turn to cook, his request is that I wear nothing underneath my apron, but you know I have to make him stay outta the kitchen lol. Either I end up on the counter with my legs up over his shoulders, or when he cooks, he ends up chasing me up under the dining room table for dessert. Ask me was whipping cream on his face? You already know, stop friend girl. Lol ha la. After all of that playing, we would lay on the couch, and I would lay back in that chest. We would watch Netflix until I would somehow fall fast to sleep. We had created so many new memories that it gave both sides of our friends and family members time to ask lots of questions and so much for us to talk about from created moments.

We did go on our first vacation together, and it was terrific. We went to the second-largest country in the world, exploring together with one another, Canada honey. As we toured, we had taken a French class, yes we did. It was so much fun because our personal tour guide would not let either one of us speak from our native language. So the whole time, it was loving, learning, and exploring. Ask me, have I fallen in love yet? I only have one answer for you.

"Yes, Yes, girl, yes!"

On one Saturday evening, I had the pleasure of meeting six-year-old Makaila, aka Mekhi's Jr, for three months in a row now. She is a delight but something to reckon with and very well-spoken. We were alone in the backseat of Mekhi's Range Rover headed to Hick's Grand

Mall, so Makaila could have some free time in the play area as we watched.

The SUV pulled up to the front entrance of the mall, and Mekhi stepped out as a younger gentleman on a dirt bike approached him. The young man seemed to have been between the age of thirteen or fifteen; he was with a group of about four to five other young boys. As they spoke with one another, it appeared from the hand gestures that things were getting pretty heated. For me, I didn't care for the look of things.

So I tried to get the attention of Makaila to simply distract her from what was appearing to not go so well. I complimented her on her fancy nails and pretty dress, being a busybody that she knows how to be, looking out of the window, she said, "That's little Timmy! My dad's play son. My dad told my grandma. Little Timmy thinks it's my dad's fault that his daddy is in da prison for a very long time. My dad feels really, really bad for him, and now little Timmy gets to be my daddy's play son, but I don't get to play with little Timmy," she shared.

"Makaila, Why do you say that?" I asked, straightening out the front of her dress. Shaking her head back and forth, she said, "Don't touch my clothes; my granny Maxine doesn't like that!" She said.

"Lil girl! Did you just snatch your dress?" I asked her with an attitude like I will handle you like a grown woman in this backseat.

"Yep, because my dad said little Timmy has a damn attitude! So now he can't come around anymore, and my dad only gives him money to help him and his mommy; they are poor. Do you know little Timmy and his mommy?" She asked me with a puzzled look on her face.

"No, I don't," I said, rolling my eyes as I answered her.

While continuing to be nosey, Makaila said,"Well, my grandma Maxine said, she doesn't like it, not one bit! And that little Timmy is a SUCK-A, and his momma Jackie is the sum of a mother-fuck-a turning her head, I covered her mouth.

Raising my voice I asked her to turn around, and let's not look out of the window. "Come on, cross your legs, and let's be great ladies in our speech and stay out of grown men's situations."

Makaila said, "I don't get in bad situations, do I?" She took her red glitter shoe off and waved it at me as if to correct me like she was about to spank me!

"Little girl! Little girl! Makaila, you need to calm down before Ms. Eve would have to help you," and I gave her the firmest face she probably has never seen. Gently with a little applied pressure, I placed my right hand across her chest and just below her neck to help her sit back. I saw Mekhi out of my side view, he reached to settle the young man down by putting his hands in his pockets, and out of nowhere, there was this black-on-black mustang with dark tinted windows. It pulled up and revved up its engine to make sure everyone knew it was there. Mekhi being the secure man that he was, didn't bus a move, nor did he turn around. The back window eased down, and smoke elevated out of it.

One of the young boys yelled out, "Duck nine eight!"

I grabbed Makaila by the head and told her to "get low."

Getting up on her knees, she shook her head back and forth. I reached for her. She then snatched back and told me, "My granny Maxine said ducks quack low and eagles fly high."

"Little girl, when was the last time somebody laid hands on you?" I once again raised my voice.

"My granny and I don't get hands put on us, cause mother Jefferson at the church is the only one who has that demon on her," she said. So you know what I had to do, I screamed and told her it was a spider crawling on the headrest. Her little chubby self started crying and tried to crawl underneath the passenger side of the backseat. Mekhi turned and looked over his right shoulder, and instantly the car sped off after noticing that it was Mekhi Henderson. I really don't know how this blending of our families is going to go—trying to be like her granny Maxine, with her little bad mouth butt, chubby red glitter shoe wearing, eating animal crackers, and jolly ranchers all day, she and her grandmama will find themselves checking coats at my wedding.

11

Blow Wind Blow

Gathering my sketches and appointment book as I prepared myself to leave. And the phone was ringing off the hook.

"Eve, I've been calling you," Jayden O'Connor said. As she stayed focused, walking out of her office door.

She said, answering back, "Not now, Jay, I'm rushing to meet with a client. What's a good time for me to call you back?" She asked.

"Call me back? Why I've never heard these words spoken to me from you. It seems as though lately, you haven't had any real-time for me."

"Well, what would you like to hear? I'm busy these days more than ever."

"At least let me ask, Do you need anything? You know I'm always here for you."

"Nope, I'm good."

"Well, what about your allowance?"

"What about it?"

"For the last nine months, you haven't touched a penny of it. It's still sitting in your account."

"No need too, as long as you gave it to me, I know it's mine. Right friend?" I asked, being sarcastic.

"Well, yeah, as long as it's sitting, then the compound interest should be good whenever you need to use it. I won't touch it."

Then he gathered the nerve to ask…"Friend? Have I done something wrong to turn you away?"

"Nope, I'm good, How is Morgan these days?"

I started skipping down the sidewalk to my car that was parked across the street from in front of my house. I usually park inside the garage. But I hung out with the ladies last night, and boy, did we have a ball. Catching up was an understatement. We went past it all. For about four and a half hours, we talked about our childhood and how typically before school gos out, each one of us would take turns passing one another notes while we were being dismissed from class to class. We couldn't wait to get to the next class period. So we could read each other's tea. The tea would either be about which boy liked us. If we loved him back, who we wanted to kiss, which boy asked us to go to the dance, how well we did on our test, setting the next hair, clothes, or shoe trend for all the girls or sometimes it was just about our friendship. If any of us girls received a note with a smiley face that had red crossed-out lips. That only meant two things. One, we snuck and had on some of our mother's red lipstick. And two, we didn't have anything good to say. But at the end of every note, we would always put it; P.S. Queen. I hope you can make it to the Sisterhood Honey Hive and bring some honey, which meant a treat to eat or something good to share. Or even some hot news.

Like my mama would always say to her best friend Yo, "Now that's hotter than cayenne pepper and sweeter than a Georgia peach." The news would be so good. It'll burn you but, good enough to have some mo. Then we would become ten-year-old Artists and draw our own personal map leading to our private Sisterhood Honey Hive. We never called it the girls club. So we adopted Evelyn's sophisticated way; she refers to her man and her home as the honey hive. Only because growing up, my mama was the stuff, and it seemed as if everyone wanted to be like her. So we did too.

The Sisterhood Honey Hive wasn't even two minutes away, but it was hidden, and no one could find us. We all made sure of that. If our parents were calling or looking for us. We had a lookout girl our Mexican friend Juana. We also talked about Olivia's drama at her new job at the Half Black Coffee Shop. The meeting grounds for gays and lesbians. Kayla's been having new conversations these days with Sebastian, who's been on vacation. So he says, but when he got outta jail, he came looking for a set of wonder twins nobody knew about. Oh! And Kayla did confess that she had been struggling with alcohol and waking up in strange men's beds. She was the reason we all went out last tonight, to support and celebrate Kayla two weeks of being clean. However, she has a long way to go on dealing with how her grandmother Sweet Lady Mrs. Hannah Mae, died, the acceptance of who her real mother and father is, and why Kaysie gave her up in the first place.

We talked about how I had fallen in love with Mr. Mekhi Henderson and had no time for Jayden O'Connor these days. The ladies were so happy for me. They congratulated me on finally having a love of my own. One that I could be proud of and had no back talk about another woman.

The ladies wanted to know If I thought Mekhi would pop the question? If so, How long did I think it would be? Since he's the only person getting all of my time these days. Even from the ladies. I was frank about my feelings for Mekhi and how I couldn't see myself without him. He's a keeper, and I'm grateful for this man being in my life. I started to wonder if God had forgotten about me. I was experiencing everyone sharing a love for one another, but for me, I talked nothing but about how soon Jayden would leave Morgan and come busting through my front door with the words on his lips. It's you who I love and have always loved.

I need you and want you to spend the rest of your life with me. Instead, it was Mekhi who spoke these life-filled words in my spirit. At first, I must admit it was tough for me to believe him.

Because I had been in a holding cell of my own prison for so long, I didn't even realize that the life long sentence had been so long. Mekhi helped me see that I had not been living but slowly walking the aisles of death row.

"What was it about Jayden O'Connor anyway?" Lauren asked as we all set there at the restaurant last night.

"It can't be because the man is filthy rich," Kayla said.

"Of course not, Kayla. Eve has her own money." Lauren stated.

"Well, it can't be that you didn't make him feel needed. She waved her hand, circling the table. All of us have seen her yield to her; she powers in front of the man." Lauren added. They went on and on so much last night that I had no choice but to but in.

When Mekhi and I get married. Hello... I said, "All the while, I was smiling; hands down, though. I shared with them raising Mekhi's daughter Makaila is going to be a challenge for me."

"Really? Do she cut up?" Olivia asked.

I explained with caution. "Cutting up is the wrong word. That mouth of hers will downright dissect you alone. She's her grandmothers' child. I do know that. She sounds just like her too."

Lauren asked, "Where is her mother, and how old is she again?"

"She's six, and Mekhi said he wasn't ready to have that conversation with me about her mom." He says, "Just know that there will never be a problem."

"It's not the child's mother I'm concerned about. It's Mekhi's mother. I'm soon to meet her for lunch. You know Mekhi set it up. We will meet alone for the first time, just me and her at The Bobo's Chicken Shack. How ghetto is that?" The whole table cracked up laughing.

"Wait! Hold on; I'm not done, she, "Being Mrs. Sonya Henderson, honey. Who favorite line is, "I don't give two piss pots about everything." She told Mekhi on the phone, and I heard her say it myself.

And I quote, "Now Mekhi, don't be having me meeting up with some bougie bitch who doesn't want to do nothing but talk about how much she spent on her name brand purse."

Omg did the ladies forever laugh at me. They almost rolled outta their chairs. They were laughing so hard cause they know I love a good name brand purse, plus all my friends know how I take pleasure in going to the thrifty Boutique. My specialty is finding one of a kind designs. They give me ideas of signature fashion pieces for me to create for my clients.

All I can say is, "She's in for a surprise. I might just come without combing my damn hair. And with some leopard house shoes on. Oh! Don't let me outline my lips with some black liner. Let me see what smart she got to say about that—Mrs. Ghetto Sonya with a capital G. With her two pissy pots full of bougie jokes."

Here's Kayla putting her two cents in, "Naw, wait now. Back to Mekhi popping the question. We tired of hearing about hot messy mama Bobo's chicken eating butt." Kayla, so slow she missed the whole joke. I had no choice but to laugh at her goofy butt.

"What are you laughing at? Answer the question," she said.
I shared my truth and gave my best answers.

"I can't spend another day without knowing that we share the same space in life. And to answer your question, no Mekhi has not popped the question yet."
Placing one finger in the air,

"However, I do know it's going to be real soon," I shared.

Olivia asked. "How can you be so sure?"

"I caught him looking at the inside of my shoe, because of my size," Eve said.

"So, you really believe that's true?" Kayla asked. "Yes, I do. I've heard many men and women say that was how they were able to determine the true ring size. I didn't interrupt him. I just walked past him as if nothing was wrong. All I can say is your girl is in love and waiting."
We continued laughing, snacking on appetizers, and occasionally sharing more stories.

I reminded the ladies how Mekhi calls me his shining star, he says I give him energy that he just doesn't have. And without me, he has no star player. Right about now, I would have you take a side note, of how to be in love with the one loving you.

My phone started ringing and it was him. OMG it's him my one year man! I whispered and told the ladies *tomorrow is a critical day for him and I.* Walking away from the dinner table at Donavan's to have a moment of bonding with Mekhi my man, his my high peak. Yes, I said it! "My man, he is my honey, sweet tea, and my happy face." The one-man I'm not sharing with anybody. And it's here our one year anniversary. For the past twelve months, we have been a fantastic power couple. We are on one accord, getting an understanding, disagreeing with balance, giving gifts just because, being a helper one to the other, affirming the need for each other's presence, quality time day or night, and learning the power of touch. From financial goals, new business ideas, family planning, groundbreaking on the corner lot, and wedding bells swinging and banging. The lady is ready, do you hear me? Blow wind blow. I can't wait to be with Mekhi and catch my next breath.

12

Two Kings

Listen here; I consider myself to be wealthy as an independent African Luxury one of a kind Custom Fashion buyer and designer. Six months on throughout the year and six months off being a Published Event Designer. With all of the elaborate event planning that I partake of around the world, my mind is blown. But this one right here... Andrea is the rich of the filthy rich. She struck silver and gold when she married the young Prince Paul Posh Sire, who is also known as the most accurate Plastic Surgeon alive all around the world. I heard about the wedding because it made the news. I would have you to know of his homeland East Hashen near the Bay of Bengal. The front page of the newspaper, magazines, and CDS News all reported the same story. Young Prince Paul Posh Sire, son of Ruler Gullo Hashen Sire II, and Queen Juliana Le Fallon Sire soon wed United States West Asian Airlines flight, Attendant.

You see, Andrea is by-racial; she was raised with four brothers and one physically challenged little sister. Although she has always wanted to fit in, she tells everyone that she's from the island of Barbados but is really from New York, born and raised as a New Yorker until she was old enough to apply for a job at West Asian Airlines. She got hired, left her parents home, and with all the money she had saved up, moved to Seattle, where she was based—after living in Ebenezer's Community Homeless Shelter for months, she cramped herself in a studio apartment with no furniture for almost two years. Her daddy is all the way Barbados black, and her mother Lou is Eurasian. European and South Asia mixed. Andrea's mother and father meet while on vacation.

Andrea is never shy of sharing how her parents meet on the island of Barbuda in Antigua simply because she wants people to think that she's from the Islands. Her Mother Lou was on a three-day cruise that her doctor sent her on because of a severe stress test from working and never taking a break to just live in the moment of now. She fell in love with the islander Abdul-Rahim which means one who serves or a compassionate man. Andrea's father Abdul was the island's top Chef, and her mother Lou likes to think she's one of the best at cooking as well. So while on vacation, eating at one of the top resorts, the Sanctuary with pink sand between her toes and all. Lou calls for the manager to have a personal word with the Chef who prepared her main dish Cou Cou and Flying Fish. It's the national dish of Barbados, and because Lou would visit the island from time to time, she noticed that the recipe was missing something and wasn't prepared as always. It's one of her favorite dishes to have while staying at the Sanctuary. So she asked to speak with the Chef.

As bold as she could be, she asked him, "If there was a change with the time frame of cooking the ingredients?" Usually, the dish is plated with fresh okra covered with cornmeal grain. The stewed flying fish is prepared with green onions, garlic, a mixture of tied herbs and thyme, tomatoes, and Himalayan pink salt and fresh black pepper.

And there it was. It happens all the time, but not for the ones who are expecting it. Mr. Rahim fell in love with the moment of boldness and control of the conversation. She handled him from the inside. Andrea's mother, Lou, began to share with him. Maybe you rushed today with her European accent. Because you did not allow the mixture of herbs to cook very long within the stew, you cook all the time the same but not this time. You have to bring out of the fish the best taste possible like times before. So Andrea's family holiday dinners always consist of Cou Cou and Flying Fish. Every holiday Mr. Rahim tries his best to get it right and keep sweeping Lou off her feet.

Relaxed in the backseat stirring out the window as I viewed the scenic route. This is all so twisted and beginning to become complicated to figure out. Because after graduating, the rumor had it that Andrea was secretly dating Paul Anderson, who formerly was the Assistant Principal of Brooklyn High. I guess she's just gotta have a Paul;Tall, clean-cut, dark, and sexy, Mr. Paul Anderson. Yep, he would be the one to mess with the ugly duckling. I don't know why this always leads to the same damn question. How did she get him? Mr. Anderson was twenty, and Andrea at the time was only fifteen soon to be sixteen. Now, if he's still there, I have no clue. Even the Special Education Teachers and the Student Aids were happy to see this man strutting down the halls. With that crooked right leg and that big bulge in the front of his zipper. Believe it when I say even the lunch ladies weren't too far behind either—having nasty gazing eyes. For some reason, everyone would always wonder why Mr. Anderson would speak to Andrea first out of any crowd. With his baritone voice.

He would ask, "You being good, Ms. Hunter?" And with her old paralyzed tongue, she would always look down to the ground, giggle awe heavy and speak back, "Hey Mr. Anderson. As good as I know how."
She would forever come to the second hour late with that ole nappy bun in the top of her head, and all messed up. At least twice a week, if I remember, Andrea correctly and Mr. Anderson would meet in the lower level of the basement in classroom one-twenty-one and for what reason. In-school suspension. Then there were the times when the bell would ring and seven minutes after everyone was seated. Andrea

would ask to go to the nurse's office, claiming that her stomach would be upset from the flow of her red valley. One time after asking if she could be excused. She came rushing back in the class three minutes before class was out carrying one of her shoes in her hand, and the other one twisted up around her ankle. She had no choice but to sit in the front row because all the seats were taken, and everyone noticed that her shirt was inside out. The whole class was full of laughter and started catching on that she was having private meetings in between classes. Now, this was the wrong part of Andrea and Mr. Anderson's sexual escapades. In the last week of school, Andrea found herself running downstairs to meet with her boo. Much to her surprise, surprise! As she hit the double doors passing the commercial kitchen. She heard the same line that Mr. Anderson would always say to her, spanking her on her butt cheeks while making love to Andrea in the doggy style position.

He would say, "This is my good loving," and make her repeat it back. "Now, be good and say it!" As sad as Andrea was, she witnessed Mr. Anderson's strong black back laid between the legs of a blonde freshman Claire Vnetchy. You see, Andrea assumed that after high school, the two of them would become a serious couple and skip in a field of daisies with two kids carrying a Yorkie dog in a name brand purse.

Two weeks ago, Andrea called me to catch up on old times. She said she reached out to me through my business website months before that. She says, "I joined the Fan-club Newsletter and left a message asking, was this the Eve who went to Brooklyn High and was raised in the subdivision of Grand Chester Place?" Once I had the chance to respond back, I was very brief because she left only her last name Mrs. Sire. I thought she was a follower of my social media fan club. So I did nothing with it. I shared that with her. I didn't know it was Andrea with the smushed face and big lips who lived in the house kiddy corner from me on Grand Chester.

My childhood friend and I talked for hours, and we talked so long that she invited me to Europe to come and meet her young Prince; she says she fell in love with.

"Eve, I'm sending a plane for you to come here!" She said, "You must visit here, girl. I'm living my best life." I assured Andrea she did not have to go all out, and that seeing and spending time with her would be enough. You could hear her excitement. It came from within, especially about how she became Mrs. Sire.

She shared how Mr. Paul Anderson burnt her so badly through this whole ordeal. That he sent her on an all-inclusive paid vacation to Los Cabos San Lucas, Mexico, to ease her broken heartbreak. Supposedly Mr. Anderson promises to join her for the week-long experience, which would have been the tip-top trip of their love affair. You guessed it; he didn't show up, but Mr. Anderson did leave a letter of truth at the concierge office explaining that he wanted her to enjoy herself after everything that he had put her through. And because of his position in the school system as the Assistant Principal; soon to be Principal, he wasn't going to be able to join her for his job was on the line. Plus, he has three small children at home to take care of. That night after reading the letter, Andrea was in a sunken whirlwind. She sat at the bar, thinking of all the times she had put her reputation and education on the line just so Mr. Anderson could have what he would call bust a nut. Andrea got wasted. All drinks and food was inclusive on the trip, so she diffidently had her share of mangos with red chili sprinkled on top and bottoms up Tequila Sunrise drinks. Andrea thought instead of jumping ship with her heartbreak. She might as well celebrate her new chapter of being alone again, even if it was only about sex.

So Andrea said, "Eve, girl, I decided to take advantage of the trip my good loving paid for." After making a shift in her thought process, she was able to put the past behind her and enjoy the blueish-green waters that carried the beach's white sand back to the shore. Rows and rows of sailed oversized Platoon Boats leaving trails of waves in the ocean, she watched the tourists enjoy laying out in the sun while brown pelicans soar high in the sky.

Two days later, the feelings of being rejected started to surface once more. Although it was time for Andrea to leave the island and she met young Prince the Dr. Paul Sire himself on the bottom of the ocean floor of Lovers Beach, scuba diving under the Arch of Cabo San Lucas. The weather was beautiful, and it was another day in paradise, she explained. It was around eighty-seven degrees. People were splashing in the pacific ocean right off the side of the anchored water taxi they had taken far out. Andrea shared with me how the sea was so beautiful, and everything she laid eyes on was a camera ready shot for a postcard. Being at Lovers Beach was a moment of peace and serenity she shared. Andrea described it as a wide variety of colorful sea life just waiting to be encountered. With intensity, she told me all about how she was wearing her two-piece black and white swimming suit for the very first time. For her wearing a two-piece swimming suit was very courageous because Andrea has never been one to feel beautiful in her own skin. So in life, whenever she had the opportunity to meet others, she found herself greeting people who she felt was not so pretty, but not so ugly too. It made her feel as if she belonged. And as always, whenever scuba diving is in season. Andrea found that makes her heart happy. Being underwater with not so many people to deal with, she challenged herself from time to time to dive deeper in search of unique and unusual rocks and seashells. I listened to the story of her life. Inside the parts she chose to give. She hopes to be found by a man who would find the hidden beauty in her heart and not her physical appearance.

An array of schools of fish swam all around her. To her surprise, she wasn't alone. As deep as she decided to lounge, someone was lying on their back close to the floor of the ocean. She assumed that he required help, so what did she do? Took it upon herself to be a Good Samaritan and made her way right through a cloud of yellow and white male Betta fish, causing them to disperse. At that moment, she knew she had just gotten in the way a perfectly good camera shot. The man waved her out of the way and shooed her off.
Making her way towards him, she tried to approach him and explain through hand movements her intentions. But, straight away, two men with Security on the back of their swimming gear came rushing towards her from behind a big rock in the ocean. Frightening her, she turned around and made her way back to the water's surface. With the unknown man, Andrea had just disappointed and the security officials not too far behind. Andrea came up out of the water, snatched her headgear off, and gasped for air. The man who is now known as her husband. Young Prince Sire who is also a Plastic Surgeon. Snatches off his headgear and, treading in a circular motion, remained a distance away as one of his security men shouted,

"What were you doing down there?"

She said, "Eve, I took the time to apologize for disturbing what he called as a bloody crime for ruining an entirely significant shot." The more she tried to explain that, the more she thought he was in trouble, and her actions were to only help. Now you listen to me, you dirtbags, she said to all of them, including the Prince. You will not talk down to me or bully me because I'm a woman waving in the water.

You are not allowed to approach the young Prince in such a manner. The security man said with boldness,

"So if you intend to enjoy the rest of your vacation, find yourself out of the way of Prince Sire's presence."

Andrea told the young Prince security, "That her father was a King too!" And she dared them to disrespect her father's bloodline with such vain hypocrisy. Young Prince Sire called out security! Hold your childish tongue and allow the lady much room to speak.

Andrea said, "Eve, for the first time in my life, a man saw fit to stop what he was doing to hear her freaking heart and what she had to say without taking advantage of her or the situation.

"Carry on, my lady. Do you continue to share the kindness of your father, the king?" He called out and asked Andrea.

Andrea said, "Now Eve, you know damn well my father is not a royal King. But, from my mother's home screen cell phone picture, when my daddy calls, girl, the phone lights up with "My King" written across the top. My daddy has been viewed as the king of my mother's home. Since he rocked her boat on the island of Barbados."

"Andrea, no, you didn't tell that man that," I said.

"Yes, I did!" She said. "We weren't in court, and I didn't have my hand on the Holy Bible. What were they going to do to me? Sentence me to outer darkness, lol lol." We both laughed at her crazy butt. One thing for sure, she still was ghetto as heck. You see, when Andra's mother got a better job, they moved to Grand Chester years later. From the time she was born in Lincoln heights projects from the West side of New York on Coopers Lane. Andrea's father worked; however, her mother was already working two jobs and was hardly at home only to eat and sleep. She was determined to give her family a better life after one of

Andrea's brother, gave their dad Mr. Abdul-Rahim, one of his kidneys. It wasn't how her father was raised to live. He believed in being the breadwinner in the household. With a house full of boys, two daughters days of always not having reminded him to get up and fight to live stronger than yesterday. All while Andrea's baby sister was born with a hole in her heart.

She said Prince Sire asked once more. "Who's your father, my lady?"

So she said,"Eve, he left me with no other choice but to speak well of my father as King Abdul-Rahim. Shouting across the waves, I asked him, "Now young Prince, what more do you have to say?"

Andrea is so crazy she left me no choice but to continue laughing. I laughed so hard I couldn't even stop her from talking to click over to answer the other line from Livia, who was calling back to back.

She said Eve, girl; you know I shut him down. He and all that royal talking out the side of his neck. Girl silenced him to the lambs, and he told his security to pardon him as he made his way to face and ask me out for dinner because he would love to hear more of my father's royalty.

This blue-blooded rich, fancy young Prince is rich in every kind of way. He has looks, style, and inescapable charm. Coming from the royal lineage of the Hashemites, he is the son of the Ruler Gullo Hashen Sire II and Queen Juliana Le Fallon Sire of East Hashen near the Bay of Bengal.

Continuing to share some of her life stories, Andrea broke down, just shy of crying aloud, and told me that her husband is no longer accepted as royalty from his father's lineage and bloodline because he chose to work in the world system as his father calls it. He became the doctor he has dreamed instead of ruling under his father's leadership as the young Price. To order over his father's territory, business affairs, and marriage from within his own family was not in his future. So now young Prince Sire has no claim to his father's total inheritance but only an acquired allowance from what is left of monthly occurrences. He can only hold the title as Prince with active security to protect the family's royal name because Prince Sire made a decision to love and marry outside of his parent's pre-marital arrangement. To his father, King Gullo II, first cousin Sir Parsons daughter Princess Lillia. Young Prince Paul Posh Sire helped Andrea understand that as long as he's married to Andrea, his dear cousin Princess Lillia will remain a single woman within their culture and be frowned upon. This is because Prince Sire was not in agreement with both parent's decision of bloodline marriage; he abandoned the grooming Principles from a childhood of loving and marrying the only Princess to uphold both the family's bloodline. Andrea's voice began to change as she continued to share. I cut her off and changed the subject because she became saddened over the fact that her husband has not seen or heard from his family in years. For he loved Andrea for some reason more than his rightful place as an heir. And that was all she wrote.

"So how long have you lived in Europe, Andrea?" I asked, changing the subject.

She said, "No, Eve, you are going to have to come here to start asking all these questions. If you want to know about how my whole life changed after two weeks of graduation day, it's called come to Europe first." Andrea chuckled and waited for my response.

I said, "Okay, hold on. Let me check my calendar."

Andrea asked, "Are you free within the next two weeks, Eve?"

I told her to, "Hold on, Andrea." I said, "I'm checking things out now."

Luckily to your surprise. I'll actually be off work for the next three weeks."Are you serious, Eve? She asked.

Andrea, your girl is free according to my calendar,"I said.

I had an appointment scheduled with my clients, a young couple. They had plans to wed, but I'm sad to say for whatever reason, the wedding has been called off.

Oh, Wow! I hate when that happens when two people decide to spend the rest of their lives together. End up going through all of this event planning. Spend all of this money, and everything comes to a paralyzing haunt. So does this mean that you go without getting paid for this event?"Andrea was curious to ask.

"Oh no, Andrea, I'm smarter than that, my friend!" Sister girl gets all her money honey upfront. Simply because of situations like this. Yes, my pay is already in the bank, according to the contract signed by Lisa the finance and Mr. Haynes himself.

"So, I'm all yours, my love!" I said, with much excitement.

She said,"Yes, Eve, I'm sending for you right away. I miss you so much, come to me darling and plan on spending at least two to three weeks with myself and Paul.

"Okay," I said,"Plan on seeing me around to have one hell of a good time.

Andrea said, "Eve, I have some much to share, and I promise you will have a marvelous time, my friend."

Andrea, so guess what I'm on my way to Europe, and I can't wait!" I said it, yelling on the phone.

We both started screaming like old times when we would be jumping on the bed after both of our parents would say yes to us having an all-night girls slumber party.

For some reason, it always started with Andrea and me. Then once we would get our parents to agree, so no one would feel left out in the Sisterhood honey hive. We would run through

162

the backyard up the sidewalk and throw pebbles at the back bedroom window until Olivia would place a crack in the window just enough to hear us whispering. Andrea would always want to be the one to invite everyone over as if it was her home and not mine.

She would find herself saying...*see if you can come over to Eve's home, her mom Mrs. Novae noted that I could stay, so let's have girls sleepover ev*en though my mother had just agreed for only Andrea. She didn't know that the other girls Kayla, Lauren, and Olivia, were soon to make it over. Standing on the front porch with sleeping bags and overnight pillowcases stuffed with popcorn, candy apples, and Rice Krispies treats. After we would get done running from house to house, making sure that everyone in the clique knew the plans. We would be sitting in the middle of my bed with the bedroom door shut with the lights off. The floor lamp leaned up against the nightstand. Allowing the lampshade to make a designed shadow over the ceiling of the bed, and as each one of our friends would make it into the room one person at a time, the door would open. We would all start jumping on the bed with much excitement and laughter because our play circle had just gotten more robust, bigger, and tighter.

13

Flying Around Work

Boom! Boom! Whiney Houston singing."Don't cha wanna dance say you want to dance, with somebody who loves you." The song was playing in the back speakers as I was sitting and enjoying the smooth ride of this black stretch limo that was sent to pick me up by my childhood friend Andrea Hunter. I haven't seen or heard from Andrea in over ten years.

This girl sent me a limo to my front door, and her very own private jet to receive me from the Magnus Airport. I can't believe I overlooked Sire, who and wherever he came from. As I was having a phone conversation with Lauren about the process of her husband's adulterous affair and divorce, the phone rang from the middle console of the limo. I watched the frosted windows that divided the front seat from the back immediately lowered. The limo driver Dan, shared that it was Andrea calling checking on my whereabouts before I took off by private jet. "l assured Mrs. Sire soon you'll be in Europe less than seven to six in half hours." The limo driver Dan said.

Hello, Andrea, darling," I said
"Eve, hello friend girl, can you believe in less than six hours we will be in the company of one another?" Andrea asked with excitement.
"Well, Eve, allow me to warn you that I'm not the same person." She said.

"Andrea, come on please for the last time. Don't start saying that I have a love for you no matter what or who you have become," I said without judging.

"No, really Eve, there's a lot that has changed about me." She said once more, assuring me that the Andrea Hunter that I once knew was not the Andrea Sire that I was about to meet.

I said, "Andrea, darling, soon I shall arrive, letting the window down to get a breath of fresh air, soon, my lady. I'll see you then."

"Yes, safe travels Eve," She said, "I must go to prepare for your coming, so you should be arriving soon."

I'm trying to put the puzzle together because, in high school, Andrea was one of the funniest in the class. But not at all pretty, according to the men on the basketball team. You know the list that floats around the athletic department that not all women make. It was the top ten girls list that all the best football and basketball players put together and passed around from time to time at the end of the week. The men would get together at the end of the hall, compare notes on who did what and with which girl. They would even go so far as to grade each woman they had kissed, touched, or sexually been with. Whenever you saw a line drawn through any of the women's names, that meant only one thing; mission accomplished. Yep, that woman was graded either with a passing grade. Which said you were either passed on to another guy, or you failed, and the experience the guys had with you was not successful at all. Now at the end of the month, the man with the most names crossed off meant he was to be crowned by all the other fellas. So by right, he would get the first choice at which woman he wanted to stake his claim, and she would be pulled out of the bet and off-limits from the rest of the other fellas.
It was time to make her his woman and parade her around the school proudly. I'm guessing Andrea, once again being rejected by the young men in school, must have started her love affair with Assistant Principal Mr. Paul Anderson.

She claims he hit on her, and because he put the bait out there, she knew what to do with it. Use it for her good and help build her self esteem. All because she had the interest of an older man.

The limo driver Dan opened the back door to assist me out. Your private jet has arrived, so Ms. Eve, allow me to introduce you to Mrs. Sire's Pilot Mr. Charlie Rogers himself. Standing there, all strong and confident, not to mention the wings he had standing on the back of his shoulders from working out. I mean, Mr. Charlie had this white Pilot suit standing up and not by the starch or the crease in the front of his pants. This man's body was talking all the way to the back of my spine. Instantly looking at him made me become even madder with Andrea. It's not ladylike at all. To have me sitting in the back of a jet looking at all this here of a man. Mr. Charlie Rogers was every bit of the whole bottle of chocolate syrup you squeeze on any banana split.

All while, Dan helped me with my luggage, loading one piece on the jet at a time. He watched by leaning back around the open door of the limo.

As Mr. Charlie greeted me with a "Welcome abroad, it's my pleasure to be in your company, dear lady Eve." He said, grabbing me by the hand as I took one step at a time up the stairs onto the jet. I didn't speak a mumbling word—a simple nod to the shoulder with a bashful winking eye that said it all.

Make yourself comfortable, dear, and I should have you there in no time," Charlie said

I said with a soft smile on my face, "Take your time; I would like to safely arrive if you don't mind." You know that one smile that Janet Jackson always gives when she sings a new song and does the happy dance because of the new man in her life? Yeah, that one, that's the one I gave him. This moment just made me think of me falling in love with Jayden

O'Connor or Mekhi Henderson. My history is longer with Jayden than my new found love is stronger with Mekhi. I'm going to have to go ahead and marry some Jayden O'Connor. Even if he still has Morgan Portland in his life because my lust radar is all the way to the right, for real, it's on ten. It seems as if it's reading love on me as an all-time high whenever I'm away from him. Especially for an extended period—and being within the company of men who can measure up to his quality of being a man. It also makes me realize how many more great men I am missing out on.

"Being a Pilot of twenty-one years, by all means, your care is my first concern," Charlie said with much ease.

As I paid attention to his mustache that so perfectly outlined his top lip. All at the same time, I rubbed the inside nameplate of the private jet that read Global Sire six-thousand Bombardier. Charlie turned to walk away as I investigated the privacy of this fancy sixty-million dollar jet equipped with exceptional premier cabins, shower options, two full windows, and LED lighting. The very modern and comfortable atmosphere seated six chairs in the front. Two rows of four seats in the back, with one long couch, styled with decorative pillows that outline the whole end left wall. I was surprised by a Thank you card for coming. It was placed on my seat, with a red velvet drawstring jewelry bag that had a dangling diamond pendant that read Inhale and Exhale...Welcome, you are needed! And a fresh bouquet of flowers that was wrapped in one of the most beautiful gold bows anyone had ever seen. I was floored with everything thus far and speechless about such class and taste. The crew consisted of two Flight attendants, one male and a female willing and ready to serve me with a gourmet meal. A let out table with a white table cloth was prepared before me. Along with a full place setting as if I was sitting at one of my favorite places in the world to eat like cozy Donavan's. The place where you would find me alone or in the company of my favorite ladies' friends. I was served something lite to eat with a round glass of white wine. Hickory smoked skinless Walleye Filets, Fresh butter roasted vegetables, and a side dish of mashed sweet potatoes with melted marshmallows and sugary crushed pecans on top. The jet has a large enough kitchen with all of the appliances to prepare for both flight attendants to work or to break down into a rest area if need be. Everything was top notch and straight lines. Nothing was off, not even the color scheme; everything was perfectly designed with taupe leather seats, dark grey carpet, light grey walls, and the beautiful almond wood grain cabinetry that accented the whole jet. The seats were most comfortable with a wide range of parallel movement. I was able to sit, dine, or relax by reclining all from one chair. The jet had a fiber optic system that allowed me access to high-speed internet. And one of my required requests for Andrea was in my spare time I needed to continue to work. Simply because, for one, I absolutely love what I do, and my assistant Nigel Navarro was off work due to his wife's first pregnancy, and all the work must go on. So Andrea sent me her business jet and because I had nothing but time on my hand at the moment. I pulled out this hidden side table from the almond wood armrest and decided to go to work three hours into the trip. I made a few more notes about the guest list and decorating the Renaissance hall for my client's upcoming women's luncheon. I go all out for my favorite clients who've been with me since I've been in the event planning business. And one of them is Coleen Clark. The woman is bad. A jazzy preaching machine of a woman. Who would preach any preacher under a pew? And Coleen knows. One of her gifts is how to pull men and women from anywhere. From all over the world for a conference or concert. She often shares with me how church women are most jealous and envious of her because of her known relationships with the men of the cloth. She assured me,"Eve, it's a lot of women sleeping around in the church from the pulpit to the back door, but that is not my testimony! Many have slept their way to the top. To only preach for fifteen minutes is not my strategy. If you only see one back door, that's the one you will always walk in. Her platform is beyond worldwide significance; it's internationally known as Coleen Clark Miniseries. Healing for the wounded souls of the total man and woman.

Here I was in a soundproof jet with the singer Khon singing about love all over the wind that's caring this jet. I love this man's voice! Sing to me, Khon baby, you can sing to me all day. I said, raising up my glass to make a toast to the best life I'm about to transition into. New plans, stable connections, much discipline equals a better experience. Feeling all happy, I stood up in the center of the aisle only because I've had one too many and not to mention the attention of one mighty exceptional Pilot Mr. Charlie. I didn't want him, no, not at all. But when you're the center of care. My mother would always say, "Take the bow off and let everybody be surprised!" There is never any dull moment with Evelyn G. Novae. The woman who could build anybody's confidence from ground zero to the twin towers of one person being two people you had never seen or met. I was torn up. Yes, I was. But, I heard Charlie say this was the second time of the day that he was training the standby pilot for Andrea's jet for the new runway landing regulations, and procedures, Mr. Charlie was checking me out over the top edge of his glasses from the view of the side mirror positioned out of the dashboard control panel. Twirling with a soft spin, I had on my notable look; an all-white long sleeve, wrap-around fitting all together lovely pencil dress. Held together by way of a white belt tied and laid to the left side, front pockets and smoothly fitted pleats dangling just below the knee. My nude shoes by L.C. Golden. The famous gold tip Stilettos with diamond jewels breaking the center landing on a gold heel cap. Matching with my lovely all-day wear undergarments. Khon was singing the song, "I Didn't Need Anybody But You," reaching for the headrest. Taking my seat and resting my head back just for a few. I believe I've gotten a little too tipsy. So to the point that I didn't realize I had fallen asleep. And the stewardess was standing over me, asking if I'd like something more to drink other than wine.

Two hours later, with one hour to go. I finalized the plans for my client Coleen's all Women's Max Out with Purpose Luncheon. So I decided to host a live private meeting that went successfully with the business owners who will have their hands in the pulling together for this great event.

"Hello... Coleen, love." I said, tapping the eraser of my mechanical pencil on the edge of my laptop.

Coleen said, "Hello Eve, I was planning on calling you first thing Monday morning to see how everything was rolling."

"Well, Coleen, with one month away and everything winding down, I just had a successful live group meeting to finalize all loose ends with my team and yours. I also received all signed contracts from the other vendors who will be joining us for the Max Out With Purpose Luncheon. Last-minute decorations have been ordered."

"The main speaker Janice Owens and her assistant Angie will be joining you and your team. You all will meet the day before, for lunch at one o'clock at Ralph's on ninety-fifth. Her assistant Angie has been informed of new flight changes. And the Renaissance Hall is expecting us the day before to set up. I have your seating list arranged with the total RSVP paid seats of three hundred dollars apiece. For guests at two hundred and seventy-five as we speak. Did I leave anything out?" I asked.

She said, going over everything in her head. "Not that I can think of at the moment, Eve. It sounds as if everything is covered." "I'm so glad that you're handling everything once again. I leave you all of my business to handle, and no one else will do. And I must say after every event I get nothing but amazing feedback." She went on to say. "I'm sure If I had done it, something would be left out."

"Well, Coleen, what's meant to be will always find a way. With that being said, thank you once again for being one of my best clients and for entrusting me with your vision and desires. Take care, and I'll be speaking with you after I arrive on vacation." I said.

She said, "Good day, and enjoy your vacation."

"I will do that!" I said.

"Oh, Eve, Wait!" She said, yelling back into the phone to get my attention. "I forget to ask...What about the head table?" She said.

"I have it all figured out, Coleen, don't worry. Ten at the head table seated priced at one thousand dollars, including yourself, and there's two that don't walk in agreement with one another as you shared before. So you'll find them both at each end of the table in God's peace." I said. Coleen laughed and called on Jesus.

I said, "It's okay. I get it always in grace, and don't worry; all is well."

"Thank you, Eve, for you are the best!" She said with peace.

I heard the music speakers softly fade into the background as the male stewardess began to say our time for arrival is at hand. We will touch down at Entally Airport in the great land of Europe. To prepare for landing in thirty minutes. You will find yourself in warm waves of seventy-nine degrees weather in Europe today. Fasten your seat belts, bring all reclined chairs to an upright position, turn all electronics off and store them away safely. Tray tables must be stored away securely. And once again, thank you for choosing to fly Bombardier Global Sire Airlines.

Just before landing, my girlfriend Andrea's face timed me live from the jets overhead tv screen. "Hey, how's it going?" Andrea asked.

"Hey lady, all is well. I've just been told that I will be touching down within the next thirty minutes." I shared.

She said, "I'm so excited right now for our meeting, Eve. You have no idea."

"Yes, I do. And I can't wait either." I assured her that the same twelve years that she's been waiting to see me, I expected as well.
Oh! And how thoughtful of you to have graced me with such warmness. I said.

Andrea said, "Girl, that jet ride ain't nothing. I'm living my highest ride."

"No, Andrea, I'm speaking about the Thank you card, the flowers, and my diamond charm necklace," I said with a question mark about my face.

"Oh well, I can't explain the gifts, nor will I take any credit for them. Perhaps my assistant Phoenix arranged the gifts. All I can say is if they were there, then they were there for you," Andrea shared.

Now a few more things just before you arrive. Just so you would be in the know, here on Chesmar Lake. Paul has a few friends who usually every Saturday night, we join each other for dinner, dance, and a high swing of a time. So if you're not too tired from the flight and all of your shuffling, please make plans to join us. Tonight Paul and I are the hosts for the evening.

"Okay, let me think about it," I said. "I'm sure of it... Paul will ask of your presence. And the others would love to have the experience of meeting you."

"And one more thing, once you have arrived and received your luggage from the baggage claim at Entally Airport, there will be a woman driver who's name is Joanna, and she'll be holding a sign with your name on it. Please look for her, and she will get you here in my arms safe with no harm. Just like childhood times when we would lay in the bed together fondling all of our toes as we shared truth and dare stories in the shadows of the lampshade, Andrea said explaining all of the last minute details mixed with memories of old."

I laughed because she and I both know that the memories we shared were not all good but not altogether wrong either.

"Okay, great Andrea, let us just play everything by ear tonight just so I don't make a commitment that I can't fulfill later," I said with a little bit of hesitation.

I wanted Andrea to be understanding because, really, I only came to meet this Paul man she called herself marrying and running off to Europe with. Also to catch up on old times with my homegirl.

14

Chesmar Lake

Jazz music was playing in my ears while the driver gracefully drove me down a winding pathway with trees that lined the property on both sides. I couldn't help but notice that the path took us totally off the grounds of the neighborhood.

"Are we on a private island on the Lake? I asked the driver Joanna. Please tell me that I'm seeing right?" I continued to say.

Once you reach the actual Lake itself, you see all of the meticulousness carried for lawns of each household. You can tell the houses have been well maintained and not an uneven shrub or brown patch of burnt grass in sight.

"Yes, that is right." The driver Joanna said, "There are a total of five homes, and the frames of three are being built as we speak. Before you leave, I'll see to it myself that you receive a full tour of the Chesmar Lake grounds."

I said, "Yes, see to it that you do, Joanna. I would definitely like that."

"We will be pulling up at Dr. Sire and Andrea's home shortly. If you would like to gather all of your things, you may do so at this time." She said.

The Sweeping drive takes you up to Andrea and Dr. Sire's beautiful home leaving behind guards securing the private property on the right and one on the left. Their home is set on a knoll surrounded by seven point five seven acres. From the cd player, I could hear the sound of the keys from the piano as I was listening to the music while watching the vision of one man's dream Dr. Sire. I fell in love with Andrea's and Dr. Sire's home the moment the driver Joanna brought me behind the secured gates attached to a stone-wall.

There were two great Wooden gate posts on each side of the gated wall as we entered very slowly. The two colossal flower pots were full of greenery and dangling vines.

"Wow, this is some kind of palace!" I said—Peeping through the smokescreen windows from the back seat. I leaned forward, taking a good look at this altogether fantastic home that's seated in the heart of this gated community.

Nestled back on the hidden waters of Chestmar Lake is known and catered to some of the highly paid affluent men and women whom you may see from day to day. Chesmar Lake is also known for its ease and access to convenient and exclusive shopping, fine dining, tennis, and golf clubs, as well as newly built and established private schools. The heart of the Lake carries with it high waterfalls sweeping down and away into three heated cozy swimming pools. Nearby are multiple international airport choices, along with commuter rail stations located in the neighboring towns of Chesmar Lake. Including several putting greens, small landscape beds fed by streams of lakes from the main Chesmar Lake waterfall known as the Wealthy Well of Gush.

The Wealthy Well of Gush waterfall is known to be the wealthiest waterfall of all times. Simply because the five families of Chesmar Lake take privilege once a year in opening the gated community, it's open to tourist groups of any and all kinds to come and tour. What's called and revealed as the Array of Homes as tourists visit the luxury of living at its highest peak. They never leave the grounds of Chesmar Lake without going to the Wealthy Well of Gush. Making a wish and casting their coins into the water. To hopefully, one-day receive an overflow suddenly of living the dream life that they had just been exposed to.

All of the houses are expertly sited from their own estate to maximize the park-like setting with water views over the lawns. The Lake and various gazebos throughout with formal and casual spaces that embrace the outdoors. By flowing seamlessly to private courtyards and black stone terraces with huge fire pits and dance floors for entertaining.

I've been told by Andrea that every morning on her nature walks, it's nothing like listening to the running waters from the streams, hearing all of nature casting its purpose for living yielding back to Mother Nature.

Built by craftsmen from around the world, for any family to create on the Chesmar Lake grounds, they must purchase the land grounds starting at the cost of no less than nine million dollars. The architecture details of the homes here at Chesmar Lake modern amenities that create each home of its own as a timeless masterpiece. The eye-catching home is red brick with a sharp edge, ornamental coins covered over each pentacle. An added circular wing for family and friends met you from the right side of this mansion. Filled with nothing but a balcony followed by windows and an excellent overview of all five homes of Chesmar Lake. The sidewalk pavement following the curve of the house brings you clear of a double archway right above the top of the four-car heated Garage. The height of volt ceilings from each side of the home was plainly seen. You can tell that this eight-bedroom home was designed with uncompromising quality and splendor

15

For the Love of Beauty

The back door of the limo opened, and all I heard was. "Get out of the limo! Get out of the car right now. I need to see your face." Andrea yelled, coming out of the front double doors. She was holding her long maxi gown in her right hand, making sure she didn't trip on her way to meet me. It was as If everything was happening in slow motion. Placing my feet on the ground and proceeding to get out, I lifted myself out and looked up.
And she, my childhood friend Andrea Hunter was standing there waiting to place her arms around me.

She was gorgeous. My mouth was open, with not one word to speak. Andrea was every bit of the stunning face and body you would find on the monthly front cover of Black Beauty On Black Magazine. I couldn't say anything at the moment because I was captured by her beauty. She grabbed me and held me so tight and repeatedly said over and over again and again.

"Eve, my girl Eve is here." She said, "I've missed you more than words can say." She then asked, "What about the other ladies? How are they? We must bring them here, Eve." She continued to say, "But for now, it's just us two of only one kind." We both laughed, for we have really missed one another.

I heard her voice speaking in my inner ear, but I was mesmerized by this tall Hashen stallion of an Indian man standing in the door frame of the house. His skin was like that of evenly melted butter with a golden hew, with one hand rested up against the door. Young Prince Paul Posh Sire made eye contact with my stare.

Andrea said, "Eve!"

I said, "Queen...Andrea, darling, you are so beautiful." Immediately Andrea pulled me away and hugged me even tighter the second time. It was in this hug that the young Prince Sire made his genuine connection with me, letting me know that I was there with two feet planted on the high ground of London, Europe. By that, I meant my welcome from him was not at all lukewarm or hot for that matter, but it was very cold, and he made it known. Dr. Sire turned and walked away. Without even coming to greet me or answering the call of his daring wife, Andrea.

She called out. "Paul, come quick Eve is here! One of my truest childhood best friends is here. Hurry Paul, hurry!" Andrea, whom Paul calls a trooper because she gave him complete control over creating her beauty under anesthesia and several scalpels. Andrea reached back, assuming he was there waiting to greet me next. There was no asking him to join her in the reunion of our childhood love affair. He made his presence known and vanished like a vapor. Perhaps he waved, and I missed it. I thought to myself, wanting to give him a pass.

"Eve, what's wrong," Andrea asked, calling out to me? Snap out of it, girl."She said. I had to shake it off. As I said, being very apologetic.

"I guess with all of the excitement, Andrea, I blanked out for a moment. Forgive me, Andrea, for my unpolished behavior."

My childhood friend grabbed me by both of my hands as we twirled around, just like Sisterhood Honey bees of old times, making the dust fly high. As little children, we were too young to know that having grass was essential and added value to your house. We didn't know any better. All we knew was across the street where Ms. Lena lived. There was grass, and the grass was always green. Every other Friday, the "Queens Bees" from the Honey in the Hive would be swinging our legs off the front porch, waiting to see what kind of honey we could make out of all of this. And which businessman would be leaving Ms. Lena's house after two hours. One of us would run in the house and look at the clock on the wall in the kitchen. To see what time it was. We would come back out and time old man Rutherford the Pastor of St. Peter's Catholic Church, from two blocks over on the corner of Ambrose and Holland. Sometimes it would be the insurance man. That had the words Targus Insurance For Life written on the side of his vehicle. He would pull up and two hours later pull off. He never did take any papers in the house.

Kayla was always the bold one. She would yell across the street.

"Ms. Lena, are you and Pastor Rutherford having a prayer meeting at your house tonight?"
Nothing would stop all of us from laughing. We would be rolling all over the porch. Mr. Rutherford would drop his head wrapped in all kinds of shame and hurry along inside the house. Carrying a briefcase and clenching his hanging cross from around his redneck.

Ms. Lena's answer would always be. "No little girl, and if you must know my business, my elderly mother and I will be partaking in communion this evening.

Something you all's mother didn't teach you about. Now stay out of my business and off my grass.

And if you don't! Need I remind each of you that I have a weeping willow tree in the backyard. And trust me, she knows how to make you cry." She would slowly turn and walk across the porch with her daisy duke shorts on and shiny black patent leather high heel shoes with a white tee shirt tied in a knot from the side. Hours later, the Pastor would be running off Ms. Lena's porch dashing for the church's van. Seconds following, Ms. Lena would come to the front door wearing a see-through white gown, calling out,

"Pastor, pastor, you left your briefcase."

The very next day, the lawn care man would be pulling up in his work truck, spraying Ms. Lena's grass. She would make sure that someone in the neighborhood heard the balance on her invoice for having such well maintained green grass. Andrea and I twirled, we laughed and hugged one another. She touched me, and I kissed her. It's been so long, but we were so happy to be in each other's arms. Even though for years without reason, none of us were liked by many. I have to tell you Andrea is now a goddess of a woman. I was mesmerized by her well-apportioned body. Everything was in harmony as far as my eyes were concerned. She was a perfect size four. And I am a seven and if I eat wrong for one hour. Like instant oatmeal, I'll be wearing every bit of a lumpy nine-under two good girdles. As we walked into the house, I tried to be as discreet as possible and not stare. But Andrea's voice did not match the face of the young girl who was teased with the low self-esteem I grew up with. Nor the one that joined all the other teenage girls who tried to have a boyfriend from grade school to high school.

Overall this time, I had been speaking with Andrea. I failed to ask her, "What did she mean?"

When she said, "She's not the same person?" And in what ways has she changed? I guess I had not been listening over these last few weeks of us getting reacquainted.

I just knew that I was coming to meet the face and body of Andrea Hunter of whom at all times when any one of us Queens within the beehive would get mad at her. For her lack of confidence. She would cover her face instantly, not wanting to reveal her ugly cry of being sorrowful and weak-minded of her own beauty. She didn't feel as if she ever had what it took to be bold or beautiful. Each of us would say, "Stop crying and don't be so hard on yourself." We would affirm her that her inside beauty was enough. However, down through the years, men played over her heart just to get what they wanted from her body and then cast her away. They called her easy in school because she would have sex with them, thinking that this would be the one young man who really liked her out of all the others. She tried to make the girlfriend's boyfriend list. The list when some young boy would send his friend over to you to see if you had a boyfriend. Before he came and asked you out? Or the list in class when everyone would be passing around folded letters behind the teachers back. Asking you to check the box yes or no if you would go out with them. Well, Andrea never got one of those letters. After being left out of the dating scene, this made Andrea bitter, and she carried her hurt feelings on her chest and desired that all men pay for her beauty that was never known. So she had no problem stating how she hated boys because one particular guy told his friends that he had been with Andrea sexually and how he told her to look the other way and not to look back at him as he had sex with her from behind. Andrea was known for one to have and give great sex, but no one wanted to claim her as a girlfriend. The boys would say we want a pretty girlfriend, but the cute girls didn't know how to please their boyfriends in bed like Andrea. The young men didn't realize that they had an erection, and they would run and tell the other guys. Man, she made my power pack stand up. She just wanted to fit in and have a boyfriend to say to her like all the other girls had how beautiful they were. And prance her around the school grounds during all the sports games while she would be wearing one of their sports shirts, or coat with their name written across the back. Everyone knew Quinn Jenkins number forty-five. I was proud to wear his jersey because he was so good at sports. He was known as the Knight Rider. The school commentators of all the sports games would call him out on the turf, and Quinn would run out there with the speed of one hundred on the dashboard liken to a black two-door Corvette. You would hear them announce Jenkins; Knight Rider number forty-five once again comes out of nowhere, scores, and wins the game! Andrea would take a high seat from everyone and sit at the very top row of the bleachers, away from us all. We would go up there and try to get her to come down and sit with us while we cheered our men on. We wanted to assure her that no one would tease her, but she would say I just don't want to cuss anybody out tonight. That said, all her trust was just not there anymore. So her mouth got her in a lot of trouble. She started down talking and belittling men as if they were all dirtbags with little penises. It merely became the defense mechanism she had on most of the guys.

Andrea's face was glowing. Her nose was no longer full, nor was her face pushed in around her mouth because of her overbite. She now had high cheekbones, and the arch within her brows was to die for.

I asked her. "Girl, what makeup are you wearing? It's flawless?" She didn't answer. "I did hear that it was a new technique out now for women to airbrush on makeup. I asked, "Are you aware?" She laughed very hard.

"Eve, please, really," She said in her newly found European accent with a strong comeback of pretending to be shy.

"Andrea!" Grabbing her by the shoulders, I said, "You ain't never had this many tidy's ever! You were the only one in the hive of the Sisterhood Queen Bees that had nothing but speed bumps and a flat ass that we all could sit on and stay balanced."

"Nope!" Andrea said, "These titties's are all of me!" We laughed, pushed, and played with one another.

But you know I knew better. Better than the way her husband, Dr. Sire, lined up her two eyes and made them even, especially that left eye, the one that used to be lazy. She would be just talking, and the right eye would know precisely what to do. Make eye contact.

Then we would say, "Girl! Andrea, your left eye." To help us deal with the slow movement of her left eye. She was so used to saying back to all of us.

"Don't worry about it. It'll catch up. It always does." And we would burst out laughing so hard until we all would hit the floor. One thing for sure, I believe Andrea dealt with so much rejection and being teased over her looks all of her life. That nobody ever had to tell her when she was the butt of the joke. Most of the time, she would be so funny responding to us that all of us would forget what the conversation was really about anyway. Andrea laughed at everything. And kept everyone laughing to keep herself from always crying over poured out milk.

Her daddy would always say. "So what? You look like your daddy. I'm from Barbados. My genes are strong now stop crying because we don't have any milk to pour out."

Meaning stopping us from doing things that would cause us to waste our time and listening to people who had a hard time with the way we looked and carried ourselves as young ladies.

I gloried over her hair; it was naturally waved soft and flowing. It hung about the middle of her back. Reaching out to feel the strength of Andrea's hair,

"What are you using on this hair? It's so healthy and full of body," I asked very seriously with every intent for the truth to be given.

She said, shaking her head. "Come Eve, come on and allow me to show you to the East wing of the mansion. Just so you are aware. Paul and I call the East side of the bedroom wall "The Burning Wing" It's where you are going to be staying for the duration of the time here with Paul and me. I promise you we have more days and nights to gather and catch up on all the girl talk you want to have."
I had a million questions, and she picked up on it. But I wasn't hiding it. Really I wanted to know these things.

"Share it with me again. Why do you call the bedroom wall, The Burning Wing?"
I asked as I walked through the bedroom door and saw nothing that resembled the scenery of a wall on fire. I was puzzled, but, if both the Sire's say so.

Andrea said, "It doesn't always happen, but whenever it does, around six-thirty for about twelve minutes, you'll see why Paul and I have named this room that."

Rubbing the outside of her arms. While she stood there with them folded. As if something was bothering her all of a sudden. I couldn't help but ask one more question, so stepping close to her to get a very good stare into her eyes.

I asked, "Andrea is everything okay?" She dropped her head while taking the deepest breath rubbing down the side of her arms once more.

Wondering if she should or how to even find the strength to say whatever was troubling her.

Leaving me with no words to say, trying not to force

my way but like always to just be present an old-time friend would. I read her eyes that something was wrong, and it wasn't the time nor day to share it with me. I gazed in upon the frowns of lines that just so suddenly appeared and assured her that her peace in the matter was more significant than any issue that she might be facing. "Andrea, listen to me, Is this why you called for me to come so eagerly?" She didn't answer, but she started to turn and walk away, and I grabbed her. "No! I'm here now." Bringing her attention back to me and our trust we have always had since we were five years old. Lifting her face from a downward position.
I said, "You will not do this to me."
With a long pause, I asked. "Shhh...Are you being abused?"
And I waited for a reply. Andrea's eyes filled with tears but still not a mumbling word.
Below a whisper, I said, *"You can still trust me. Andrea, you are my queen, from the Sisterhood Honey Hive, for I am yours. Talk to me that we may make honey in the hive... I'm here for you and only you. Whatever storm that has you disturbed... and has touched down upon your life is no storm that can't be tamed or ceased."*
Eight-seconds into our silence. And we stood there as if we both were suspended by God's own gravity and the one earth we were only a part of. The world around us wasn't spinning but, the one world she and I had hold of was. Andrea's world that she could not speak of had consumed me within a matter of zero-seconds, and her inner being was made known before my very presence. She was all spent out. Her boldness was emptied and broken. To a place where worry was carrying her face and scars of uncultured beauty had manifested instantly as a hump came in her back, and her shoulders dropped, but still have no words, tears fell.

Reaching out to embrace her fall, I said, "Andrea, you know you can trust me with this." As I laid my hand on top of her obviously shaking hand that was running up and down her chest with firmness, I demanded her silence to become broken.

"What's wrong? I raised my voice and asked once more as I reminded her of sister code number seven. To withhold my truth is to not be trusted. I shared under my breath. We are Sisterhood Queens! Do you hear me? Queens, who have been trained to make honey out of any hidden secret in any threatening space. Make sweet honey with me, my sister. Who may taste and see that all is good? Remember! What has crushed you?"

She leaned in my chest from her left side and said very softly,

"Eve, I need you...my beauty is scarred."
I felt the presence of Prince Paul Posh Sire standing behind me, but there was no sound being made as I made eye contact with the black and white rug centered in the middle of the room from my side view. Paul was there. Andrea cleared her throat and quickly wiped her face from the soft tears that streamed down.

He called out to her, "Andrea!"
She hid her face in front of me, not allowing Paul to see it.

She answered tenderly, "Coming."
Andrea locked eyes with me as she turned around to walk towards the man who has been her provider for all of her shattered luxurious lifestyle—closing the door behind her. I stood still to hear if there were shared words, nothing. Now I'm wondering if Paul believes that I have come to invade his and Andrea's agreed space?

Walking out towards the circular patio that was designed with four single panel doors to step out onto.

Taking a deep breath to regroup from all of what just happened, I stretched my arms out to release everything that had held me as a prisoner of emotional bondage. I focused on one of the most amazing views from where I was standing. I was able to see all of the beautiful works of Chesmar Lake. All five homes were in plain sight. The mastermind behind the planning of this outward view was a Disneyland for adults. Whatever you could imagine it was before you.

As I laid back onto one of the patio chairs, I called Lauren. I wanted to check on her, and this pulled apart marriage situation she and her husband had going on.

"Hey, Lauren, Eve," I said as she answered.

"Well, hello, Ms., I always need a vacation, and I'm always gone on vacation." We laughed.

She asked, "How was your flight?"

"Everything has been lovely; from the time I was picked up, all the way up until now. But, I can't wait until you all get a chance to come to Europe to spend time with Andrea and her husband. Lauren! Girl! This heifer Andrea is rich, honey! Do you hear me? She has struck gold on boatloads!"

"Really, Eve?" She asked.

"Yes," "And she's fabulous all over the place with her body and beauty, I assured her."

"No!" Lauren said.

"Yes," "Lauren, our Andrea, is queening and swirling around at the top of the hive,"You didn't hear me!"

"I did," Lauren said. She continued to speak. "Well, tell Andrea I said make honey with all that money!"

I said, "Andrea and this husband of hers, Prince Paul Posh Sire, is really living a marvelous life."

Lauren stated,"I wished I was there with you, ladies.

I'm sure you both are about to have the time of your lives being together, and plus it's been so long since you've all seen one another too."

"Well, before you go, allow me to ask how's things going with you and Robert?" I asked her with concern in my voice.

"Eve, no, I will not do that to you. You're on vacation, and you need not worry about me and Robert's situation. Just know that I have my eyes on things, and I'm watching from a distance."

"Yeah, you're right Lauren, and as much as I would like for you and Robert to work things out."

"We'll have much to talk about when you get back," Lauren said.

"What's up with Olivia and Kayla? Have you spoken with them?" I asked her.

"Well, Kayla is taking up meditation to help with the healing journey of her loss. She claims to be burning sage to get rid of evil spirits and repeatedly says how she has a hate relationship with her grandmother Sweet Lady Mrs. Hannah Mae's God. In the midst of all of that, one of the mothers from the mother's board over at Greater Spirit of God Missionary Baptist Church set up counseling sessions with Kayla and First Lady Madeline Rose Mason. But for some reason, Pastor Henry said Kayla's issues are far beyond the healing ministry there at SOG-MBC. And she needs to be encouraged to seek help elsewhere."

"Well, that doesn't make sense," I said, "Kayla's been going to her grandmother's church since she was a baby. What better church to administer healing than that of her own SOG-MBC?"

"Your guess is as good as mine, Eve," Lauren said. It's obvious Lauren's not aware of the dead cat on the line about who's Kayla's father.

188

"Now Olivia, she's been running down to that Parker Joyner Workout gym. She says that the steam room is something else. It's got her hooked chile. But she's working and keeping it going."

"She says an old friend of hers was about to bless her with a Rolex watch. You know she's been preparing for the swimming torment down at the gym. She's excited about this watch; she'll be able to wear it underwater and that it could monitor everything but the truth from what she told me."
"Listen, enjoy your trip, and don't be cooped up in the house working either. Promise me you will get out and have the time of your life?"
I said nothing to that question because I know me.

She states again, "Sister code number ten. Excelling is who we are and not what we do. We are the force. No limits! Do you hear me?" Lauren asked with firmness.

"Eve?" She called me.

"Yes, I'm still here."

"You didn't say anything about Andrea's husband," Lauren said.

"I already spoke about him, what more do you want me to say?" I asked, and she paused.

Okay, listen, he's sho nuff handsome but strange,"Eve said.

Lauren asked, "What do you mean by strange?"

"Well, once again, he didn't have much to say."

"What do you mean, and what were you expecting him to talk so much about?"
I said. "Lauren, Paul has been silent the whole time that I've heard thus far. Now that's strange, or do you think I'm overreacting?"

"Yeah, it could be a little off if you say it like that. Perhaps it'll take Paul time to warm up to you." She tried to make sense of Paul's silence.

No, Lauren, you are not listening to me. It must be within his culture. Because this man never came to greet me as if I was unimportant.
There came a knock on the door.

"Yes, come in, please," I said, "Lauren, I'll have to go, love. Talk with you soon."

"Okay, Eve, take care," Lauren said. *"I will, bye for now."* I whispered into the phone.

It was one of the maids coming to introduce herself to me.

She said, "Hi," with the biggest smile on her face. "My name is Winnie with a very strong accent. I'm here to be of service to you." Pointing to the intercom system on the wall next to the door, she began to share with me how to operate it. Well, hello, Winnie, so lovely to meet you. Winnie said, "If I am unavailable, the green light will stay on until I can fulfill your request. But please don't worry, it won't be very long. You can just leave a message for me, and I will make sure that all things are taken care of for you promptly, my lady." "Thank you and will do," I said, "Would you like something to drink?" She asked, "Yes, that would be wonderful, clasping my hands together. Thank you for asking," I said, "What is your desired choice?" She asked.

"I would love to sip on some hot herbal green tea, with a little ginger, lime, and a small pour of honey," I answered.

Winnie said, "I will go and prepare it and soon return. You must know shortly in about an hour; dinner will be served in the dining room.

You may find us there either by taking the East wing elevator to the right of your bedroom then straight down the hall. Or perhaps you don't mind the stairs. Once you get to the first floor soon after passing under the overview, make a quick right, take that hallway midway, and there you will find us gathered. Oh! And Eve, Walleye is on the menu, and we will not eat until everyone is present.""Thank you, Winnie, once again. I will find my way,"I responded to her. Closing the door behind her, she left with the smile she came in with, and instantly I was whistled away in a different mood, my reset button was triggered by the glory of Chesmar Lake. The sun had begun to set, and it was so breathtaking and being fully aware my own strength I decided to walk over to the balcony to see this firsthand. The sun was settling in the distance. Far but very near. It appeared on the face of Chesmar Lake as I watched for a full twelve minutes. Reminding myself to breathe and live in this moment as well as others that was never created for me, but sensitive to the given opportunity. Just as Andrea said, the hues of fire reds, mandarin orange, and shades of golden yellows were cascading over the waters of the lake and reflecting onto the back wall of the room that I was occupying. The East wing room became still but peaceful and warm from the glorious rays. The burning wall had just appeared in the most abundant form of an angel's wing. Turing my back towards the sunset, my breath escaped me as I let down my hair, laid back, and watched it rest as it covered all of me.

16

Hide & Seek

The friends of Chesmar Lake have arrived! Checking everyone out as they pulled up in front of Paul and Andrea's home with their fancy name brand cars and SUVs, from the Bugatti Chiron, Maserati Gran Turismo, Aston Martin DB11, a Bentley Mulsanne, and the Porsche Macan.

As I watched outside the window, I saw everyone being so polite to one another; a hug and a kiss, a smile, and a handshake. It's about to go down, and I have no idea, but I'm so ready to meet every one of Chesmar Lake, coming away from the window to prepare all of me to join in on what the evening had to offer.

As I made my way down the hall, I wore my very own design—the one of a kind long maxi Afrocentric gown. Of course, my whole back is naked.

And one strap that gracefully revealed the bareness of my right shoulder. I named it the Safari Wild. It was flowing from behind. My body is rubbed down with Miss Sassy's Scent called Private Room. And my hair was gently pulled away from my face into a messy high bun with gold beaded chopsticks embellishing my finish look of the night.

My face was made up softly with light shades of pink, emerald greens, and gold. Feeling good about the night, I made my presence known by landing on the last step of the staircase.

All of the couples had gathered together in the foyer. As appetizers and wine were being served by the waiters, the lights were dimmed down slightly low. Conversations were being had by groups of merely two and three, but everyone was engaged in the friendship of each other. The music of Lem Okies, one of the finest singers in the world, was heard by all of us. His smooth sounds traveled tastefully from the center staged gazebo arranged in the backyard. The framed wall behind Lem was wrapped with nothing but lights and hanging lanterns. With his chest hair exposed, Lem wore all white. The earth smell of Mother Nature was endless with fresh-cut grass, patchouli, and sandalwood underneath our nose. Candles were lit, and windows in the house were open, just enough for a gentle breeze to bring a chill and yet remain warm inside. And out of nowhere, Paul raises his wine glass, and with as much celebration, he could muster up. He got everyone's attention by posing a toast to Andrea's childhood friend me. Speaking under my breath, I said, now ain't this about a sucker full of surprises. "To the friend who has been friendly! Everyone help me welcome for the first time to Chesmar Lake Ms. Eve Novae." All of the couples came and circled around the bottom of the last stair where I stood, and they patiently waited for me to respond. I thought to myself, Paul has never greeted me. This punk ninja! Immediately I looked over at Andrea, and she smiled and dropped her head to keep from reading my mind. Oh, so we are wearing faces tonight, I thought.

And I did. I responded with... It's my pleasure to have embraced all of you. I look forward to getting to meet each of you in a more personal way.
Seeing all of your faces tonight allows me to know that Chesmar is full of awesome people and many surprises.
And I deem to unwrap every bow as I said that each of them raised their glasses with lots of cheering.

Afterward, we celebrated together. For the night was young and awaiting us to arrive at every whatever.

Walking upon this rather odd Couple,

Andrea said, "Allow me, Eve Novae, meet my great friends Aiden and Chanel."

"Good evening," I spoke and nodded my head to them both. Andrea was called away, and the conversation carried on.

The two of them were a little different, I might say. Aiden was very talkative but handsome to be a bi-racial man. Tall and muscular with dreads hanging from a ponytail in the back of his head. The first biracial man I've seen with gold-tipped dreads, in a suit with bow legs. He asked me several questions. Such as, if I had any children? And If I was married? Then I was respectfully given a chance to answer by Aiden. However, Chanel, who is a Physical Fitness and Obesity Coach to top celebrity children. She flies all over the world, hosting boot camps. As short as she was in height, budded in with a rather small attitude. She took a glance at my shoes, sized me up and down. Ms. Sherlock Holmes is here to investigate all the business she doesn't need to know.

Chanel then asked. "Where are you from, and what is it that you really do?" Bringing her eyes back to my attention. I raised my glass, letting her know I see through you just as much as I can see where this is going already. Off the tracks!

Awe...Chanel feels threatened and has, for a brief moment, unleashed her little girl syndrome that is intimidation

I said as if I was feeling sorry for her, "Really, Chanel, my life is not that complicated. I'm from around the way, and for the most part, I seem to live in a drift from time to time. My ruby red slippers have paved me many yellow brick roads."

I simply raised the front of my gown and clicked the back of my heels together, making sure the both of them noticed I had taken the time to get my feet manicured. I carried on by making a clicking sound from the side of my mouth. Click, click, click.

"Now enough about me, please share how tall you have been in life? I'm eager to hear," and I smiled. She quickly swallowed what was left in her glass and stormed away. Like Toto, the little puppy from the Wizard of Oz who ran off and got lost. Being sympathetic, I turned and asked her soon to be husband.

"I'm sorry Aiden, did I say something wrong?" Walking past me, he whispered by leaning in from my left side.

"I want you first leaning over the upstairs balcony." Just in the nick of time, the Waiter walk passed with a tray full of oysters mounted on top of wine glasses filled with champagne. You know I grabbed one. As a matter of fact, I swallowed two of them smothered in hot sauce and all. Tasted the body of the champagne for a moment, tossed it to the back of my throat, and pondered on Aiden's silent words.

"Well, hello...Mrs. Ms. Eve Novae." "Hi!" as I was greeted with a warm hug from the married couple. Sage, who also was Africa American, and Huston, who is from Nigeria and one of the world's top OBGYN's.

"Eve, would be fine and thank you," I shared with the lovely couple.
With his rather strong accent, Huston asked, "How long will we have the pleasure of having you here on the lake?"

Sage says, "Yes!" Rubbing my shoulder while rocking back and forth. "I hope that we can keep you here in a hideaway, Sage says you're so darn cute!" I don't know if it was me but, I'm almost certain Sage just zeroed in on my breast.

She tried to kiss me on the lips, leaned back, looked at my facial expression, and gave me a slow and steady wink from her left eye. Placing my hand on my forehead, slightly wiping the flyaway hairs away, I answered the question. "As much as I would hate to return home. I must. To keep all of my clients happy and satisfied." I stepped back two steps on guard. With that being said, "My stay is only for one week." From behind, Huston just so happened to bump into Bailey Kevas. A white chick who is mad wealthy. Her father owns the first and largest Stock Market ever—Kevas Stocks. Bailey is in love with Dawson, who is black. She wants him to marry her, but Dawson can't deal with that mother of hers. Who he calls the Ace of Spades because she has a black heart, and Dawson is the top leading Lawyer for Chesmar Lake. Dawson was also wrongfully accused of raping one of the neighborhood daughters in his teenage years. He served nine years in the Dept of Correction and became good friends with Paul by way of another inmate Marco Sanders. Through much research, Dawson tracked Paul down. Which after all, charges were dropped he paid and used Paul with his expertise to do some minor face changes to his appearance after he was found not guilty.Do to the diary of the little girl Kerry Hensel which was discovered and hidden in the library at her grandparent's home out in the country years later. She wrote about it, built lies, and buried the truth. What a little sugar cookies and warm milk right before bed would do when talking to nosey Grandmas. So the state had to pay him for the nine years of wasted time and abuse from the prison system he occurred while being tried and locked up. Naomi's father couldn't care less that she's with a black man. Oh! But that mother of hers is heated. Mrs. Kevas keeps dirt turned over on Dawson and could bury him alive if need be. The good in it all is, Dawson used the money the state of Arizona paid him for retribution. He made a wise decision and invested some of it in his future. Achieving his goal, Dawson attended Crimson Law as a law student. One out of every five people is accepted in Crimson Law.

"Pardon me, Naomi, my apologies," Huston said, embracing her with care and catching her fall. Not a problem Huston, you're such a tease; she continued to be funny. We all got acquainted very well. Except for the very last couple, I did not have the pleasure of meeting. Because the dinner bells were ringing softly from the dining room, one by one, we all walked in the dining room, and three male waiters dressed in all black and white gloves were pouring water in our water glasses. The room was stunning. The decor was white linen with crystal bright place settings, black and white name cards, a side menu printed on black with gold lettering across the top that said welcome to the Sires—offering each of us two choices of sides and desserts along with seasoned herbed Walleye. The table was long and square, running down the center of the room. Four large fishbowl vases full with an arrangement of exotic red flowers. They were so vibrant in color that it placed love in the air automatically. Even though I was in the room, I had begun to feel alone. Missing Mekhi to the tenth power, I needed to hear his voice and see his face. I love how he makes me know that I'm wanted. It's so exciting to me that Mekhi comes to mind way before Jayden O'Connor does. Boy, how time brings about a change. You never really know until you're stuck in it, and dinner was served. I was being stared at by the husband of the couple that I did not meet. The conversation started with how well everyone was pleased with the City hall officials having such a well-planned winter event of Christmas. It was talking all throughout Europe about the spectacular event. Every downtown storefront store and restaurants participated. Windows were decorated, and Christmas lights, trees, and holiday music were enjoyed by men, women, and guests from around the world. Each of them shared how stages of different artists performed some of the most exceptional talents you would ever see from across the globe. Little children walked around, holding cups of hot cocoa and cotton candy at the same time. It's not often that the families of Chesmar Lake go into town, but when they do, they are always noticed as the rich wealthy people of Chesmar. Then all of a sudden, out of nowhere. By the wife of the husband that I keep seeing stirring at me every now and then. With his punk ass, I was being kicked from underneath the table before I knew it. I shouted out. "Hey!" "What was that for?" My whole body quivered as I held a strange face.

"Are you all right, Eve?" the unknown wife asked, Looking over her glasses as if I'd just peed my pants. Andrea gets up and walks off to speak with the kitchen staff. I feel as if I'm being tested or something. Almost like some of them would like to know what it is that I can handle. Okay, well, I'll just check this old muddy water that appears to be so crystal and see how quick and precise we can get it to change. Leaning my head to the side, I spoke. "Wouldn't you like to know. I do apologize. Somehow time didn't allow for us to meet. I missed your name. Not that you're not important, I just didn't catch it." Very carefully, I made my point to be understood. Simple because she was of Asian descent, and a sister will whoop her ass up in here. Up in here! Batting her eyes to make sure I saw her lash line from Tokyo, she said, talking to me but stirring Paul in the face from the head seat at the table. "My name is Nicole," She then quickly, without turning her head, pointed her finger to the right of her. And this is my man Cree. Not that it matters. The main thing is making sure you're enjoying your stay on top of the lake and not under blowing bubbles. Stabbing three pieces of the orange garnish that laid so beautifully on the side of my half-emptied plate with a twirl, I placed my fork to the bottom of my water glass and made her a high class of freshly decorated water floating with ice and fruit. One cold one coming up! I thought. I tasted it just to be sure. Reached across the table, replaced her water glass with mine. And I said, "There's no need to thank me, your kindness has to be noticed. And one more thing Nicole, I snapped my finger and blew her a kiss. In Cree's silence with his black ass, I can tell that he's been well kept. Since I was a little girl, my mother has always taught me great table manners can tell a lot about someone. It shows your refinement and upbringing for yourself and other people. It's a respect that's given and taken when you're seated with or without the best."Nicole's eyes got wide as a stray cat falling off a thirteen-foot building landing on its back. "I don't know, what do you think, Nicole? I mean, It helps when you are raised with table etiquettes, right? You do know that It could never just be about the money we're raised with. Do you agree? I'm sure you know...It saves you from all embarrassing moments."I said to her gracefully as I crossed my legs and set straight up. Everyone stopped eating and began to take notice that I knew I was the only pink elephant in the middle of the room. Who had just bagged up against the wall to defend me? Andrea returned and said while taking her seat. "Now that all of that is taken care of. "What did I miss?" I motioned for my server Winnie to fill my wine glass up, as she poured, I closed with making sure the whole table knew that I lived in the moment and was very present. Slowly looking around the dining room table at each of them. From face to face in their absence of speechI said,"No, Andrea, I'm glad you returned and was able to join us. I continued with... "Now, I do understand that we all do things differently. Because we're all from different parts of the world, this is what makes all of us so unique and very much needed. There is no need to feel threatened or guarded. For all of us have something to give to one another.

I'm not here to take but to give what I can." "To only help what you have accomplished here to become more delicious." And we all burst out laughing. All around the room, we raised our glasses, and I made another toast.

I said, "Here is a good place to learn from all of you. To us!" These women had become so stiff and hard-hearted that their husbands were turned on over the fact that as a woman, I was free just being me, out of all the money that I had made and was soon to have. It was just paper with someone's face on it. The space of life that I was in was living moments of change. In the open view, they all knew that money had not consumed me or the experience I had decided to live. I had not become a woman of wealth who had lost her way of living. It's never my job to oversee who God has already sent in my life as a provider, protector, and a promise giver. For me, it wasn't about money, having money, or the status of who I had become with all of the money I had made, at the end of the day. The lesson at the table with all of the exotic red flowers was everyone could see the same red exotic flowers, whether we paid any attention or not. They were not hiding their original beauty as we all finished dinner, the men hurled talking about sports and the close of the evening. The women gather-ed around, and I reminded them first and foremost, how love always has to lead.

17

The Mountain of Regret

The night had become spent, and half the week had passed. I've noticed, and there's no doubt in my mind, that Dr. Prince Paul Posh Sire fell in love with Andrea's flaws and the needed correction of her female anatomy. But, on the other hand, Andrea loved the idea that Dr. Paul Sire presented endless possibilities of the lifestyle of the rich and famous.

One evening I couldn't sleep, so I decided to get up and take a cruise down to the bar. Just to get out and to make some sense out of all of this. Winnie, my server, reached out to me through the income system that was in my suite.

She shared, "Your driver is here to take you around the lake."

"Thank you, Winnie,"I responded with kindness.

"Will you be traveling alone?" She asked.

"Yes, indeed," I answered back.

When I arrived downstairs, Winnie had surprisingly prepared a driver and a tour ride on one of the Chesmar Lakes thirty-two eighty-five CR Avalon Pontoon boats for the night.

It was beautiful out on the lake. Lights outlined the entire lake.

You could see the fronts and backs of people's homes. Winnie had prepared me a picnic basket full of goodies, some blankets, and a bottle of Carmile's red wine called Red Crush.The label on the bottle was red.

Suede on the outside, and on the top was mounted a
red diamond. That had been crushed to its own unique shape.
Although the bottle was so cute and feminine, the mature
taste of the brick red Cabernet wine was every bit of three
hundred dollars per bottle. Red Crush is definitely a woman's
drink. The rich blends of Cherry, Cassis, and Vanilla on
lonely nights like tonight is what every lady needs in her life
when she's away from her man. I went from cheese, nuts to
fruit and bubble up Red Crush.

As we sailed, I laid back and took in all the nature
one could find. I put in a request to the driver Monte.

"Please take me to no man's land." Boy, did I have a
laugh on that one? Monte had no idea what I was talking
about.I yelled back and said, "Take me to the middle of
nowhere. I don't want to be found!"
I think he caught on that time, cause Monte laid the waves to
the side.

I could have got out and walked on water in the name
of Jesus.

The radio was on, and Sade was cruising with me
along the lake.

It was so peaceful that after a while, I was just out
here. Monte cut the motor off, and we just drifted.

I heard grasshoppers and lightning bugs glowing on
and off. In the stillness of the boat, I remembered as a little
girl how I would run as fast as I could to reach out to catch
the lightning bugs. Just to take the light off the back of the
bug and put it on my ears. I made my own earrings.

I wandered off into a dream. Jayden O'Connor was
asking me for my hand in marriage, and I had refused.

In the dream, we were on this very high mountain in
Hawaii. The Jackson Davis dance company was there
dancing in all white. They even had white turbans wrapped
around their heads, male and female.

Then there was half an orchestra singing from the heavenly side of heaven. Three women dressed in white goddess apparel were playing the harps. There was also a dinner table prepared. Off into the distance, the meal was ready for two with a lovely bouquet of yellow roses. Jayden O'Connor came out of nowhere, and his best friend Kass followed in behind him with the island's wedding official. They both had on suits and were smiling from ear to ear. I stood there in mixed feelings because my heart was crying out for Mekhi as we were proceeding to partake in communion. My mind was saying yes to Jayden because we were finally here. A moment in time when our love for one another would become one and no longer two. But every time I looked down at the yellow roses, I saw my dad's face but my grandmother's Tilly's voice.

She said, "Baby girl, he only appreciates you. He knows that you bring him delightful cheer and filled moments of joy." She continued to say, "Now that ain't enough. You get down off that mountain right now!" And within seconds, the opposite happened. My daddy's voice was heard, and I was viewing my grandmother's face.

I heard him say, "There is no real romance.

Platonic love without passion is just friendship. Baby, follow your heart. What does your heart speak?

"No, Jayden, I don't want your flowers. I don't even like yellow flowers; you know that. I love Mekhi; I love Mekhi, Mekhi loves me; he really does love me. No, I can't marry you. Take me off of this mountain. Please take me back, take me back."

"I don't want to be here!" As I was coming out of the dream.

Monte, my driver, was standing over me, asking, "If I was okay?" He said that I was having a bad dream and waking up.

As I saw past Monte broad shoulders, the sky had become midnight blue with sparkling stars here and there.

"What happened?" I asked.

He said with a strong accent, "You were having a bad dream about your dad, my love."

"I recall bits and pieces of a dream, but not all of it," I said.

Monte said,"It sounded like you didn't want to marry a Kass man who didn't get you the red roses, but, only the yellow ones. I shook you like this,

"Hey... you're trying to run away from your grandmother." For yellow is not your favorite color.

I was so exhausted, not to mention embarrassed. At this point, the only thing I could do was cover my head with the blankets and cry while I was laughing it off.

Wow! I'm done, I believe in my heart that I have fallen in love with Mr. Mekhi Henderson. Today I know I cannot marry Jayden O'Connor even though in the dream, I felt like I marred him. And my father gave me away.

But for some reason, I heard grandma Tilly say, "We have only been at a friendship level all these years. And not to give in."

I enjoyed the girlfriend's three-way telephone call on the way back. Livia, Kayla, and Lauren joined me on the phone as we made honey to put in my tea. I had to call them to share the dream. And what did I do that for? Oh, they teased and made fun of me.

"Girl, you were trying to run off the mountain," Kayla said.

"Naw, get this," Lauren says,"Eve along with the whole dance company dancing around up there, about to come tumbling down the side of the mountain trying to get away from O'Connor."

"You are trying to marry that ole young thang who has tapped that ass and rocked that sleep down on you," Livia said, full of laughter.

"Stop! Y'all, making my stomach hurt, I said, "I miss you, ladies, so much. Y'all some dirty bees, but I'm happy I called you all, and I can't wait to get back." "I really needed this laugh.

Kayla burst out and said, "At least we all know not to get you any yellow roses for your birthday or your funeral." They talked about me and tore me up so badly. I had no choice but to laugh at myself for calling them.

18

The Private Party

As we headed back and Monte docked the boat, the house had become dark for all the lights on the inside were off—all except one or two. The cars from the Sire's circle of friends I met a few days ago were parked outside. I wonder what's going on tonight. We've already had the time of our lives—all in one week and three days. Every day has been fabulous—yoga each morning on the upper balcony, a pig roasting, fireworks, and jet ski racings. A tennis court full of ice sculpturing for a day, food, drinks, and a lawn backed up with horses, donkeys, and pink colored ponies for the children with blue hairspray and painted faces. We hopped from plane to plane shopping for shoes, purses, and jewelry. Private concerts are ranging from Lem Torres, Angela Speckman, and Ernie Larousse. What the hell could be happening tonight? I'm tired and miss my own bed. You know what? Rich people need to get a job! They ain't got nothing to do. I figured this thing out. They sit back and pay the expert to make them money while they fly all over the world, spending it. Forget a man I've got to get myself in a better position of living.

After walking up the sidewalk from the dock. Sandals in my hand. I came in the back door of the house. I stood there in the door frame of the mudroom.

Just as I thought, the lights were off, and the lighting that I saw was all from night lights placed in the hallways strategically here and there. All the shades were pulled. Soft romantic music was being played through the intercom speakers throughout the house. There was not one server or waiter to be found. Besides the music,I heard whispering from around the corner. But I didn't see anyone. So I listened because I listened to my name in the conversation. This was one conversation I probably should not have heard. It was Andrea's husband, Dr. Prince Paul Posh Sire, speaking to Dawson.

Dawson whispered and asked Paul, *"Will Eve be joining us?"*

Paul answered back. *"Naw, man, she's out for the night."*

Dawson asked, *"Out like she's not here, or you failed to invite her to the private party?"*

Paul said, *"No, I didn't fail to invite Eve my wife did."*

Paul responded as if he was teed off. *"Andrea claims she doesn't want Eve to know this side of her life."*

"Oh!" *"So you and your wife are ashamed of being swingers of love."* Dawson made a smart remark.

"No," *"Don't get it messed up, Dawson,"* *I told Andrea to make sure that Eve was well aware of the games ahead of time. So I left the invitation to give up on her. Besides, you're not the only one who wants to share the same bed with Eve. "*Paul said very sparingly, trying not to be heard.

"Who?" *"Who else wants her?"* Dawson asked. I tried to understand, but Paul said nothing.

Dawson said, *"You!"* He asked again, *"You want your wife's childhood friend?"* *"Yes, why not? She's gorgeous, and there's something about her spirit that draws me to her. I find myself staying away from her. So I don't give myself away. It's like I did all of this surgery on Andrea. To make her this beautiful woman on the outside, hoping that it will have some effect on her inside spirit. And she's this divided woman. I'm married to two different people. There's this side of her I told you about before. When she's not polite but insulting, Andrea has no idea of manners or the use of wisdom in handling me or our business affairs with other people. Eve is a woman Dawson. I've watched her. She's all woman through and through, and I want to taste and experience her love."*

Dawson said, *"You are breaking the rules, Doc."*

"I make the rules D. Remember?" Paul asked with his place of authority.

Dawson asked, *"Well, what happens if she makes it back? The night is still young, and the games have just begun."*

By this time, I was bent down on all four. Knees and hands. Trying to make my way past the refrigerator and the helm of my skirt got caught on the metal leg of the garbage can that was the shape of a pink flamingo standing on two legs— looking at me like stop tripping. So I backed up. There was no way around it. I had to go back, or I was about to be butt booty naked in three-point two-seconds. The whispering continued.

Paul finished his sentence by saying, *"All I can say is, If Eve gets in the game Dawson, I'm going to need you to cover for me."* Like we did one time before for you. You go in and quickly come out without one word spoken. I'll replace you. And do not! I repeat, do not touch her. She's mine. Secretly I'll have her, and she'll never know.

Dawson told Paul, *"I gotcha. Don't worry; this is how we roll. You had my back when Chanel's little ass Auntie Tangela came. Talking about she didn't know what to do. Man, when her little ass got done with me, I ran and hid in one of y'all closets. I was scared like a Mother Rucker. I was so tired I fell asleep and didn't come out until the next morning. You remember I didn't get to make it to any other rooms. Tangela put that leather whip on me and spanked my ass. I thought my dad had beat me."*

Paul asked, *"How did you know it was her? Did she not wear her mask?"*

"Man, she took it off! She said she wanted to be remembered. She made me look her in the face as she beat me."

After I heard this, I had no other choice but to leave my skirt behind laying at the flamingo's feet. Yep, you guessed it. A ninja's ass is out, and I'm on an island by myself under this circle breakfast nook table curled up on this shaggy DA rug. Evelyn G. Novae's advice keeps me in trouble. "Real women don't wear panties all day everywhere they go. Just don't be anywhere you can get caught." I can hear her just as precisely as soon as Dawson walked off.

I heard Sage say with her singing voice, "Do we have any special guests joining us tonight?"

"Nope," Paul said, "just us and the theme Wild and Wet."

Then Sage drops her voice and sends an indication that she would be in the garage lying in the back seat of his black Rolls Royce, wearing blue shop towels for a cover-up. Just Incase, he wanted to find her.

Paul says, "Sage remember, I'm the man with the vision, and then came the followers."

Paul walks off with her and says, go hide and watch how fast I find you.

Not even five-seconds went by, and Andrea came into the kitchen, grabbed a bowl of fresh fruit out of the refrigerator. Cree then walks up and grabs her from behind, holding both of her butt cheeks.

Cree asked Andrea the same question Dawson asked Paul. "Will Eve be joining us, Andrea?"

"No, Cree, I'm sorry to say Eve has not been feeling good these last few days?" She responded.
Cree grabbed Andrea about the neck and started threatening her about me.

He said in a very stern voice. "I want the record set straight and make sure that if anybody in this house was to have Eve first, it better be me. Or else Andrea Paul will not be a happy husband when he finds out that I know his little secret and bye-bye to your life of luxuries. Don't think he won't be mad when he finds out that is was your idea to break all the rules when it came to sharing my bed. Should I tell him, or would you like to say to him that you love me naked gun? And for the second time, you are carrying my child."

"Watch yourself, Cree; she said,"You are dancing on the wrong floor."

"I want her alone and without you, Paul, or Bailey. Do you hear me, and have I made myself clear?"
Snatching Cree's handoff from around her neck, she rolled her eyes and said, "Yes! Now take your ratchet hands off me, you double-crossed low down dirty backbiting dust eating rattlesnake."
Cree rubbed his fingers through Andrea's hair. She looked off to the side, trying to ignore his foolishness.

He spoke, "Well, make it happen and get her down here. Now! I know how to make her feel better. You should know that, or does big daddy need to make you call his name again to help you remember?"

He then bent down and started rubbing Andrea's stomach, kissed it, and said, "Daddy can't wait to see you." Pushing Cree as hard as she could. "Take your filthy hands off of me." With anger coming from her voice, she immediately reached for the kitchen drawer.

Cree leaned in with his hip, slammed it, and said, "I wouldn't do that if I were you," and walked off.

She dropped the bowl of fruit and almost saw me. I bagged up against the wall in a snail-like position. Because a pineapple ring rolled right underneath the table, and wouldn't you like to know I started having an allergic reaction? My mouth got watery, and my tongue began to swell along with my face. My eyes began to run like the Brown's River Falls, and a sneeze was coming with a mighty force as I balled up. Hives broke out all over my body.

Paul walks in and says, "Andrea baby is everything all right?"

Caught off guard, Andrea jumps and says, "Baby, what baby? Yes, Paul, It's just me being clumsy."

"Here, let me give you a hand with that," Paul stated. "No!" "Your help is not needed here. Go find something to do. I can handle my own mess up. Plus, I don't want to hear your punk ass mouth about it later. How this was one of your Grandma Ci Ci's antique bowls that I shattered."
With my mouth wide open. I couldn't believe I heard Andrea speak to Paul this way. My lips moved with motion without any sound. Andrea! What is really going on around here, I thought? Here was my chance to escape as Paul stormed out and headed towards the inside garage door. Andrea dropped the broken pieces of the bowl in the garbage and started crying. "What have I gotten myself into?" A swingers quarrel. I love the way Cree loves Noelle. She has no idea the lover she has. Paul tries, but Cree knows precisely what to do to put me to sleep. Paul wants children that I don't care to give him, and his family will never receive. For the second time, I have to get rid of a baby Cree wants me to have and mess up this badass body I fight every day to maintain. She walks out and says, "Never!"
The cold air hit the crack of my butt as I scooted out from

under the table backward. I snuck out of the side door and ran around the house with the kitchen towel flapping between my legs. It wasn't comfortable sneaking in through the back patio door leading to the side hallway to go upstairs.

   I heard Aiden shout out. "Let the games begin! Find yourselves wild, and you better get wet!" I tipped passed the staircase and looked out into the living room, and much to my surprise, all of them that were there were dressed in black sheets with fancy masquerade masks over their faces.This is one private party I will not be a part of I said. Shutting her bedroom door; the curtains were open, and she witnessed three people run past her bedroom balcony, with he-he and a haw-haw giggling as they chased one another. Not knowing who it was because of the costumes everyone was made to wear before they could make it back passed the balcony doors.

   Eve was feeling weak because of all of the excitement and the pineapple allergic reaction. She lost her balance, hit her head on the wooded arm of the love seat couch in her bedroom, and was knocked out instantly. Coming out of her daze, she couldn't make out the voices. But she knew she wasn't alone.

   She heard, "We found you in a position we couldn't refuse to get you up,"someone said.
Fainting in and out. Eve was nervous. She went into a memory lapse of her childhood. In the vision, she heard someone praying in the closet. It sounded like her Aunt Roxanne but could have very well been her grandmother Tilly. Roxanne was the mean aunt who was partial when it came to Eve's mother, Evelyn. She couldn't stand Evelyn from the time she was born. Eve was told when Evelyn was just a baby, and everyone would come over to see the pretty bundle of joy. Roxanne honey would go outside, fall off her bike or go in her bedroom and break something to bring all

the attention her way. It always ended out in a whooping. Out of all the sisters, it was these two that never could get it right. Roxie, as the family called her at times, was older than Eve's mama. Whenever Evelyn would walk away, Roxie would say in front of whoever was present; I can't stand her. She had no problem hiding her true feelings; it sounds like the spirit of jealousy to me. She had a keen sense of humor, though; however, she was very wise and did not play games when it came down to handling any type of business. Roxanne has never worked a real job a day in her life. She has been well taken care of by one man in particular named Toby. Whatever Roxanne wanted, needed, or had a taste for. Toby was there with one question to ask,"Whatcha need, Roxie?"
Her favorite line was, "A stack. Two if you got it. My Mama needs one." She ran Toby like a Hebrew slave for her greed for money and things. Toby kept Eve's Aunt Roxanne dressed in name brands, animal print shoes, and fur coats. You could see clear through Auntie Roxanne brick and glasshouse, trying to set the bar to be the Jones' and bitter about wanting to be the first in the family to marry the wrong man. Every now and again, Roxie will bring her whip out when she finds out that Evelyn has something new. Toby not knowing he's the man of the house running around her tide tongue, scratching the back of his neck with a pink pleated skirt on. He says she is the only woman who can bring the tamed lion out of him.

To Eve everything had become blurred. Trying to get out of bed. She said, "I smell frankincense and myrrh." Precious anointed oils that her grandmother Tilly would rub on her body before she went to deal with the saints at the church. Grandma Tilly would always say on Sunday mornings. Please, Jesus, keep the demons away from me and my young-gins. So, I don't have to deliver anybody with grace. And she would hold her hand up with her fist open as if she's getting ready to slap somebody down to the altar. Eve would sit outside the closet door with her knees up and her back against the wall. For hours she waited for her grandmother Tilly to come out. And every time she would try to look in the closet, it was a glory cloud that filled the little space, and her grandma Tilly would be laid out on the floor. Eve heard her grandmother praying in a different language to Jehovah Jesus, and in her silence, at times, she laid waiting for an answer. It was a private meeting as far as Eve saw. She saw and heard Tilly. Having an encounter with the man she identified as, the delivery of the Red Sea. The best healer of arthritis and Mr. Bengay had trespassed way too long. He is the God of the show nuff touch! Grandma Tilly would tell the other church mothers who attended the prayer meetings. The touch of a cold towel laid across Eve's forehead woke her straight up out of the blurred vision. Grandma Tilly, can I get some cookies and cream now? I did all of my chores. Is what came out of Eve's mouth as she set up in the four postered bed. Naomi and Huston were planted on both sides of her. At the bottom of the bed, Cree stood with his hands positioned on both of her ankles. They started laughing. Eve laid there with sweaty palms, a laced rose petal tee-shirt on, and naked from the waist down, for she had no idea that she was no longer in the vision waiting for her grandmother Tilly to come out of the closet from having an encounter with the Lord. Eve scanned the room, bringing her legs up in a tent position, for she tried to hide her private kitty girl in the company of Chesmar Lake hellions. "Did anything happen to me while I was out?" She asked. Cree snatches her forcefully by the ankles and pulls her down to the edge of the bed and says, You're about to meet your new lover boy. She flipped over onto her stomach and tried to crawl back up towards the headboard. Huston having the support of Cree, says, "Oh no, you don't!"Naomi says, "What's the matter Eve, my lady, don't you want to play? We can both hide in the closet." Eve yelled out, "I'm not a swinger! Now go and get the hell outta my room." The door opens with a burst. It was Andrea to the rescue from the vouchers, which was ready to run up in her childhood friend. "Eve!" Andrea yelled. "Yes," I reached out to her and gained strength instantly just by her grasp. "Take your hands off of her and get out! I told each of you, Eve was not invited to Chesmar shenanigans. She is my best friend, my childhood friend, to hell with all of you in your greed!" Andrea said, raising her voice. I covered my body by gathering the sheets pulling them to the center of the bed to cover what had been exposed. Each of them walked out, Cree being the last, placing his hand under his throat, he said, "That she had just slit her own throat without haste." Andrea did not hold her tongue, "Do what suits you. Just remember you built on my property." Andrea was once again speechless. She fell down on the bed and wrapped her arms around me. "Girl, what is this you've gotten yourself into?" I asked her. "It's Paul Eve," shaking her head as she carried on to explain, "this mess has gotten way out of hand. It's the lifestyle that comes with the rich and famous. Everything is perverted; Perverted! Fucking perverted! You live well. Damn good. But, at all costs of your deepest and life lived morals and values." "Andrea, they were about to rape me! How did all of this get started was my next question?"

"Eve, you should know this... Paul wants children. Children that I don't care to give him. I came into the marriage, thinking I could live my best life. We talked about children but never really decided on having any. Well, look at me. I've never had such an amazing body or life."

With speed, she kept explaining, "Children...changes the dynamics of everything in a relationship. I have always been told that," and she hesitated.

215

"And what?" I waited for the rest.
Because of what I've heard with my own two ears while being trapped under the dining room table, I starred her in the face. I wanted to know If I could trust my childhood friend to give me the truth and nothing but the whole truth so help her God.

"Eve,...my sister, my fear of having children has caused me to become very distant from my very own husband in our bedroom. He didn't turn me on anymore. Lovemaking came with pressure from his childhood. I began to feel like he only wanted to make love to me to make a baby girl, which would mean from his culture that his biological mother had died when he was four years of age. If she had come back to him. For him, it means a long life of pleasure, peace, and prosperity. I hate to say it, but Paul has no forgiveness in his heart towards his father for the death of his mother and for marrying another woman. His Grandmother Ci-Ci told him the truth about the woman that raised him is not who he thinks she is. The truth for him came out. However, for me having a baby means stretch marks, sagging breast, and postpartum depression from a baby I do not want to bond with."

"So you're telling me Paul wants a baby and you don't. Right?""Yes, and because I said no. Paul's suggestion was to bring another woman into our bed, bobbing her head up and down, I agreed yes, I did."

"Andrea!" I called out her name, "What were you thinking? You know that you can't compete with that. Andrea, you brought another woman into your bedroom to wrestle with the spirit of adultery and division?"
Andrea started sobbing underneath her breath.

"Eve, I thought that It would take Paul's mind off of me having his baby. If I could give him his long time fantasy of being with two women," Paul, in his obsession said, "that

216

It could only be with someone whom both of us knew and trusted. So It started with Dawson and Bailey."

I spoke up and said, "To hell with that! Paul is married to one woman, and when he married you. Look at me, Andrea! You were enough. However, you have to know that selfishness can't be apart of your marriage."

Andrea shared, "Watching him make love to another woman made me feel like I wasn't enough anymore. He wanted me to invite you tonight. And I told Paul no! This is just a phase we were going through, and you could not be a part of sharing our bed. Or anyone else's bed here at Chesmar for that matter."

She dropped her head. And there it was…"Paul is attracted to classiness."

"Andrea, you are classy."

"He asked me last night, why can't I be like you on the inside? A real woman's beauty comes from within, he says." "Well, Eve, Paul doesn't understand that I was never that woman. You know me, I was and have always been dirt poor. I came from nothing. Outside of my parents, I was raised with four brothers and one physically challenged little sister. There are times depending on who Paul is going to meet; I just can't go! I've tried to be the woman he wants out of me. But I don't know who she is. I've never met her myself. My mother was not her; she was a work alcoholic because of our lack. There was no one to groom me and to teach me how to have confidence when I walk in the room. Or to hold my head up and stand tall. I tried to glean from the fields of your mother as she poured into you with wisdom and class. But sometimes it's hard when you're gleaning wisdom from a distance."

"So Andrea, is this why you called for me out of all these years?"

"Yes, I don't know how to be that woman. I need you, or I'm going to lose my life." She grabbed me by both sides of my collar as she spoke through her teeth.

"Eve, Paul is my life. I have nothing outside of him. I was the ugly duckling that followed and lost her way. Eve, my greatest secret, I fight every day looking in the mirror. I'm still that nasty duckling on the inside. Sure, I can make everyone laugh, but I don't know how to love myself. How Am I going to enjoy a baby? I need that love. I need it damn it! Eve, I have never purchased my own house. My credit has never been good enough to buy a car. I stole clothes from Jan's Thrifty Boutique. Was teased all threw school, you were there, you saw it. You witnessed it all. My life was hell on hot flames."

"What do I do with my nerves? When I'm in the face of who I have always been and nothing better. I get nervous about Paul and his friends. The power and influence they have. And he doesn't understand. I'm not used to nor have I ever had to walk in this much power."

I rubbed her back with comfort and spoke, "Andrea, when you don't know the purpose of who you are and what you have, you will abuse it." I gave her all that I could that my father gave me at that moment.

"We abuse what we have no knowledge of."

Broken as she continued to say,…"I thought I was becoming a better wife." And here goes Paul asking me,

"Why did I have to be so rough and edgy and out of control?"

"Eve, Paul gets so frustrated with me at times," "He says I never have the right words to say, and that I don't know how to carry myself in public or around his wealthy friends. Now that Paul has made me this great masterpiece of arm candy. He says that I'm nothing more than a turned over diamond that he shined. And an uncontrolled bitch who always wants to control what I did not work for."

"What!" I yelled as I got up, wrapped the white sheets around me like a skirt.

I had to walk away to pray from the inside as Andrea's conversation was tempting me to become very bitter. Something on the inside of me said, Eve, stay calm. This is not your game. Know your place. You are here to be a sideline cheerleader. To encourage her from base to base until she makes it back home. The place of being redeemed, for she has an umpire, who will catch her every strike.

Andrea asked in a whisper, *"Eve, what Am I to do with my husband? I love him, but I don't like who he's become. Paul beats me with his words. Eve, I don't have the mental strength to fight him anymore. I'm worn out. It's if he's been punching me in the throat for these last three in half years. I can't breathe any longer. He verbal abuses me, and to me, there is no way out! I feel as if I'm not wanted within our marriage vows anymore. He constantly reminds me that his investment in me will pay off one way or another. And I must be honest my thoughts and words have become harsh like target knives towards him."*

I turned and walked back towards the bed to make sense out of all of this.

I asked, "So basically you're telling me Paul is pimping you out to fish women? So you will bring him another woman to keep his sexual appetite at bay until you fulfill his need of granting him children."

"Yes, and I don't want to do it anymore. I can't do it. My heart is torn in two now," she said.

I asked, "Wait, what do you mean?"

"When Paul became bored with Bailey, I feared for my marriage."

"Fear is of the enemy, Andrea. And it opens so many other battle doors that you have no time to war with," I shared with her being sympathetic.

"Eve, she's young and pretty. I mean, come on, did you see her? She's every bit of the baddest body ripping the New York runways. After our rendezvous, Paul shared with them that it wouldn't be a bad idea for them to invite some friends that they trusted and knew would hold the secret fantasies of Chesmar Lake. I insisted that Paul stop and cut it off before we got in way over our head. Then it became this once a weekend thing."

"Wow," I said.

"I knew it. We had gone way too far because suddenly I found myself desiring Cree outside of the private Chesmar parties."

"Andrea, no, please tell me you didn't."

"Yes, Eve, I did; Paul became so abusive whenever I tried to pull out."

"Where is he? I will take him down with my own bare hands? How dare he put his hands on you!"

"No, Eve, Wait!" "He's only slapped me around a few times. But look at me I've survived, right?" "But he makes me stay in the room and watch while he has sex with the Chesmar ladies from time to time."

"So this punk has a fowl mouth towards you, is slapping on you and makes you watch him cheat on you?"

"Well, Eve, really, he's not cheating on me."

"Yes, he is!" I yelled.

"Well, you know what I mean. Come on, Eve, listen to me, I allowed it. And I deserve every negative word his heart chooses to call me. I just couldn't hear him continue to rave on about his dead ass mother anymore. It's not my fault she's not here," as she started to cry. Andrea, with a sobbing voice, said, "I couldn't bring her back."

"No, Andrea, you can't. It's not your place, nor do you have the power." She stood in silence.

"Now what?" I asked.

"Wait, Eve, there's more."

"You gotta be kidding me." "What more could be added to this jungle?"

"I started meeting secretly with Cree. Nicole and Paul have nothing to do with our own love affair."

"Well, cut it off," I said.

"Eve, come on; it's not that easy."

"What is easy when you know what's right?"

"Eve, I'm pregnant." She said.

Andrea gets up off the bed and walks away, leaving me to look at her back with a dangling masquerade mask hanging. It had two faces. On the left side was of a black joker, with feathers and the sound of bells dangling. And the other hand was of a beautiful white woman one would dare to look at with gorgeous long flowing hair.

"It's not the happiest thing in the world I want to share with my childhood best friend. That I'm pregnant for the second time by a man who's an Attorney and is waiting to take my ass to the wringer by blackmailing me with every chance he gets," she shared.

"Why because you got rid of the first baby?" I asked as if I needed permission to.

She turns, walks back towards the bed, and kneeled down on her knees on the side of the bed. Before she spoke, she turned and glanced back at the open door. Making sure not a soul was standing there. Andrea started sobbing.

"*Eve, I'm such a terrible person.* She softly cried out. *I killed my baby. Eve, I had no other choice but to have an abortion. I had no idea who I was pregnant by.* She whispered even the more. *I opened one of Paul's safety deposit boxes in his office downstairs. Underneath his desk is a hidden drawer. I dropped my earring as I was taking him some coffee, and he had stepped into the shower to prepare for a meeting. As I bent down to retrieve my earring, my head hit the secret drawer under his desk. And there it was the safety deposit box. It had taken me three weeks to locate the key. It was hanging on a hook behind the painted portrait of the woman who his father says is his mother, Queen Juliana Le Fallon Sire, in the upstairs hallway. I read everything."*

Andrea's hands had begun to uncontrollably shake as she rubbed them.

She stated, *"I saw all of the images of Dr. Paul Sire and who he really is. Cree came over to drop off some paperwork he needed Paul to sign. I couldn't hide it, Cree saw it in my face. He knew something was terribly wrong. I trusted him, and he swore to my husband's privacy. Cree knows who my husband really is. Out of trust, I shared with him, and Cree took advantage of me and the situation. After his consistent threats, I just couldn't take a chance to share it with anyone else."*

I took a chance and asked…"Who is Paul, and should I be concerned for you?"
Andrea talked right over me as if I said nothing. I don't know if I can trust her story.

"Truly Eve, I don't have friends here. And this has been eating me up inside. These bitches aren't my friends! Some of them want me out of the way to have my husband and his wealth, is not for them. Nor for their hungry sisters and friends, and now I'm pregnant again for the second time. Cree is blackmailing me into keeping me to himself as his private side piece. He won't protect himself when we are intimate, nor did he care to protect me. Cree is controlling me, my husband, and our marriage. Cree wants me to have his baby to make Paul think that it's his daughter, and then I'll be out of the picture for good."

"So Cree is after the legacy of Chesmar Lake?" I asked.

"Since Paul married me, abandoned from his family has been his life's lot. He made Cree Chesmar Lake's attorney. Now Cree wants me to talk Paul into making him a trusted beneficiary of the grounds of Chesmar. So if anything happened to me, Paul promises to raise me and Paul's baby girl and take care of Chesmar with the utmost respect."

"Andrea, I heard some of what you've been going through downstairs in the kitchen, and I want you to know that Nicole knows."

Andrea's mouth fell open; *"She knows what?"* She asked.

"Nicole knows that you were pregnant by Cree. I don't know if she knows from the first time or if she knows about this pregnancy." I told her.

"How do you know? And where are you getting all of this from?" She asked, being full of questions.

"I overheard her speaking to Chanel about some text messages you sent Cree. About whether or not you were going to keep the baby. Apparently, he stepped out of the car, and she read them coming up on his cell phone laying in the driver seat."

"Are you kidding me?" Her eyes were wide open as she asked.

"You need to know Chanel told her to take you down until every window in your glasshouse is shattered, leaving nothing but the stairs to your front porch that leads to nowhere."

She dropped her head and broke down. I grabbed Andrea and hugged her as tight as I could.

"Eve," she said as she cried, "I was happy at one time. I was, I promise you I was. But I have to be honest.

Being happy now only means there's nothing to be happy about."

Andrea sobbed until her voice became faint.

"My sister, my queen, let's make honey. Hold your head high and be confident in all the woman you know how to be. My grandmother Tilly shared with me years ago. There is an answer to every problem. I'm not the problem solver. However, I know someone who is. I actually call on Him more than a few times a day because I find myself in a better place when I allow him to fix things that I have no control over. He's the man my grandmother Tilly has forever found herself petitioning. She called him the problem solver."

"Who is he?" Andrea leaned in close to my face and asked, "And what's his price? Name it, and I got it."

"No, Andrea, He doesn't entertain for the highest price or bid."

"Well, can you introduce me to him?" She found herself desperately asking.

"I can tell you who He is, but you're going to have to make an appointment to meet Him on your own. For he has delivered me out of so many situations."

"It doesn't matter, if he can make all the difference, then I need to know him," she said.

"But it wasn't always easy going to Him. At first, because no one shared with me that He's a father. A loving father. Not a judging father but a forgiving one. Then my perspective changed in how I would go and meet with him privately." I shared with her the greatest passion.

"Okay, well, where is this man's office? I could use a good Counselor."

"He's far more than that, and for your sake, He takes private sessions." Two taps were lightly made at my bedroom door; it was Andrea's husband Paul. Andrea became silent instantly.

"Well, well, well. Here is where the two of you have been hiding out all night," he said, "Andrea, come please, our friends are leaving."

Bracing herself to get off the floor, she leaned in once more with the stare of desperation and said without being heard, *"Eve, Who is he, and where can I find him?"*

Quickly I pointed toward my bedroom closet and whispered...

His name is Jesus.

You can find Him behind any closed door. Open your heart and give understanding to the healing that needs to take place in your life and the deliverance within your marriage. And He will keep it a private party between just the two of you.

Paul spoke up to challenge me and asked, "Excuse me, Eve, did I miss something?"

"No,...Paul, not at all, the both of you enjoy your night and sleep well," I responded.

Paul walked out, and Andrea followed, looking back at me. Then towards the closet door with tears in her eyes. For she knows there are some decisions she needs to make. And one of them is privately behind closed doors without anyone else.

19

Breathe

It's a beautiful morning today. I thought, why not. I'll just sit out on my back patio listening to the birds chirping, eating leftover shrimp and grits for breakfast. I'm already full, stuffed, and need to get up and run around this block. But not today! Hearing the sound of the traffic keeps me on track with all the work I have to do. Think of it as if you're moving. You got to be going somewhere. Now, if it's the right place, you need to be. I don't know but, you better be finding that out. Wearing my white silk pajamas, enjoying the slight breeze moving the leaves on the trees swaying them back and forth.

I'm in some kind of mundane mood, though. I don't know about you. But waking up to Saturday mornings have been the best days of the week for me, simply because my weekdays for work have become so demanding. Traveling to meet clients for custom fittings has been the joy of my days and nights. I love what I do. Yes, I do. Not to mention, I take it with pride, and I do it well. Evelyn's famous words growing up were. If you're gonna do it. Do it right. Or don't do it at all. I made it up in my mind a long time ago. Never to do anything else that I will not take pleasure in or not having the love for doing it. If I don't love it or get any joy from it. It's not happening. I will not do it; life is short. Period; and I promise every given day to live with purpose on purpose. So now you have it.

Pretty much the only days I've been able to have to myself and soak in the bath with lit candles, shave and sleep in, is Saturday mornings, I haven't been available to hang out with the ladies in weeks—one thing about our friendship for sure.

We can be away from each other for days on end, but, somehow, that connection between us all is never lost.

The backseat of my car is full of the latest magazines, sketchbooks, and material.

Dinner? Who has time to sit down to dine? For me, breakfast, lunch, and dinner have been on the go. I can't even begin to tell you what the inside of Pandora's Lounge looks like anymore. And most of my Saturday nights that I'm with Mekhi is fast asleep in his arms from being exhausted. And the times that he brings his daughter, I end up falling to sleep even more quickly. Ask me why? You already know. I take enough Benadryl for two nights. And whenever I wake up. And he was gone. She made sure I knew she was there.

Even though our nights have been short, and our time together has been brief. We talk through text, and FaceTime. We are yet very much of each other's world. A few times, while flying in between clients. I was able to give him a surprise visit to one of the SkyLoft Lounge. One more question. Ask me, was your girl naked and wrapped in black mink? Oh, yes, she was. Un-apologetic, she went there all the way.

Believe it or not, I'll be heading out in the morning for the rest of the month to meet three new clients. First to New Jersey to comply with Toya for an all-white fiftieth birthday party. Then to meet up with Sharlene in Atlanta. She's married to Quarterback Wallace Anderson. Whom she's taking the pleasure of being on the front cover and centerfold of Winner Ways Magazine with her hubby. Lastly, my final destination will be to North Carolina. Congresswoman Cynthia Black will be interviewed live by Josh Gibson from the Gibson World News Morning Show.

My alarm on my cell went off to remind me that I have only ten minutes to finish getting dressed, grab all of my things, and make it out of the house.

Right on time, out the door. Wait just one minute; I need to double-check that back patio door, back in the house. Like I thought, patio door wide open. The last time I left the patio door open. I came home late, and a bird flew in my house, and I had a panic attack trying to get out. Just reset the alarm. I got my peace in the proper place. And I'm ready to go.

"Hello, Jay."

"Hello, my love," Jayden O'Connor said, "I miss you, and I really need to see you," He said.

"Jayden, I'm headed out as we speak. What's the problem?"

"I'm on my way," He said.

"Jayden, you're not listening to me." Giving him my reset warning.

Being persistent, Jayden said,"I miss you, and I really need to see you. Right now Eve, I've been longing to see your face and touch your body." Trying to swindle my way out of giving Jayden any unwanted space in my head or face.

"Really, Jayden, I'm running a few minutes behind, and this client is quite the boogie man. Honestly, he has a hissy fit whenever I arrive at the meetings late."

"Okay, well, I guess I have no other choice but to let you go. But, before I go. Promise me, Eve, that I'll hear from you later tonight?" He asked.

"Jayden, you know, I do not like making any promises that I have no control over keeping. Does that sound familiar at all to you?"

"Eve," "Do you really want me to respond to that?"He said.

"Good Morning Eve," Faith said in the surround sound speakers."

"Good morning Faith," I responded.

"I just placed your order for your grande, Chai Tea Latte, with two pumps of hazelnut cream from Half Black's Coffeehouse."

"Thanks, Faith."

"Eve, I'm talking to you. Can you turn her off?" Jayden O'Connor asked harshly.

"Now, Mr. Jayden O'Connor, that is rather rude of you." Faith replied.

"How would you like it if I just so happened to end this call? Due to your faulty thinking," Faith asked him with power under her automated voice.

He said, "Power Faith down now!"

Trying to calm him down, I said, "Jayden be good, would you please? It's too early in the morning for all that. She's just a car."

Faith came with a strong comeback and spoke, "Mr. Jayden O'Connor; I do apologize, you may have purchased the vehicle, however, due to the manufacturing guidelines. I only have one master to obey. Should I go any further?"

"Faith!" I corrected her not to come out of pocket.

"Yes, Eve If you're wondering If I ordered your pumpkin spice bread along with your grande Chai Tea Latte. I always do."

"Great Faith, Thank you, and please leave Mr. Jayden O'Connor to me."

"Sure thing Eve," pulling in the drive-through of Half Black Coffee House to pay for my Latte.

"Eve, please be advised. You're due to your next appointment in less than eight minutes," Faith says.

"Thank you, Faith, for keeping me on track."

"Eve."

"What is if Faith? And It better be good."

"I don't know if Mr. Jayden O'Connor can still hear me," as she lowered her voice to belittle him, knowing that he was very much present on the call.

"The Bible says That one can chase a thousand to flight, and two can chase ten thousand."

"I know what the Bible says, Faith. Be kind, and stay in your lane!"

Faith said, always having to have the last words, "Two is better than one Eve. I am always on your side and your team only, have a good day."

Jayden O'Connor said before hanging up, "I expect to hear from you tonight, Eve. Take care of yourself." He hung up, not giving Eve or Faith any last words to speak.

The door swung open. I heard Teddy playing in the background, Singing *Close The Door and Come A Little Closer.*

"I thought you would never get here," Mekhi said.

"Oh! Am I that late?"

"Two minutes and thirty-five seconds," He said, looking down at his watch, "You know how I am about being on time."

I took three steps and walked right out of my wrap-around dress. He ran his fingers down my face taking his time to pass my lips. Covered in all diamonds, there I stood in my favorite Von Sha' ShaVon's six-inch heels, with a stethoscope laying down gracefully in the front of my naked birthday suit. Waiting for Mekhi to take me in his arms, quickly, he snatched me in and pulled me close. He asked me gently with his very manly voice.

"Nurse Novae, are you or are you not on the clock?"

"Yes, Dr. Henderson I'am, but, on my way to work, Sir. It started storming, and I've seemed to have caught a really, really bad cold behind it." Just as I said that the thunderstorm made the lights in the house flicker. And the sound of the lightning-caused me to fall right in this man's chest. Help me, Lord! All these pecs, triceps, and biceps got me wrapped up in all this love. I grabbed Mekhi. And he made sure I knew it was him who had me.

Forcing me to speak with his hands wrapped around my neck in a chokehold. My body became cold with chills. This ninja is a demon! That I don't want to be delivered from, Jesus please baptize me! Right here and now with the water, blood, and the cross.

"What is your ID number, Nurse Novae?" He said, bringing my head to his attention, front and center. He continued to speak.

"For now, on you will no longer be needed on this shift."

Talking with my voice that says, don't make me beg, "Please, Dr. Henderson" making sure he was reading the stance in my eyes, "I really need the overtime."

Stern and black, he read me my proper rights, "You do know, according to article number Four, five, three nine three in our rules and regulations handbook that we just can't chance the risk of all other staff members catching a cold and running a fever."

"Now let me ask you again, do you understand the policies that are in place?"
I inhaled and exhaled, quickly assuring myself to please the man that had me captive.
Listen to how this man makes me respond to his love and leadership.
I then responded by dropping my head to get the lover's side of his attention.

"Yes, Dr. Henderson, I do. I have no other choice but to take this harsh punishment lying down. Four, three, zero, two five is my badge number, Doctor," I spoke with my most submissive surrendered voice.

"Because of your condition, Ms. Novae, you must be made aware of your overdue checkup as well as I'm checking things over. Your temperature appears to be rising, even as we speak."

Mekhi grabbed my breasts. I felt all the muscle in his chest, and the firm grip of his hands tighten. What? You didn't hear me. I'm captured. Ship down. There's no need for a life jacket, rescue helicopter, or nine one-one. Don't save me; I'm going under. I don't want to be saved. All the honey in the Sisterhood Hive can't slide me out of this position.

"Here, allow me to touch your lips while I get your mouth wide open," Mekhi whispered.

I pulled back to gather myself, for I was in too deep. I asked Mekhi amid my tease.

"Excuse me, Dr. Henderson, just one more thing. Do you know if you would be sending me home from work today?"

"No!" "Not today, I'll have to monitor this rare case of cold. Soon I'll know if this sickness take a turn for the good or the bad. I will say this, though. It's good you were only a few minutes late. That storm out there has really gotten nasty. It seems as if you've made it out of the rain just in time, young lady. Allow me to apologize now, because I know about you and needles, and you don't take much pleasure in being poked." I was silent and patiently waiting.

Mekhi, who likes to play the role of my doctor at times, said, "Nurse Novae, I've noticed you've become shy of words," Then he repeated himself, "I'm going to have to examine you and give you a strong dose of my prescribed medicine. But don't worry. I'll have you feeling better in no time."

I said, "Doctor Henderson, I trust you with my last breath."

"Fine then. Would you like to take your medicine bending over? Or perhaps as I'm examining your lungs on the operating table, I could slip it to you then."
The door closed softly. Mekhi kissed me. The sound of the lock clicking echoed in my ears and all throughout the house.

Before I knew what was happening, I was lying under the dining room table locked up in a-position that I only had the strength to whisper.
I called his name, *"Mekhi."*
"Yes, he said, I'm here."
There were no words to be spoken after that. Other than seeing one another eye to eye. As he changed our position, turning and pulling me close, placing the left side of my head in the palm of his hand, I felt his allowed touch. My head fell back as my body relaxed. I felt the rise of his man as I became needy and wet, tapping my g spot softly as he awakened my inner woman.

"I've been waiting too." Once again, I tried to speak.

He said, "You've been waiting for what...go here? Where only I can take you."

My eyes closed, and It didn't matter where I was for the moment; all I know is I was there in a place where only Mekhi could find me.

He gently whispered.
Breathe.

20

Live

I just wanted to roll over, curl up and snuggle under Mekhi's underarm. It's nothing like smelling the natural scent of the man you love. I love him. Smile. He holds my hand with care. And it drives me so crazy when he rubs across both cheeks of my back end. You are talking about a good feeling. Girl, please, you know it makes my toes curl. He likes doing it as much as I want him to. But when he gets done. Your friend is ready. Stop laughing, you heard me. Go on and say it! This woman is nutty for some Mekhi Henderson honey. Pour the tea! Smh with a good laugh...

Reaching over to feel the smoothness of his back, but for some reason, he wasn't there, and the sheets on his side of the bed were chilled. Snatching the covers back on Eve's side of the bed, she glanced at the clock on the wall. The clock read one eleven in the morning.

She wondered what would drive him out of her presence for so long, that cold settled in and was allowed in their bed. This was very strange coming from Mekhi. Typically he's the one asking. Where are you going? I need you next to me. Every time Eve made her way out of the security of his arms. Most of the time, Mekhi would find her in low lighting with candles, soaking in a hot steamy tub with a book in her hand. Although she kept her own home that Jayden O'Connor bought her. She seemed to always find her way back in the king-size bed wrapped in the arms of her lover, boy Mr. Mekhi Henderson. She had her own keys, garage door opener, and teapot with the matching his and her mugs. That read soon to be husband and wife.

As I made my way toward the stairs, leaning over the balcony, smoke was ascending fast. I heard men scuffling and arguing with Mekhi. Three clicks from the sound of guns were made, and my heart started beating fast. I heard Mekhi trying to reason for his life.

"Baby!" I yelled out, "Baby! What is it? What's going on down there?" I asked.

It sounded like his mouth was being muffled. And the only words I can hear him say over some man threatening him was…"I had nothing to do with it!"
They kept asking him over and over about things that didn't make sense—wearing all-black clothing with a gold sword hanging from the middle of his necklace. Eve saw and heard the lookout man standing at the front door yelling.

"Two minutes left, let's get out of here; this place is about to blow. Fire is everywhere!" He said.
She then saw on the back of the neck from the raised black skull cap. Engraved on the tall, dark-skinned guy bent to the ground where Mekhi was lying. A tattoo of a woman's body, with one finger, raised to her mouth, given the expression of enjoying the time of silence.
On the other hand, she raised the edge of her dress that implied come and get it. The tattoo of the woman's body had the head of an octopus, with many raised tentacles, and a compass for the face that only had one shiny emerald green eye and a bold letter S for south that was on her chest.

Even though Eve couldn't hear it, she wondered what was being said. She watched the expression on Mekhi's face, and it wasn't right. She tried to read his lips to make out what he said. But nothing was made clear. As the gunman held the barrel gun to Mekhi's face, the house continued to burn on all four sides.

He gritted his teeth and demanded an answer, "Who kicked in Baldacci's doors and killed his one and only daughter?" He asked.

Eve wanted to know what was being said. But all she heard was Mekhi pleaded and pleaded that it wasn't him. He said, "He didn't know her and had nothing to do with her death."

Then one of the gunmen shouted out, "How do you want to die, punk? You are about to take your last breath!"

Then I heard another man with a profound raspy voice say, "Yeah, go ahead and make your request known, "Which side of Baldacci's daughter do you want to be buried on?"

I had no choice but to yell out to say, "No! No! Leave him alone, you bastards!" I shouted at the top of my lungs.

Mekhi said, "Baby, stay put!"

"If you come any closer, you'll be dead before you take your next step," said one of the gunmen with hostility in his voice.

As he pointed his gun right at me, she yelled out to them again, "Who sent you here? Who? Was it Jayden O'Connor with his bitch ass? Get the hell outta here and leave us alone!"

"Baby, stay where you are. Everything is going to be-alright. Go back to the room and lock the door!" Mekhi yelled back, trying to calm her down.

I ran back into the bedroom to grab my all-white housecoat hanging from the back of the bathroom door. I opened up every dresser drawer to see if there was a gun in the house. Returning to the stairs,

I warned all the gunmen, "I'm coming down, you sons of bitches!" I said, making sure every one of them heard me as I made my way downstairs to be with him. I had my cell phone in my hand trying to dial nine one-one. I ran down the hallway towards the wood winding staircase. I could hear things were getting turned over, and glass was being broken.

And there it was. The first shot. Pow! The gunshot wrung all throughout the house.

One of the men yelled, "Mantella! Jue! A., Jueleus, come on, man! He said no one is supposed to die. Boss said, bring him alive. You guys know the plan. Man, y'all stick to the plan!"

Pow! Another shot was fired, and I heard Mekhi pleading once again to someone named Adonis.

"Stop-'em man, Adonis, we go too far back. Man, you carry my blood." And his voice was no longer heard.

"No!" I screamed.

Trying to make my way to him, I saw the men through the opening spaces of the stairs as my climbing down was a long way from coming to an end.

"Hello, nine one-one, What's your emergency?" The operator asked.

I said, "Help me. Please!" Yelling on the phone!

Pow! "Don't let me die like this, Adonis," Mekhi said faintly.

Tripping over the belt of my housecoat, I fell down the last two stairs from the upper staircase after taking my fall. I ended up on the floor of the lower landing twenty-five feet from the man I dreamt of marrying in front of all my family and friends.

Pow! Pow!Pow! More shots were fired. This time the echo sound of "Baby!" Boomeranged back at me like a slap in my face, and my bottom lip shivered.

"Mekhi no!"

"God, no! Please! God of Grandma Tilly let him live. Lord, I'm calling on you now. Please, God. I'm begging you with everything within me. Please spare me his life! I will serve you for the rest of my life. You can have my life, Jesus, you can have it. Just let him live. I'm nothing without the love of this man; he gets me, and he has always accepted me. I am beautiful in his eyes, and I know in his heart. I have always been the rejected black sheep and hated by so many. I can't be another man's throwback."

In Eve's devastation, she cried out. Her pain surfaced, and the daring of her heart began to speak out loud. Experiences of the hidden place of pain was speaking of being turned down, abandoned, deserted, shun, and a failure for the most and a loser for the rest.

"God, you don't get it!"

There was no number count to her tears.

"Nine one-one, what's your emergency?" The lady operator repeatedly said in my ear. Exhausted, she replied, "My name is Eve G. Novae, and my Fiancé Mekhi Henderson has been shot. I believe six times in his home. Please come fast."

I tried to stand up. But the strength of my legs was not supporting me. I fell without having any balance, "My leg is broken. I shouted!" Through my blurred vision, I saw four men run out, leaving Mekhi lying in a pool of blood. The operator's voice calmly said from the cell phone laying on the floor beside me.

"The nearest ambulance to your location has been notified, and it shows that they are two minutes away. Ma'am, Are you there?" She asked.

"Yes, please hurry. I'm here!" Why in the hell are you asking me, "Am I here? I can't lose him. I'm here!" I responded.

The operator continued to say, "Please stay on the phone with me until the EMT has arrived. Eve, I need to ask you where he is located in the house?"

In full pursuit of her role, she continued on. But my fight was to get to Mekhi. I wanted him to know that I was going nowhere.

I slid down the rest of the stairs on my belly. I crawled over to the body of the man who has been the wind of wonderland, *"No, baby, don't leave me. I need you."* I whispered.

Kissing Mekhi all over his face and lips, blood was everywhere, but it did not matter too, Eve. It was important that Mekhi knew and felt that her love was real even unto death as much as she poured her love out on him. She needed him to wake up and take it in. If it was only for a moment, she wanted to look him in the eyes just one more time.

She desired to hear him tell another funny joke. Like the one he shared about how he thought he was the great American hero as a little boy. His mother, Sonya, would threaten him about her shade tree. If she caught him swinging in her weeping willow tree again, tearing up her branches one more time. She had something for him. Every Saturday, he couldn't wait for his mother to go to bingo with her gambling buddies. So he could swing on the weeping willow in the backyard and yell out like he was the master of all heroes. Eve wanted to hear him share again about his Uncle Joe, who was a professional taker, according to him. He would always come into the house and place his hat on Mekhi's head. One time Uncle Joe made him a Batman costume. He let Mekhi wear one of his black wife-beater tee-shirts and his black ski mask from the glovebox of his pickup truck.

His superpower instructions to Mekhi was before you swing back and forth in these trees. Take this black button-down dress shirt I gave you and tie it around your neck for your cape and beat your chest like a grown man. Like you know, you just saved the day, nephew. He later found out his uncle was just trying to get him out of the house because he had the neighbor's wife upstairs in the spare bedroom, and every now and then, his uncle would look out the window and say, "I see you, nephew; keep on swinging. Do it again."

Everything was moving through Eve's mind in a matter of seconds. And even though her faith was excellent and reliable for Mekhi to rise up. Not forgetting, she believed and began to wale out once again to the God of Grandma Tilly.
The God she knows has manifested much and many miracles for their family since she was a little girl.

Seeing Mekhi lay lifeless. She thought. I don't know where to stop the bleeding. Eve opened her mouth and began to encourage him to fight for his life.

She spoke, "Don't give up… Mekhi, I gave up too much to be with you. And I can't go back! Baby, I need you, please hold on." Mekhi's eyes fluttered back and forth. Sadness came and structured the front of Eve's face. Tears fell, and the tightness from her throat swelled.

As flashbacks came about the last telephone conversations between her and Jayden O'Connor, the first man from her teenage years, back and forth, he called again and again. He wanted Eve to pick up. We need to talk. Only to speak her truth, she answered. She left him feeling once again released and released by a woman he has put on hold for years. She waited on purpose to serve him and honor his last name. Oh, how she has played second to the addiction he had for Morgan. Having the courage to walk out of other relationships just to be the side chick without a promise ring, her love dangled as she watched the women around her travel the coming and going tunnels of love. Eve, the woman he thought he could trust and forever have only by his side and not of his whole heart.

She told O'Connor without any hesitation, "Go your way! And move on with your life." He said, "I have never met this Eve. Who is she and where did she come from?"

Giantess became Eve's middle name. Strength carried the thunder of her voice.

"Jayden, you told me yourself. You could never do life without Morgan. Well, here you go. Have at it! Finally, I realized Morgan needs you more than I do. Thank you for everything you have ever taught me or gave. But, my love is for Mekhi now."

"Eve, Stop it! You're going too far with this," He said.

"Jayden, I will not put you before him. Ever! Don't even ask me why. Because he never places me last. Don't you understand I want to be happy, O'Connor? And you need to be. Let go! And live the best life you can buy with all your money. That I may be free to love Mekhi wholeheartedly. I'm not in love with you anymore. I had to let go of you and the old relationship that did not serve me purpose."

The last words she heard Jayden O'Connor whisper and say for the first time in her life. Was... *"Eve, never come back. Not even on your knees."*

Leaving only air on the line. They both acknowledged the lingering wanted and unwanted space from one another. Taking a deep breath, Eve took note that out of all the times, she was worried when O'Connor would become silent during their conversation. Well, this time, she wasn't at all concerned about asking Jayden O'Connor, "What does your silence mean?"

The smell of burning wood and furniture filled the air as the room began to flash boldness of bright emerald green, reds, and hues of cobalt blue. Eve's mind traveled from place to place. For the hurt in her soul for Mekhi was wandering. The hope for him to live was a great question. Will he survive? As she watched the low rise and fall of his chest.

She went back to how she's been there for all of her girlfriends. And them in return since childhood. The Sisterhood Hive has always been her one reality of understood love. Times when they may have thought they would have died and never lived to tell it over a cup of hot tea. But somehow through it all, they have been one another's celebration, Kayla, Andrea, Lauren, and Olivia. Eve, too, had been there during the times of their filled spaces of pain, uncontrolled addictions, and empty moments of rejected love, for she knew their story. Cheating men, abortions, poverty, lies, hidden jealousy, dancing for money, and crying for relief. They didn't see that person of Eve, but only the Eve of the surface, for out of the loins of the women from which she had been called out the women of her family. They had already pulled the air out of the lungs her friends were struggling to live with. Deceitful rape of purpose, the lack of trust, and wanting to be loved, sleeping with men for loveless sex, how they faithfully lugged around mental and emotional garbage. The vicious habit of paranoid loneliness, being un-loyal women to verbal commitments, having fed the greedy appetite of selfishness, the refusal to be led by a God they could not see. Competition between highs and lows of happiness, jealousy from a dead place, catering themselves to never satisfied wants. Small-minded thinking with the shield of anger, and the repetition of sleeping with married men for unmeasurable gifts.

Many years of being the abandoned black sheep with a broken spirit with no truth, sharing the testimony of how each of them experienced significant loss and was left to only grieve unhealthily. Eve herself came face to face with the legacy of the great women in the root of her family tree and kissed what they lived as well. Her friends were unaware. At times she did not bring forth good character. The core of her laboring pains was for not only her family and friends but for all women. Here is where Eve herself was strengthened to give and speak life into them and their circumstances reminded of their every struggle. They're lies a decision to be made. To live or die, she would ask them? She did not always see life from this end. For in time, she grew to this point to understand. Her life purpose could never be just about her, for her journey was to be made known to all, especially to women, because she had experience and was exposed to unconditional love, which is universal. Applicable to all cases. Eve or someone of her family had already experienced what they carried. Eve also knew at some point her submission to brokenness would surface. And in the back of her mind even though there was the greatest struggle of self-doubt. How can I speak life when at times, I didn't have enough courage to open my mouth; She began to question whether she would be healed from even this? What appeared to be another dead relationship. How could she embrace the strength to live again? Or also face the women of Grand Chester Place and beyond.

Lying with her face to Mekhi's chest, the fire in the room had formed a circle around their love. She had never experienced this moment where life laid before her, fighting the call to die.

The Lord revealed to her a portion of her purpose. In a still small voice from her inner being, she heard the Lord speak to her heart…

"Your given name, Eve, carries the birth of all living. For you are not one, but many. For many have and will come out of one. Give life, and life will be known. Speak, experience, and life shall be. Life lives even in death. Not even eternity can hold back the breath of life. For all things are my daughter... love is love, for life was created out of love, for I-AM love. Be brave and only strong. Perfect love casts out fear. It's not your fight; it's every woman's win.

Stand on my Word Galatians 2:20 You have been crucified with Christ. It is no longer you who live, but Christ (the Messiah) lives in you, and the life you now live in the body you live by faith in reliance on and complete trust in the Son of God, Who loved you and gave Himself up for you. Strengthen what remains." Then the voice she heard was no more.

It was more about them fighting to live beyond what appeared dead. Even in times when she encouraged them to take a deep breath as each one of them battled to live inside their own journey. They exhaled, and she inhaled. At the tingling of her numbing fingers, she too required the strength of Eve. Why does she have to experience losing who she loved alone?

She viewed the room as it looked back at her, very small and full of burning walls, in the corner of her mind. She sat at the bottom of a dried-up well in the darkness of pitch black. No one was there to be found as she became weak by experiencing a lack of love, the lack of respect from a young man who came and stole her heart, and has loved her all-inclusively.

Finally, Eve was courageous the day she stood up to the dead relationship she carried for the love of Jayden O'Connor. She no longer wants to do life without self-control, and her spine renewed its own posture. She was empowered to say no and walk away to the only man that has ever meant so much to her. Jayden O'Connor, he was King! And her testimony of him became law to everyone. Long live the King! Mr. Jayden O'Connor, he had been right there through all of her naked moments of living. But in her waiting Eve, realized she had become lifeless herself. She wanted her love to flow and her inner peace back. She looked forward to being kind and faithful to a man she desired to call her husband.

Outside of many, she now knows that the one man who has been the strength of all her broken and rejected places of weakness. That Jayden O'Connor never gave credence to. The love of God demonstrated from Mekhi. He loved her out of all her fears and insecurities—concerns she had of being and forever becoming more like them. Mislead women of old. Stuck in an illusion waiting to be saved and hopefully resurrected.

Out of nowhere...She yelled out, "I cannot lose you!" She started beating him in the chest one pound at a time, Bam! Bam! Bam! Screaming to the top of her lungs with the hope that he would respond by hearing her cry.

"You gave me living life out of a stagnant cesspool. You found me in a parked car with Jayden O'Connor with a back seat full of gifts going nowhere." Eve cried out.

"Baby, you know this!"

Rubbing his hands that were laid still on both sides of his brick body. She snatched him up with all of her upper strength and demanded him to look at her.

"Look at me!"

One response after the other, "Mekhi, Don't you dare die on me!"

Feelings of panic were all over her body. The hairs on her neck were standing tall. Grabbing him by the open bloody black housecoat he was wearing. And his lifeless body answered back by the falling of his head and the extension of his neck. Eve cried out in desperation of losing the one man that gives her so much joy. She shouted and moaned to the top of her lungs as she watched life escape his body.

All of a sudden, she heard the dripping of water from the kitchen faucet—drip,...drip. The sound was so far but very near. Coughing, as she spoke, come back to me, catching her breath, and hitting him profusely in the chest.

As she looked passed the flames that began to burn the designer rug, they both were stuck on. Throughout the open door, the shooters left open. Eve heard and watched the North Park Emergency Ambulance fighting their way through the burning doorframe of sixty-three fifty-nine Mountain-way Trail.

"Baby, they're here," exhausted by the smoke, "the rescue team is here," she said, seeking hope of his response.

Everything appeared to be moving in slow motion. Stand clear...Beep... one more. Stand clear... beep... was the sound that filled the room. Feeling faint, while inhaling baby breaths, Eve watched as the rescue team came in to try and revive the young man who rescued her from all of her fears she'd never dared to face—living in the space of love all alone.

One of the EMT workers shouted out, "Come on! I can't get a pulse. Come on! Come on!"

The other EMT worker said three words, "Nothing is happening."

Eve reached over his back, trying to fight the fight Mekhi needs to win as they shocked Mekhi's body one last time. She hollered and slapped his face with all of her strength. "Wake up and live. Mekhi!"

Before I knew it, I screamed from my bowels until I felt the strain coming up out of the pit of my sunken soul.

Mekhi…Mekhi! Wake up and breathe you, MOTHERFUCKER!

Hey, it's LuGina here and
I'm the book's author.
I hope you've enjoyed it, finding it both
intriguing and delightful.
I have a favor to ask you. Would you consider
giving it a rating on Amazon, please?
My desired goal is for this book to be considered
"a New York Times Best Seller," and one way to
help establish the book's status is a mass of
social media love that speaks to why it's valued.

Many thanks in advance,

LuGina C. Horton

To all my exhaling readers near and far.

Thank you for everything.

For all love notes!
LuGina C. Horton
6260 E Riverside Blvd
Suite #134
Loves Park, IL 61111
Luginac.horton@gmail.com
Visit www.luginachorton.com

Sisterhood Honey Hive Chat Guide

1. What are your thoughts about Eve having an alter ego? Do you have one? If so an introduction to the Sisterhood Honey Hive would be nice.
2. Do you agree or disagree with Eve's and Jayden O'Connor's relationship? To you how long is too long to wait for a man or woman to commit to marriage?
3. Do you think Jayden O'Connor is holding back his true feelings about Eve? If so, explain why you think he is doing that? Or would you say that Jayden O'Connor was never right for Eve in the first place?
4. Is being with a younger man the right way for Eve to go? What's your preference?
5. Like Eve and her childhood friends. How important is it for you to still have and hold on to your childhood friends?
6. What are your thoughts when it comes to growing out of childhood relationships? And should the boundary lines that were created in childhood still exist?
7. Why do you feel the need to create more friends?
8. In today's setting of broken marriages, would you say Lauren's best bet is to stay with her cheating husband?
9. Because Lauren made such a large investment and now living good in her husband Robert's future of success should she remain silent and lose her voice?
10. How many times does it take for you to forgive someone who has a repeated cheating pattern?
11. Are you open to interracial dating? Which nationality?
12. She has not been honest about her lifestyle and knowing that Olivia is struggling with her true

identity. Would you say Olivia has trust issues with her childhood friends?

13. Should Olivia share with the Sisterhood Honey Hive about being raped in her childhood or should she struggle in her innocents alone?

14. How do you feel about materialistic friends?

15. Do you think that Young Prince Dr. Sire would have still married Andrea, had he known the truth about who she really was from her childhood beginning?

16. Do you think Andrea should stay in her wealthy way of living and her husband's love triangle?

17. Now Eve has met Mekhi's daughter Makaila. If Mekhi marries Eve, do you think Eve has a chance with grooming her mindset to be a little girl when her grandmother keeps her in grown people's business?

18. Who do you think is going to share the business with Kayla of who her father really is?

19. Do you believe that there were ever any twins Kayla gave birth to with Sebastian? If so, do you think that anyone from the Sisterhood Hive is going to investigate along with Sebastian's quest to find them? And should they? Or do you think what's hidden in the dark should remain hidden?

20. Do you think Mekhi is going to live? If so, what if he's lost his memory and doesn't remember the love he's built with Eve?

21. If he live without his memory of them, do you think she could convince him that what they had, was real? Or will this be just another spill about a dead relationship over hot tea at the Sisterhood Honey Hive that she doesn't want to swallow?

CPSIA information can be obtained
at www.ICGtesting.com
Printed in the USA
BVHW031242290621
610723BV00001B/36